Jennifer *away, watched until he was* *out of sight.*

Trouble. He looked like big-time trouble to her. An outlaw with a gallant streak. A battle-scarred warrior, from the looks of him. Thief of hearts if ever she saw one. She needed to steer a wide berth around him while he was in town.

It was safer for her.

Safer for her heart.

Safer for her sanity.

She let her breath trickle out. She didn't need any more outlaws in her life. One had been enough. Plus, Corey Rainwater was running from something. It was in his eyes. The law? The past? Love? It fit with the image of him. Weren't outlaws always running from something?

And weren't there always women who wanted to help them or reform them?

Well, not her. Not this time...

Dear Reader,

By now you've undoubtedly come to realize how special our Intimate Moments Extra titles are, and Maura Seger's *The Perfect Couple* is no exception. The unique narrative structure of this book only highlights the fact that this is indeed a perfect couple—if only they can find their way back together again.

Alicia Scott begins a new miniseries, MAXIMILLIAN'S CHILDREN, with *Maggie's Man*, a genuine page-turner. Beverly Bird's *Compromising Positions* is a twisty story of love and danger. And welcome Carla Cassidy back after a too-long absence, with *Behind Closed Doors*, a book as steamy as its title implies. Margaret Watson offers *The Dark Side of the Moon*, while new author Karen Anders checks in with *Jennifer's Outlaw*.

You won't want to miss a single one. And don't forget to come back next month for more of the best romantic reading around—only from Silhouette Intimate Moments.

Leslie Wainger
Senior Editor and Editorial Coordinator

Please address questions and book requests to:
Silhouette Reader Service
U.S.: 3010 Walden Ave., P.O. Box 1325, Buffalo, NY 14269
Canadian: P.O. Box 609, Fort Erie, Ont. L2A 5X3

JENNIFER'S OUTLAW

KAREN ANDERS

Published by Silhouette Books

America's Publisher of Contemporary Romance

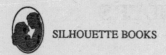 SILHOUETTE BOOKS

ISBN 0-373-07780-7

JENNIFER'S OUTLAW

Copyright © 1997 by Karen Alarie

Printed in U.S.A.

KAREN ANDERS

lives in northern Virginia with her two children. She is the support person for a psychology graduate program at an area university, and the graduate students refer to her as "the goddess." She earned the title for her infinite wisdom, which comes from nine years of service to the department.

She believes that a book is a gateway into an exciting world, and feels lucky to bring this world magically to life with her own unique way of telling a story. She enjoys creating unconventional characters with unique personalities. Her first book is the realization of a nineteen-year dream. She calls herself a true, dyed-in-the-wool romantic, and is not ashamed to admit it, so it comes as no surprise that she writes romantic stories.

Her many interests include country dancing, cross-stitching, horseback riding, book research and, of course, reading. She'd love to hear from her readers, who can write to Karen c/o Silhouette Books, 300 E. 42nd Street, Sixth Floor, New York, NY 10017.

To my family and my daughters, Meghann and Briana, for their precious love. To the supportive efforts of my fabulous GMU fan club, especially Jim Maddux for his marvelous support. To Ruth Graham for her undying faith. To my agent Joseph Anthony for his wonderful expertise. To Ruby Sheradsky for her help in a trying time. To Donna Broshek, the sister of my heart, for listening, editing, critiquing, pushing and just plain *believing*. To Debra Robertson, my gracious editor. And to Lisa; she knows why.

Chapter 1

Jennifer Horn stood her ground, daring Jay Butler to hit her. The sun-drenched parking lot sweltered in the late-morning heat, ripples of hot hazy vapor rising from the black asphalt like steam from an overheated kettle. The wind blew swirling dust around the lot, rattling the leaves on the trees with a dry papery sound.

A crowd had formed to watch the quarrel between the two prominent Silver Creek citizens. Jay's angry voice rose in pitch and the people watching stirred nervously as he raised his hand to slap her. She could almost feel the sting from the anticipated slap. Backing down hadn't even occurred to her.

Her eyes shifted to Tucker who stood behind his father, his eyes bleak and filled with dread. The boy's body was rigid and ready to spring forward. Jennifer implored him with her eyes to stay put. If he interfered, Jay's wrath would be turned solely on him and she couldn't bear that. Her eyes slid to the nervously shifting crowd.

"I wouldn't do that if I were you."

A hand came out of nowhere to clasp Jay Butler's wrist, and a solid barrier stood between her and Jay, eclipsing the sun. The stranger towered over her, and Jennifer noted that his deep, husky voice had been soft with menace.

The anxiety that had churned in her stomach when Jay raised his hand slowly disappeared. And when the stranger moved sideways, bringing Jay with him, she stared up, searching out his eyes. Her father had told her that she could always gauge a man by his eyes, but this one wore mirrored sunglasses, his eyes concealed. He had on a black Mexican-style hat with shiny silver conchos decorating the band. Two thin cords were cinched tightly under his dark stubbled chin.

If it weren't for his long, black hair and the missing gun belt that would look natural strapped to his lean hips and strong thigh, he would look like Clint Eastwood in *High Plains Drifter*.

He even stood like a gunslinger.

Her eyes traveled over the rest of him as he glared at Jay with a forcefulness that even she felt. With Jay's wrist tightly manacled in the stranger's powerful, black-gloved hand, Jennifer felt suddenly and unexplainably safe. Even the crowd behind her seemed to settle down at the stranger's sudden appearance.

As the standoff continued, Jennifer's eyes roamed over him again. A tan mackintosh with a brown leather collar reached almost to dusty, scuffed black snakeskin boots complete with spurs.

A rodeo rider? she wondered silently. He wore a blue chamois shirt, the top three buttons undone, showing off his elegant tanned neck and the beginnings of a smooth chest. Black jeans clung to his body, revealing hard male strength, and she recognized the gold belt buckle for what it represented. Yeah. A rodeo rider.

"Get your hands off me, chief!" Jay snarled as he tried to jerk his wrist free.

Jennifer saw Tucker stiffen, his soft mouth pull into a grimace, and she felt more sorry for the boy than she could ever show. She knew Tucker would never accept her sympathy. He was too proud.

She sighed softly and shook her head. "Jay, you're such a jackass."

The stranger smiled, a soft upturning of his mouth. He shot her a sidelong glance. "A woman with backbone?"

Seeing the two men together, she realized what a dandy Jay was compared to the plainly dressed stranger.

Jay's blond hair was curly and short. He was as fair as the stranger was dark, and he looked soft compared to this lean, tall man. Whereas Jay was stocky and heavyset, the stranger was cool, lean and sleek like a panther. Jay wore brand-new blue jeans that had never seen a day's work and a flashy red cowboy shirt with black piping. A gold bracelet sat on one wrist while the glint from a gold watch could be seen on the other. A wolf in sheep's clothing.

The only jewelry the stranger had on was a small gold hoop in his ear with a little dangling golden feather and a watch with a turquoise band.

There was something so *honest* about his appearance, she thought. A hardworking man without vanity who dressed for comfort and ease of movement. No wolf in sheep's clothing, just pure wolf.

As for Jay, he had more brazenness than brains.

Couldn't Jay see the wild danger in this man? Couldn't he feel the power emanating from him like the heat rising from the asphalt?

"You want to call the sheriff, ma'am?" The soft husky

drawl of the stranger's voice was enticing, hypnotic. It flowed over her like warm honey.

She noticed that he never took his eyes off Jay.

"No. Let him go," she finally responded, disgusted with Jay and his public display of temper.

The stranger didn't just let Jay go. He shoved him away from her.

"Why don't you go and pick on someone your own size, cowboy?" the stranger drawled as he squared his shoulders and placed his black-gloved hands on his hips. He slowly perused Jay, one hand moving to the stubble on his chin. "I reckon I'm too big and she's too small."

The insult struck home and Jay puffed himself up like a peacock. "Why don't you go to hell?" he said between clenched teeth.

"I've already been there."

The smooth change of pitch in his voice caused Jennifer to wonder what the cryptic comment meant. It sounded as if he had more to say. She could almost hear him finish the sentence, *And I've never gotten out.* Well, after this confrontation he would be gone and she would never know. She surprised herself by wanting to know, and the thought suddenly saddened her.

"Why don't you mind your own business, chief?" Jay sneered the word as if it was distasteful to say. He stepped forward but halted at the imperceptible movement of the stranger's body. He backed up, as though finally recognizing the danger he was in.

"I'm making it my business, cowboy, so you better back off."

"Jay, come on," Tucker said in a firm voice.

"Who the hell do you think you are, coming into my town and telling me what to do?" He violently brushed off the young boy's hand.

Jennifer opened her mouth to tell Jay off, when the stranger put his hand on her arm. She was shocked at the heat of him even through the leather glove. "I don't pay any mind to braying jackasses, ma'am."

She had to concentrate on not laughing, but her twitching lips gave her away.

"Bitch," Jay growled, lifting his hand to strike her.

With breathtaking speed the stranger reached out and grabbed Jay's fingers, bending them back. A tiny amount of pressure had Jay on his knees in the dust.

With soft threat in his voice, the stranger said, "Apologize to the lady."

Jay's eyes narrowed in pain and anger.

"Now!" the stranger ordered.

"Sorry," Jay said tightly.

The stranger let him go, then turned his gaze to Tucker. "You all right, kid?"

Tucker's head lifted and his nostrils flared. For a long moment he stared at the tall dark man with a look of wariness passing quickly through the chocolate-brown depths of his eyes, but Jennifer sensed he wasn't afraid of the man. It puzzled her, but before she could even think about the quiet exchange, Jay once again caught her attention.

He'd scrambled back to his feet. Eyeing the stranger with hatred, he rubbed his fingers, and then glared at Jennifer. "You'll be sorry, Jennifer, you little bit—" He glanced back at the stranger who pulled his gaze from Tucker and lifted his dark eyebrows, just waiting.

"I already am," she murmured shakily, rubbing her wrist where Jay's hold had made the skin tender.

As if with a will of their own, her eyes lifted to the stranger's and her blood seemed to slow and heat. The lethal quality she'd sensed in him hadn't diminished at all. There was deep anger in this man, she thought. An anger that went down to the soles of his boots and suggested he would like nothing better than to rearrange Jay's face.

She also sensed that he was holding back because of her. He intrigued her. Why would a man obviously not a citizen of Silver Creek, Texas, stand up for her? No one else had come to her rescue because they were all afraid of Jay and his brothers. Clovis, who was twenty-seven and the second oldest, was vicious and mean. It was rumored he killed one of his own dogs when he brayed too loud one morning and wakened Clovis after a night of drunken brawling. Jackson, at twenty-four, liked to say obscene things to women for their sheer shock effect. Emmett, twenty-one, would do anything Jay said, even hold down the owner of the feed store while Jay punched him until he agreed to a lower price on feed. And there was talk that Stuart, the youngest at eighteen, had smashed a truck owner's new vehicle just because it was better-looking than Emmett's truck. The Butlers were men who thought they were above the law and terrorized anyone who got in their way.

But not this man. He showed no fear of Jay at all. She had a feeling even if he knew about the dark rumors circulating about Jay, he still wouldn't care.

"Take a hike, cowboy," the man said. The menace in his voice was unmistakable and Jennifer felt an unaccountable thanks for the act of kindness he was showing to a perfect stranger. She had no doubt that if he hadn't stepped in, Jay would have slapped her.

Jay gave her one more vicious look, a wealth of dark promise in his eyes. Grabbing Tucker by his upper arm, he stalked away.

Jay's departure seemed to cue the crowd that the excitement was over for the moment. Some of the onlookers began to leave.

The stranger turned toward Jennifer and pushed the hat

off his head to hang by the joined cord. Pulling off his gloves, he tucked them into his belt just like a rodeo rider and raked his hands through his straight dark hair.

It gave Jennifer a moment to study his strong features, and she discovered that he was really easy on the eyes.

Loner. The word came to her mind suddenly. Not only alone, but this man *wanted* to be alone. She realized how much of his solitude he was risking to defend her, and it struck a chord inside her. "Thank you for involving yourself in my problems, Mr...."

"Rainwater. Corey."

"Jennifer Horn," she said as she extended her hand. He pushed his sunglasses up into his hair and clasped her hand, gently, but firmly. Her pulse stumbled from the electrifying feel of his bare palm against hers, as if her hand had hit a live wire instead of warm callused flesh.

But the electricity of his touch was nothing compared to the sheer shock effect of his eyes. *Green eyes.* Dark, fathomless and hot. Honest, straightforward eyes that could melt solid steel, see into the deep recesses of her soul and learn her most private secrets. Eyes a woman could sink into and get lost in. Yet she felt that in those deep glistening turquoise pools, she would find the shelter and warmth she'd been craving ever since she was stupid enough to marry that good-for-nothing, rodeo-riding, womanizing Sonny Braxton and allow him to foster a child.

No way, Jennifer, she admonished herself silently. No way are you going to get mixed up with a man that looks this good, a man that looks as elusive as the wind. A loner who clearly wants to stay alone. So stop looking at him like that. She pulled her hand away as if burned, but he either didn't notice or didn't care. He probably had women swooning at his feet all the time and was used to being stared at. Even though she told herself to stand firm, she couldn't seem to stop the quick, fluttery feeling in her stomach.

He was at least part Apache, she speculated, with his sharp, high cheekbones, his full sensuous mouth and strong firm chin. Long, straight, silky hair was parted on the side, blue-black and breath-stealingly gorgeous—a dead giveaway to the fact that he had Native American blood in him. A hint of a wild, untamed nature glinted in his astonishing eyes. A warning?

One she intended to heed.

He canted his hip slightly in an arrogant display of male cockiness, indicating that he knew she was looking and he didn't mind. In fact, she had the feeling that he welcomed her appraising eyes on him.

Dangerous.

She had never met a more blatantly sexy man since Sonny, and even he paled by comparison.

"What brings you to Silver Creek?" she managed to ask, trying to conceal the evident wonder he evoked in her.

He didn't answer, but strode away. He shucked the worn mackintosh and stowed it in the pocket of the saddlebag he had strapped to his gleaming motorcycle. She shouldn't have, but she did notice the way his tight black jeans molded to his very nice backside.

She must have been so caught up in her argument with Jay that she hadn't even noticed the noise of the sleek motorcycle's powerful engine.

Even through the coating of dust, she could tell the bike was well taken care of. He'd probably put it together himself, she mused. He looked like the kind of man who was good with his hands.

"Where's the nearest hotel?" he asked with his back to her.

Thank God, he couldn't see her eyes. She took a deep

breath. "No hotel. We've only got one motel and it's at the end of town, but it's really clean. Ellen Beaumont runs both the motel and the diner and she keeps everything spic and span. She even tries to dry the sheets outside if she can manage. We call her Mrs. Clean."

He chuckled softly without real mirth. "If it has a bed and a shower, I'll be ecstatic. I've done my share of sleeping on the ground."

An unexpected catch of pain stabbed her heart at the disheartened tone of his voice. Hadn't anyone ever shown him a little kindness? He seemed so alone and so sad. "Just keep going down this road." She pointed down the main street of town when he turned around, leaning his backside against the seat of the motorcycle. "It's next door to the diner."

"I have always wondered what the difference is between a hotel and a motel." He raked his hands through his hair and it fell back around his shoulders like a silky ebony waterfall. She wondered what it would feel like between her fingers, against her heated skin.

Realizing that she was staring at him again, she shifted and stuck her hands in the pockets of her straight denim skirt. "A motel wants to be a hotel when it grows up."

His lips twitched. His eyes traveled over her, and even though the humor glinted in them, she could still see the anger burning in their depths.

"Ah, a woman with sass *and* backbone. A volatile combination," he said huskily, his voice doing strange and amazing things to her insides.

His eyes moved slowly over her, causing that warm tingle in her stomach to radiate to her skin. The appreciative look in his eyes made her so nervous that she instantly looked away.

Softly he said, "Look at me, Jennifer."

Her eyes flew to his and her face flamed. His eyes lingered with intense force on her lips.

Self-consciously she licked them and the appreciative look swiftly changed to one she recognized immediately. Her breath fisted in her lungs. God, she'd never had a man look at her like that. It weakened her knees into jelly. It wasn't lustful, exactly. It was the intense look of a man who admired a good-looking woman and made her feel intensely beautiful.

Unfortunately, the look made her remember what it was like to be held by a man, made love to—it brought heated visions of a hard, muscular body, legs wrapped around hers and warm supple skin. For a silent moment she savored those memories with a hunger that had grown over the thirteen long years since she'd divorced Sonny.

"So are you visiting?" she managed to say around the knot in her throat.

"No." He folded his arms over his chest and tilted his head with a self-indulgent expression on his face.

"On vacation?" She thought that possibility unlikely and noticed how his eyes became distant, wary and closed.

"No."

"Just passing through?"

"You're very inquisitive, Jennifer Horn."

And you are very guarded, Corey Rainwater. Yet regardless of the shield he had erected, she could see the pain in his eyes. This man was scarred and battered by life. He was running, she thought silently. "And you're being polite. My father would have called it nosy." She could hear her father's voice. *That inquisitiveness is going to get you into trouble one day, girl. That devil-may-care attitude will, too. Mark my words.* He'd been right. The fact that she was raising a child alone showed how her impulsiveness had gotten her into trouble. "My father always called me as curious as a cat."

A smile warmed his face and twinkled in his eyes. "Well, darlin', cats have nine lives. You only have one."

"A man with backbone *and* sass," she teased. She watched the wide grin slash across his face and wished for more time with him.

What was she? Crazy? She had enough trouble. More than she could handle right now with Ellie and the Triple X, not to mention Jay. She knew she hadn't heard the last from him. Besides, this stranger was involved some way with the rodeo. She was sure. And she couldn't let history repeat itself. She wouldn't.

"Down this road, you said?" he questioned while his astonishing eyes traveled over her face, then touched intimately on her hair as if it were changing colors or something equally magnificent.

She got the strange feeling that he was as reluctant to leave as she was reluctant to let him.

Ignoring the weakness that his smile aroused, she managed to keep the breathlessness out of her voice. "Yes. You can't miss it.

"Why don't you come to dinner tonight?" The words were out of her mouth before she could engage her brain. "After all, you saved me from getting punched out. The least I can do to repay you for your help is give you a home-cooked meal." She stumbled over the words like a tongue-tied teenager. Her face flushed again.

He went very still. The raw pain that passed across his face wrenched something deep inside her. Who'd hurt him? she wondered. Who hurt him so much that a friendly invitation to dinner would make him look as though someone had ripped open a wound? She remembered what Jay had called him and winced inside. Derogatory words came easily to Jay. How many times had Corey's heritage been be-littled? she wondered.

He had been hurt enough to make a simple dinner invi-tation seem like a gift from God.

He looked at her so long she thought he wasn't going to say anything. He rubbed at his eyes and pushed his hair back again. His voice cracked slightly when he finally an-swered.

"That's very kind of you, but I'll have to decline." He paused and looked down the street as if trying to maintain his composure.

At his refusal of her invitation, she felt slightly relieved and intensely disappointed at the same time.

"You don't owe me anything, by the way," he said. "Creeps like that cowboy need to be taken down a notch or two. I don't like seeing women abused." He looked at her suddenly and the fierceness in his eyes caused her chest to tighten. "I especially don't like seeing you abused." His jaw clenched and he closed his eyes wearily, and she sud-denly noticed how tired and drawn-out he looked. "Any decent man would have done what I did."

"I'm not so sure about that." She looked away because the vulnerability in his expression was too much to bear. Why did people have to be so damn narrow-minded?

"They didn't seem too eager to help." She gestured to the men and women who were still giving them interested glances as they made their way to their cars. "Everyone in this town is afraid of Jay and his brothers. They were bul-lies in high school, and they've only gotten meaner and nastier since then."

"My advice would be to stay away from him, but I guess that's hard to do in a small town." He pushed away from the bike with a sigh.

"I would, but he won't stay away from me." Jennifer

remembered the painful grip Jay had had on her wrist in the bar two nights ago. Remembered his pawing and his sweaty face pressed to hers. She got disgusted all over again.

Corey's eyebrows snapped down into a frown. "Is he stalking you?"

"He considers himself irresistible and something of a lady's man. I bruised his ego. He'll get over it. I think he's harmless, at least I thought so before today."

He looked as though he was going to say something else, but then changed his mind. "Why don't you report him to the sheriff?"

"The sheriff? He's been trying to find evidence on Jay and his brothers to put them away, but he hasn't been able to get anybody to press charges. Like I said, everyone in this town fears him."

"Why is that?" Corey asked, drawing closer to her.

"Things happen to people who cross Jay."

"Scare tactics. Very effective. Steer clear of him, darlin'," he drawled softly, then, unexpectedly taking her hand, he brought it to his mouth and placed a soft kiss where her thumb joined her wrist. "Thank you, Jennifer Horn, for the directions and the dinner invitation." He dropped her hand almost reluctantly and slipped on the mirrored sunglasses, but then peeked over them. "Stay away from jackasses. They bray awfully loud, but they can kick pretty hard."

She smiled. She was flustered and tried not to show it. The kiss was just a brush of his lips, but she felt the contact as if it were a fiery brand. He rewarded her with a slight upturning of his mouth. Then he laughed softly. He pulled the gloves out of his belt, slipped them on, then reached back to pull the hat on, cinching it tight under his chin.

"Take care, Corey," she murmured, her regret rising unexpectedly, leaving her with an inexplicable feeling of emptiness.

He straddled the bike and Jennifer couldn't help noticing the thick, rippling muscles in his thighs. Definitely a rodeo rider, with legs like that.

"I will, and thanks again for your help and the gracious invitation to a stranger." He tipped his hat and a flare of awareness punched her in the gut. Why she found the simple act of him tipping his hat sexy, she couldn't comprehend.

"You'll be okay?"

"Yes," she said pointing to her green truck with the Triple X's on the side of the door. "My truck's right over there."

She watched him ride away, watched until he was out of sight. Trouble. He looked like big-time trouble to her. An outlaw with a gallant streak. A battle-scarred warrior, from the looks of him. Thief of hearts, if ever she saw one. She needed to steer a wide berth around him while he was in town.

It was safer for her.

Safer for her heart.

Safer for her sanity.

She let her breath trickle out. She didn't need any more outlaws in her life. One had been enough. What she needed was a dependable, hardworking, benign foreman, who knew horses and bulls. Who knew how to ride, rope and brand. One who didn't have hot turquoise eyes, hard muscles and a soft husky drawl.

Not that man. That man was running from something. It was in his eyes. The law? The past? Love? It fit with the image of him. Weren't outlaws always running from something?

And weren't there always women who wanted to help them or reform them?

Well, not her. Not this time.

She turned and walked away.

The woman had been attracted to him, but not in that giggly, irritating way most women came on to him. It was so subtle that he wouldn't have been aware of it if she hadn't flushed slightly, or dropped his hand as if it had been a hot potato. The woman was pure class. His palm still tingled from the contact; his ears still vibrated from the tone of her velvety voice, and his body was still hard from the awareness that had jolted through him. The force of the attraction scared the hell out of him.

He'd been so tempted to accept her dinner invitation, but it would only prolong the inevitable. He was just passing through.

But he couldn't stop thinking about her. Her hair was like hidden treasure. He'd thought it was dark, but when the sun had come out he realized it was a dark auburn with glinting fiery highlights.

Damn, he had always had a soft spot for redheads—sweet, classy redheads with delicate bones, wide catlike green eyes and a body that could give a saint the fever. Make him give up heaven for one night in her arms. And her mouth. Those soft, coral lips glistened, invited, beckoned.

He had never wanted to explore an attraction more. He'd never met a woman he wanted to kiss right away. No, not kiss, but savor. Linger over her lips as if they were sweet nectar from the gods. His lips wanted more than the soft flesh of her hand. He didn't want to just kiss her. He wanted to connect with her.

He wanted the right to touch her hair, her body, her heart.

A lump formed in his throat. He couldn't ever allow those pleasures because of his dark legacy.

His body had never responded so quickly to the sight of a woman. It was as if his body had a mind of its own and recognized her as the other half to make him whole.

He was so damn tired, devastatingly lonely and his guard was down. That was it, he told himself. His threshold was low.

It was a good thing he was just passing through, because Jennifer Horn was not a one-night stand. She was a woman who could worm her way into a man's heart with one soft breath. A woman who would make a house a home. A woman who deserved better than a broken-down bull rider who had turned into a coward.

Maybe if he hadn't been such a coward, his mother and little Marigold would still be alive.

He'd been wandering since he'd gotten out of the hospital two months ago, never staying long in one town except to do odd jobs until he made enough money to travel again. Right now he had fifteen hundred dollars to tide him over. It was as if his shame pushed him along, dragging him from city to town to small little burgs like Silver Creek. The shame he'd carried with him for a lifetime. Once a coward, always a coward, he said.

He recognized the look in the boy who had been with Jay this morning. They were tied by a common bond. He wondered who the kid was and what relationship he had to that vicious cowboy. Hell, it didn't matter, did it? He wasn't hanging around long enough to find out anything.

He never even went near a rodeo now. Once he had been at the top. A champion bull rider, belt buckle and all—years of belt buckles. But now he was nothing, and all he had to show for his time on the circuit were scars, painful memories and fear. He must never forget about the fear. How could he? It was always with him.

The vision of the black-and-white bull charging at him made his stomach queasy, and he pushed the image out of his head. He gripped the handlebars of the bike a little harder to quell the shaking of his hands. His hip began to throb.

He didn't want to think about the past or worry about the future. He lived for right now. Got through each day and each night in a never-ending succession.

He didn't think about the loneliness and the emptiness or the guilt. Not much. He didn't dare think about the talent he'd locked up inside himself since he was a small child. A talent that burned to be released, ached to be expressed. He didn't think about allowing himself to settle down in one place too long.

It would allow the shame and fear to catch up to him.

He'd spied the motel sign before he saw the building where Jennifer had said it would be. She'd also said it was clean in that soft, husky voice that made him think of black satin sheets. After a while, the motel, a nondescript elongated building beside the highway, came into view. It was the same as every other motel he'd ever seen, only this one was very well kept. Flowers lay in thick red, gold and purple riotous abundance. He had to admit it was the most appealing motel he'd ever seen.

A vacancy sign sat in the big picture window that could use a good cleaning. The dust from the road, he supposed. Just as he pulled in, a fresh-faced blonde came out with glass cleaner and flashed him a friendly grin as she proceeded to clean the window.

Corey parked the bike and ambled toward her, stretching the kinks out of his legs and back, rubbing absently at his left hip.

"Need a room, mister?"

"Yes, ma'am."

"It's Ellen," she said before giving the window another swipe. "I must clean this at least three times a day. The road dust makes a mockery out of my elbow grease."

He smiled briefly, liking the woman right away, then kept his expression somber. He didn't want to make friends. He didn't want to stay in one place.

"Well, come on in and we'll get you situated."

After he registered, he found his room, unlocked the door and pushed it open. "Not bad," he murmured as he stepped inside. Jennifer had been right. It was clean. So was the bathroom, which smelled faintly of ammonia. Big fluffy bath towels lay over bright silver racks, and he sighed at the anticipated pleasure of being clean.

He stripped down, eager to wash the dust of the road out of his skin and hair.

He'd been riding most of the night and a good part of the day. The nightmares had woken him the night before, and unable to go to sleep he left the crumpled grass of his camp and sought the peace of the open road on his Harley. His body still hummed from the vibrations of the powerful machine.

A while later, clean, with just a towel wrapped around his waist, his hair damp, he settled on the bed and tucked his hands behind his head. The soft scent of lilac tickled his nostrils and he smiled when he saw the freshly cut flowers on the nightstand. He closed his eyes, but sleep eluded him.

His thoughts turned to Jennifer Horn. The woman was in trouble. The man she had called Jay wasn't going to let up. Corey could tell bullies a mile away, and that guy was hell-bent on hurting Jennifer, maybe even seriously. A sense of uneasiness settled inside him and he swore softly.

He didn't want to care about the woman. Yet, to his astonishment, the rage he had felt at her possible injury flared up again, along with a fierce protectiveness he'd only felt for his mother and sister.

Damn. He couldn't seem to help himself. He was worried about her. Wondered who she had to protect her, where she lived, and what kind of trouble she was in.

Well, he couldn't help. Hell, he couldn't even help himself. How was he going to help her? By being there. You're stronger and bigger and you need someone, a faint voice he suspected was his conscience admonished him.

He couldn't fit anyone into his life. He was too busy trying to fit the pieces of his own life back together. Pieces that were almost smashed beyond recognition.

He thought back to the scene in the parking lot. Seeing a woman abused made him see red. He knew about battering. He knew what a woman looked like after a man's fist had connected with the soft flesh of her face. How split lips looked all swollen and bloody. When he'd stopped to ask the couple for directions, he thought they were arguing spouses until he'd gotten closer and seen the look on the man's face. Corey had been too little to help his mother, but, by God, he wasn't now and there was no way in hell he could have refrained from stepping in to stop that vicious bastard from hitting Jennifer.

He'd wanted to beat the man senseless, but he had resisted the urge, knowing instinctively the woman abhorred violence and would have been horrified if she'd caused it.

But the cowboy deserved it.

Thinking about Jennifer brought back the shock in her eyes when his hand had met hers, the way her soft lips had parted in surprise. His eyes had homed in on that sweet, enticing mouth. Don't think about her, he warned.

But it was easy to think about the woman. An easy excuse not to dwell on his failure or his shame. His pride had taken a damaging blow and most of the time he felt precarious, as though he were on the edge of a dark abyss losing his balance with no handhold in sight.

He had begun to unravel at the seams, slipping deeper and deeper into that black nothingness. The substance that was his spirit was leaking away like a bucket with a hole in it. Drip by precious drip it drained away until soon there would be only emptiness left. A gaping hole.

Rodeoing had been his freedom, and his ticket out of a brutal life. He had achieved the pinnacle of success and the high from riding bulls had been as addicting as a drug. Right now, though, he never again wanted to feel the surge of adrenaline that came from lowering himself onto the back of a huge Brahman. He never again wanted to experience the dizzying ride, the whirling, the bucking. Because all he remembered was the jarring impact, the searing pain and the terror of looking into two enraged black eyes and coming face-to-face with death.

He turned over abruptly, seeking sleep, and damn if the sheets didn't smell like fresh clean air and sunshine.

He closed his eyes, his thoughts drifting back to sweet, brave Jennifer Horn. He hoped she was all right. Maybe he would stay a couple of days and try to find out where she lived and make sure she was okay.

He didn't think about how dangerous that thought was as his mind closed down and sleep finally stole over him.

Chapter 2

Jennifer made it back to her truck, though she kept a keen eye out for Jay. She wouldn't put it past him to wait and then approach her once the outlaw had left.

Fitting the key into the ignition, she put the argument with Jay out of her mind.

She knew he wasn't upset with her for refusing to allow him to graze his cattle in one of her pastures. He was mad because she'd turned him down countless times. He was mad because she didn't go out with him.

Maybe dumping that beer over his head two nights ago at Jack's, the local watering hole, hadn't been such a good idea. But it had been so satisfying, and it had cooled him off considerably.

He had insisted that she dance with him. In fact, he had pulled her from her chair and dragged her out on the dance floor. She had been furious and had acted without thinking about the repercussions.

Jay considered himself a lady's man and his reputation

had been blackened and bruised by his actions. He must be taking an awful ribbing from his friends. She couldn't help getting satisfaction from that thought. Served him right.

Jay had a mean streak two miles wide and he was capable of rape. A shiver traveled down her spine at the thought.

There had been a rumor in town that Jay had raped a Comanche woman, yet the woman had never pressed charges. Jennifer had heard that she'd gotten a settlement. Gray Dove Garrison had made a "deal" with Jay to care for Tucker Garrison, the son she had conceived. In exchange, she wouldn't tell Jay's father about the rape.

It didn't surprise Jennifer that Jay agreed. He was so afraid of his father. A meaner man had never existed and Jay had learned at his knee. It was common knowledge that Robert Butler was an Indian-hater, and he would most likely cut Jay off without even a thought if he found out Jay had sullied himself with an "Indian," rape or not.

Her thoughts went back to Corey Rainwater—strong, fearless Corey. She rested her head against the steering wheel, suddenly feeling melancholy over a man who she would never get a chance to know. She couldn't pine for a guy she barely knew. Yet her thoughts stayed on him and she wished she could wipe that loneliness off his face and erase the pain in his eyes.

A longing surged up deep inside her. A longing so intense, so devastating that she almost felt swamped by it. She breathed deeply as it rolled over her in waves.

A pair of hot aqua eyes burned in her brain and the need intensified. "No. No damn way."

She clamped down the longing and stuffed it and the weakness that came with it into a closet in her mind and slammed the door.

She wasn't a fool. She knew what Jay and every other

yahoo within a ten-mile radius wanted: the Triple X, the land that came with it and her money. She had inherited one of the richest ranches around these parts when her mother and father had been killed in a tragic plane crash during their annual trip to Vegas. Her father had bred the best bucking bulls in the area. She still had standing contracts from rodeos all over the state and up north for rough stock. Her mother had also come from money, and at thirty-one Jennifer found herself quite well off doing work she enjoyed and raising a precocious thirteen-year-old daughter.

Yes, she thought, Jay was interested in her money and her land. She hadn't received so much male attention in years. After Sonny, she had made it quite clear she wasn't interested in a relationship with anyone, and they had left her pretty much alone. But now she was much too fat a pigeon for some of the lowlifes around here, and they were attracted to her like ticks to a hound.

Her hand still tingled from the outlaw's touch and dejectedly she wished Corey had accepted the dinner invitation. It had been fun to flirt with him. She'd forgotten how good it felt to be desired for herself, not her bankroll. When had her life gotten so lonely? Struggling against an overwhelming urge to cry, she clenched her fists and beat at the wheel. He's just passing through, she reminded herself.

She'd forgotten that thrilling rush when she'd been just a little bit reckless and just a little bit wild. But that was in the past. She had too much responsibility to let herself become morose over a tall, handsome stranger with painful secrets hidden in his eyes.

Well, this wasn't getting her errands done, she thought. She'd go to the bank first, then the feed store. She put the truck in gear and drove out of the parking lot.

And still her hand tingled.

* * *

Corey woke up from a nightmare, sitting bolt upright, his breathing harsh in the silent room, his hip throbbing in time to the hard beating of his heart. He always woke from these dreams with an aching hip. He looked at his watch. It was almost noon, and he hadn't eaten since last night. He should make his way over to the diner and get himself something to eat, he thought.

People looked up when he walked into the diner a half hour later. An old man sat on one of the orange vinyl stools at the bar, the overhead lights casting his face in a sickly hue. A young mother and her little girl talked quietly in a corner booth while they munched French fries. The little girl popped her fingers in her mouth every so often to lick off the ketchup she kept smearing all over her hands.

He smiled, and the sudden image of Marigold insinuated itself into his head. His sister had loved ketchup and French fries.

Taking his eyes off the child, he noticed the old man staring at him, a gleam of recognition in his eyes. Corey stared back impassively until the man looked away.

Most of the conversation in the diner had stopped, except for the mother and little girl's. The only sound was the coughing wheeze of the old air conditioner and the sizzle of hamburgers cooking on the grill. The air was heavy with the smell of grease and hot coffee. His stomach rumbled.

An old man and his blue-haired wife glanced his way. The woman leaned forward and whispered something to her husband. He could almost hear what she had to say. *Do they let them kind in here?*

Suddenly he felt so damn tired. Soul-weary, his mother would have said. The nap only seemed to have made the fatigue deeper, heavier, as if it had settled into his bones instead of relieving the mounting pressure. A pressure that was now pressing on the backs of his eyes. Finally he found an empty booth and wearily sat down.

"Can I help you, handsome?"

A young waitress in the typical light pink uniform with white apron approached the table. She snapped her gum and giggled. "You got some really purty eyes."

Unsmiling, he looked up at her and she retreated a step. She was probably only making conversation, but the compliment irritated him. He remembered how Jennifer's eyes had widened when she had seen his eyes, and the obvious admiration mirrored there had made him feel powerful.

"Can I get something for you, sir?" A new respect whispered in her voice and he glanced down at the menu, disgusted with himself. Now he was scaring young girls. What was next? Kicking dogs? He was in a black mood. He felt like hitting something. In his youth, when these moods came upon him, he'd look for a fight and God help the poor bastard who started with him.

The circuit had taught him always to sit facing the door, never to back down from a fight and always to look people straight in the eye. It had toughened him up, made a man out of him.

With the bull goring, something had changed. He didn't know what it was. He couldn't put his finger on it, and the anxiety churned in his gut. He felt restless all the time. And angry.

He thought he had put his anger to rest a long time ago, but lately it surfaced at odd intervals. He got so angry that he had to get on his bike and ride until the black rage passed.

"Coffee, black, and a steak sandwich."

"Do you—" she faltered when he looked up at her "—want fries?" She swallowed and her eyes widened. He realized he'd unnerved her so much she'd swallowed her gum.

"No." He softened his expression, but the young woman was so rattled she didn't notice.

He followed her with his eyes as she turned away and placed his order. As he shifted his gaze, he caught the eye of the old man sitting at the bar.

"I know you," the man said. "You're Corey Rainwater, best damn bull rider I ever did see.

"Saw the ride that won you the gold buckle last year. It was something to see."

Panic gripped him and squeezed. He didn't want to be recognized. He didn't want to hear the whispered voices saying, "Lost his nerve...almost killed by that bull... doesn't ride anymore...coward."

Abruptly he turned away and said icily, "I don't follow the circuit anymore, old man." The finality in his voice stopped whatever the man was going to say.

When his meal arrived, he ate, avoiding any more eye contact with the man or the waitress. When he finished, he paid for his meal and walked out.

A voice raised in anger made his head jerk up. He squinted against the blaze of the sun and wished he'd brought his sunglasses.

Wasn't that Jennifer Horn's husky voice he heard? When he spied her truck with the Triple X's on the side, he made his way across the street.

Jennifer was spitting mad. Jay had waylaid her at the feed store. Obviously he had guessed that this would be one of her stops and had planned to ambush her. Right now he had his hand around her wrist, his fingers digging into her flesh, squeezing so tightly she was sure he would break the bones.

Her lips still stung from his brutal kiss. She hoped his face was still throbbing from the slap she'd given him.

"Jay, let go!" Her voice was getting more frantic than angry, and in pain and desperation she brought her knee up. But he turned and the blow just caught the inside of his thick thigh. He laughed with malicious glee, the sound grating her nerve endings.

Just when she thought she would scream from the excruciating pain, his hold loosened and she looked down to see Jay in the dust. Only this time he was flat on his back. Her outlaw stood menacingly over him, his boot planted against Jay's chest, his thumbs hooked into a pair of worn denim blue jeans.

"Jackasses never learn," he said with such steel-edged derisive amusement she saw Jay stiffen. "But when you're dealing with dumb animals, it takes a few times before they understand what you want them to do." He shook his head in condemnation, causing his hair to swing around his shoulders. She was mesmerized as the silky mass slid over the soft material of his deep purple shirt. She wondered if the color would deepen the hue of his eyes.

Even though he had his back to her she could see the threat of violence in every line of his body. She could tell he wanted to beat Jay by the way he stood, his hip thrust out as some kind of challenge. A human-male call of the wild.

She wasn't worried about Jay, he deserved everything he got, but he was vindictive and he could cause a considerable ruckus for this green-eyed man who just wanted to be left alone. But twice now he'd risked his solitude to protect her.

She moved forward, placing the hand with the aching wrist against the steel of his bare forearm. It was a warm day and he'd rolled up the sleeves of his shirt. He was hatless and he'd shaved. It made him look more vulnerable and less unapproachable. Still an outlaw, though, with his firm jaw and the aura of danger that sparked around him.

His face was thunderous, his eyes a dark and stormy turquoise. The heat of his skin was like a shock coursing through her palm and up her arm. She wanted to caress his soft hair-roughened skin beneath her hand with a most unbelievable need. The tenseness of his body, taut like a strung bow, belied the lazy drawl of his voice.

"Mr. Rainwater," she said, "please don't. Just let him go."

Corey removed his boot and stood in a threatening gun-slinger stance, as if Jay were suddenly going to draw on him.

Jay cursed a vicious oath and scrambled to his feet, his wary eyes watching Corey with hatred.

Those angry eyes moved to her and a sudden chill of fear brushed down her spine. Clearly, she'd made a powerful enemy. "This discussion isn't over, Jennifer," he snapped, brushing the dust off his clothes.

"Just what is it you want from her?" Corey's voice was quietly cold and raised warning gooseflesh over her skin. The promise in his tone was a challenge she knew Jay wasn't ready to take on—at least, not alone. Corey's fore-arm tightened beneath her hand, his own hand drawing into a fist. She exerted a light pressure and he seemed to relax.

"I want her to pay my dry-cleaning bill," he whined.

Corey snorted in disgust. "What for?"

Jay's face turned sullen and his eyes darted to hers. "She poured a pitcher of beer over my best shirt two nights ago. I want retribution."

Corey slid a glance sideways, a smile flashing on his handsome face. "You did that, Jennifer?" His tone was so full of mockery that she laughed, knowing he was gibing Jay.

"I confess. I'm the guilty party," she replied with mock sheepishness.

His conspiratorial grin widened, and she found herself grinning back. He held her gaze longer than necessary and she floundered before the hot brilliance. Far back in his eyes hunger flickered like heat lightning. The shock of his hunger ran through her body, beating in time to her own. Abruptly he stopped being a stranger to her. The conspiracy and the possessive way he looked at her made him familiar and coveted. Jennifer's hand clenched around the warm skin of his forearm. She needed something to anchor herself right now.

"I'm appalled at you," he said in a mock-scolding voice. A shrewd teasing gleam twinkled in his hot eyes before he pulled his gaze away and fastened it on Jay.

"Your favorite shirt? That must have been awful for you. I can certainly see why you'd want to terrorize a woman, especially if your advances were unwanted." Corey reached into his pocket and pulled out a twenty-dollar bill while Jay called him the most filthy names. Corey stilled and his eyes narrowed with menace. "Watch your mouth, or I'll close it for you." He held out the bill. "Here. This should take care of your fancy clothes," he said with scathing force. When Jay reached for it, Corey dropped it to the ground.

Jay picked up the twenty, and as he rose, Corey leaped forward and with one smooth motion pivoted and slammed Jay up against the feed-store wall. "Don't go near her again, cowboy." His voice was deceptively mild, deceptively soft. Steel couldn't be harder.

Fear blossomed in Jay's eyes as he obviously realized that he was dealing with a very deadly, very protective man. In that same chilling voice, Corey continued, "If you're walking down the same street, you cross over to the other side. Got my drift? If you don't, you'll have me to answer to."

A strangled yes came out of Jay's tight sullen mouth. Corey let him go and he backed up, rubbing his beefy neck. "I'm not afraid of you," he said with false bravado, his eyes telling the real story.

Corey didn't even acknowledge that Jay spoke. Very deliberately he turned his back. The motion was as good as a slap in the face.

With his back to Jay, Corey didn't see the vindictive, hateful look that crossed Jay's face before he left, but Jennifer did and she was suddenly afraid for Corey. A thin shiver of warning trailed down her spine.

"This is becoming a habit with you," she said while she tried to massage some feeling back into her hand.

"I could say the same thing for you, darlin'. It looks like you do have more than one life, huh?"

He moved the hand that was rubbing her wrist and swore softly when he saw the beginning of a bruise. Very gently his fingers caressed the sensitive flesh and goose bumps shivered over her skin. He continued to rub her injury, a distant look on his face.

"You should have let me teach him a lesson he wouldn't soon forget," he said, his voice thick.

"It wouldn't have made me feel any better," she countered as she tried to slip her wrist out of his big capable hands. But he gently held on, his thumb moving over the palm of her hand with smooth distracted strokes.

"I would have felt a lot better," he murmured as if in a daze. He brought the abused flesh close to his mouth.

The warmth of his breath had her stomach doing tiny flips. Tenderly he kissed the red skin, his hand sliding down her arm, around her back as he urged her closer to him. "Better?" he questioned, the concern in his eyes warming her. "He didn't hurt you anywhere else, did he?"

It didn't take much urging from him to get her closer. He'd showered and smelled of soap and shampoo and a tantalizingly delicious aroma that was completely his own. Jennifer couldn't answer. The tenderness in his eyes jammed the words in her throat, a tenderness and aching loneliness that left her emotions raw. Then it happened. The deep need to hold this man in her arms stole over her. Hold him tight and rock him until the wrenching pain in his eyes went away and never came back. Oh, how she wished for that right. The right to put her arms around him.

He knew what it was like to be abused.

With that realization, she lost another little piece of her heart to this man she'd met only hours before. "No," she said softly.

He moved his head closer, his eyes focused on her mouth. "Are you sure?" His voice thickened with a longing that tore at her heartstrings. He gave her ample time to evade him if she wanted to.

"My mouth." Her answer was just a puff of air as his lips dropped to hers. His kiss was gentle warmth moving over her mouth, a sweet insistent pressure that she couldn't resist.

She was certain that he never meant to deepen the kiss, he'd only meant to brush her mouth. But unable to stop herself, her mouth softened beneath his seeking lips, broadcasting to him loud and clear her surrender, her invitation.

With a soft moan she tangled her fingers in his long silky hair, searching for the sensitive nape of his neck.

He moaned softly into her mouth. How could she know that he loved being touched there? A shiver of pure pleasure jolted along his nerve endings.

His tongue touched the corner of her mouth and she parted her lips, giving him access to such sweetness he thought his knees would buckle.

Their tongues entwined, tasting each other with a fierce need that left them both weak.

He drew her closer, his arms closing around her while he kissed her with a deep hunger that was surprising in its immediate force. One hand came up to cup the back of her head, his mouth moving frantically over hers. His body shifted to accommodate her soft curves until she was as close to him as two bodies could get without actually joining. It was an intimate kiss, a kiss of two souls who had long since been apart and were finally discovering one another again.

With a small sound she clung to him, unnerved by his desire and the silky demands of his tongue, reacting to him as she had never reacted to any man. Just as she knew she would. The intimacy of the kiss was stunning in relation to the short time she had known him. She couldn't help wanting more.

When his mouth moved from hers, she was weak in body and reason, barely able to stay upright. My God, the man could kiss the socks off her. She couldn't seem to think this close to him.

There was just this deep abiding fire that he had lit inside her with that toe-curling kiss, so deep that she felt she had just been taught by a master. She was feeling things now for which she had no labels. A powerful wanting that shocked her, the implications frightening, the impact of such *recklessness* terrifying to a woman who didn't want to lose control of the wild, reckless nature she held rigidly in check. Especially to a loner. A man who would break her heart. A man who was as elusive as the wind.

His voice was husky, almost bereft. "Does this mean that you now owe me two home-cooked meals?"

He caught her off guard, but only for a moment. She had expected him to apologize for kissing her, but she should have known better. Outlaws never apologized. Her smile was pure mischief. "How about a home-cooked meal with an apple pie thrown in?"

His eyes rolled and he smacked his lips. "Offer me a scoop of vanilla ice cream on that pie and you have yourself a deal and a friend for life."

She didn't want to be his friend. He slowly let go of her and she felt suddenly disconnected as he stepped back. She shivered and wrapped her arms around herself.

Once again the distance was there in his eyes, and maybe a flash of regret. Quickly she gave him directions to her home and he promised to be there at seven sharp.

"I do have to warn you," she said with a little lurch in her stomach. "I have a mildly precocious thirteen-year-old daughter."

The only indication of surprise he gave was the lifting of his eyebrows. He cocked his hip and raked his hand through his hair in such a knee-melting sexy motion that Jennifer couldn't concentrate on his words.

"You don't look old enough to have a thirteen-year-old daughter, but I'll look forward to meeting her."

He walked away then and left her with the lingering taste of him on her lips and his hunger burning in her blood.

Chapter 3

All the way over to Jennifer Horn's ranch, Corey cursed himself for the fool he was. Hadn't he just told himself this morning in no uncertain terms that he couldn't get involved with her? Then all it had taken was that two-bit bully to threaten her and he turned into a knight in shining armor. Ha, more like a knight in tarnished armor. This afternoon, he'd only meant to brush her lips, but her response was so hot, so sweet he hadn't been able to pull away. A knight who couldn't control his own desire. Some hero he made.

But Jennifer hadn't seemed to notice. She had looked up at him with such wonder in her eyes. He'd been stupid, giving her ideas when he had nothing to give and was losing himself daily.

He still felt the shock of his family's death. He remembered when the doctor had told him that his father had passed out in a drunken stupor with a lighted cigarette in his hand and had torched the whole house. He had to hear that his mother and sister hadn't made it out alive.

Something had died inside him that day, something that had been dying since he was old enough to understand that other families weren't like his.

Other fathers didn't beat their sons. Other fathers took their sons fishing, canoeing, hiking and riding. Other mothers didn't have to use makeup to cover bruises. Other mothers didn't have to come up with excuses like, "Oh, he fell down while he was playing. You know how kids are."

God, he hated his father. Michael Rainwater was full-blooded Apache. He'd left the reservation to pursue his amazing talent as an artist. Then when Corey was three, his father had been beaten up by some Anglos who decided to do some Indian bashing. During the beating, they had stepped on his father's hands and crushed them, crippled them, usable only to bruise and batter his family. Michael Rainwater had started to drink. He blamed everything on the Anglos after that. The money had stopped coming in, and his father sunk deeper and deeper into depression.

Corey drew a deep, long breath. He pulled off the highway at the entrance to the Triple X. The name of the ranch appeared on a beautiful wrought-iron sign with fine metal curlicues. Three X's in bold red letters were outlined in gold.

He hit the brakes on his bike, then dropped his feet to the road's surface to support himself and sat idling at the entrance. The ranch screamed money and his insides knotted.

He should turn around and get the hell out of here before he cared too much about this woman and her daughter. A thirteen-year-old. His sister's age. Hell, Jennifer must have had her when she was a child herself. He wondered where Jennifer's husband was. No man who had married such a beautiful, smart woman would ever be fool enough to leave her. He must be dead. That was the only way he'd want to leave a woman like Jennifer. Not that he was going to get involved with her, because he wasn't. He'd only come to let her repay him.

He had almost made up his mind to turn his bike around and leave. After all, it would be best for both of them. His protective instinct could go to hell. He couldn't be a hero. Didn't heroes succeed? Didn't heroes always save the day?

He'd eat dinner, he would make polite conversation and, damn it, then he would go.

Why did this woman have to be so alluring? He could feel the tug even from this distance. He wanted to gun the engine and go hurtling up that road and let her feed him and get his mind off his problems for one night. He couldn't remember the last time he'd had a home-cooked meal, with apple pie, no less.

He looked over his shoulder with a feeling of unexplainable uneasiness, as if something was following him. What had he expected to see? The ghosts of his mother and sister pleading with him to help? Well, he had tried to help. He had tried to get his mother to leave. Time and time again. He had proven he was no hero.

Hell. He decided to go forward because he wanted to see Jennifer again. Just remembering that kiss was enough to make his body hum. He wanted to kiss her again and never stop.

He was going crazy. Well, he might as well go crazy and get it over with.

"So, Mom. Is this guy your boyfriend?"

"No, Ellie. He's just someone I met in town who chased off Jay Butler after he was bad-mouthing me." Jennifer turned the heat down on the chicken and dumplings.

Eleanor Jean Horn wrinkled her nose. "You mean Tucker's dad who keeps pinching my cheek like I was a piece of ripe fruit?"

"Yes, honey. That's the guy." She chuckled. "You have such a way with words."

"Why was he bad-mouthing you, Mom?" Ellie's words got fainter as she exited the kitchen to set the dining-room table. A moment later, she came back into the kitchen to pick up the silverware.

"Let's say that I wasn't very nice to him a few nights ago." Jennifer turned from the stove and leaned back against the counter.

"Mom, you're always telling me I shouldn't lose my temper. Did you lose yours?"

"I'm afraid so, dear. I tried to apologize, but the damage had been done by then." Jennifer smiled faintly at the chiding in her daughter's voice.

"So he likes you and you like him?"

"Who, dear? Jay?"

"No. This guy who's coming to dinner. This guy you dressed up for and made apple pie. I hope he's worth all this effort," Ellie said matter-of-factly.

"Ellie, I want you to be polite." She smoothed down the emerald green silk blouse and matching silk pants. "Do you think it's too much?"

"What, your clothes?"

"Yes, my clothes," Jennifer said, trying not to sound anxious and failing miserably. She felt nervous about her appearance. She hadn't thought about her image this morning when she'd left. She'd been thinking about groceries, feed for her stock and her ranch.

"You look beautiful, Mom. What does he look like?"

"Dangerous," was Jennifer's immediate answer. "He looks like an outlaw."

There was a scratching at the door and Ellie walked over

and opened it. In trotted Two Tone, a miniature Vietnamese potbellied pig. A black-and-white runt of the litter that followed Ellie around like a dog.

At first Jennifer hadn't allowed him in the house until she realized that he could be housebroken. In fact, he liked to be clean. He loved taking baths, grunting with pleasure each time Ellie bathed him. The two of them were inseparable. He even slept with Ellie.

"Hi, Two Tone, are you hungry, little guy?" Ellie said, bending down to pet his head and scratch him under the chin. The little pig closed his eyes and grunted in pure pleasure.

"He's always hungry, honey." Jennifer smiled as she too bent down and patted his bristly head.

As she rose, Jennifer heard the roar of a powerful engine and her heart started fluttering. Until she heard the motorcycle, she wasn't sure he was coming.

All afternoon she'd thought about that kiss he'd given her. He hadn't been consoling her, although it was what he had meant to do, she was sure. Things just got out of hand. He'd been kissing her as a man kisses a woman and doing a very thorough job of it, if the sudden weakness that was traveling through her was any indication.

It was true, she had been reckless in her youth and her father had been right when he warned her that she was heading for trouble. But ever since her disastrous relationship with Sonny, she hadn't done anything even remotely rash. She had gone to college and studied animal husbandry and small-business management so that when the time came she could take over for her father—something he had always wished for but never expected would happen until his wayward daughter grew up. But she had never expected both her parents to die so tragically in the plane crash last year.

She grew up fast going through a pregnancy with no husband to help her. She went through the first year of Ellie's life in constant fear that something would happen to her or that she would do something wrong. She went through that first year falling out of love with Sonny and learning to despise him for his infidelity. It wasn't until later on that she learned the key word was *infidelities*.

The pain of Sonny's cheating passed, but the mistrust of men remained, especially rodeo riders.

So why had she invited one to dinner?

She was a seasoned mother now. She had Ellie to worry about, but she couldn't deny that she was lonely, devastatingly lonely. She had never been the type of woman to sleep around. So, after Sonny had taken her virginity and fathered a daughter, she had never been with another man.

"*Mother,* he rides a motorcycle!" Ellie's normal tone of voice was replaced with the censuring tone of an old woman's, interrupting Jennifer's thoughts.

"Don't mother me, Ellie. I told you, he's just a friend."

Ellie was at the window unabashedly trying to get a glimpse of the first man her mother had ever invited to dinner. "Oh, my God, Mother. He has long hair."

"Ellie, will you stop acting like your grandmother and finish setting the table."

"Okay, but I have one more comment."

Jennifer turned away from the stove in exasperation. "What?"

"He's one gorgeous piece of beefcake!"

"Ellie!"

"That's what my friend Mary Lou calls good-looking guys." She gave her mother her most innocent smile and peeked at Corey Rainwater again.

"Well, you're not Mary Lou, and for heaven's sake don't say that to him. And stop peeking at him as if he was some kind of freak, Ellie.'' Jennifer crossed the room and grabbed the curtains out of Ellie's hands, closing them with a snap. She turned to Ellie and in the middle of smoothing her daughter's hair back, she noted how much she'd changed. When had it happened? She wasn't a baby anymore, and she was certainly old enough to know about attraction between a man and a woman. God, she would do her best to steer Ellie away from the mistakes she'd made at her age.

''Don't embarrass me,'' Jennifer said in a firm voice, then softened her words by tugging on one of Ellie's auburn braids.

Ellie followed her mother over to the counter and picked up the glasses, then bumped her mother's hip. ''Okay, but I want a raise in my allowance.''

Before Jennifer could respond, a knock sounded at the door. With a waggle of her eyebrows, Ellie disappeared into the dining room.

''Scoot, Two Tone.'' Jennifer used her foot to usher the black-and-white pig from the door with affection. He grunted and ran across the floor.

Jennifer pulled open the door and a wave of heat rose from deep inside her, swamping her with sensations. She remembered how soft his hair had been on the nape of his neck, how his mouth had felt moving over hers and the way he filled out his jeans.

He still wore the hat and now was wearing the mackintosh, but it had been brushed clean of all the dust. He'd changed his boots for a pair of soft moccasins that reached his knees and were beautifully beaded.

He reached up and removed his hat. ''Having second thoughts about dinner, or do I need to wipe my feet?'' His tone was filled with teasing amusement and curled around her.

Heat rose in her face and she moved backward, both because of her wicked, unladylike thoughts and because he'd caught her staring.

"No, no second thoughts," she murmured. "Come in."

Ellie entered from the dining room and gave her mother that mischievous grin that Jennifer knew so well. "So, Mom, how about that raise?"

Jennifer looked up to the ceiling for guidance. So, this is my parents' revenge, getting a daughter as impish as I was, she said to herself. She faced Ellie and pierced her with that don't-mess-with-me-I'm-the-mother look. "It's going to be pretty hard to spend ill-gotten gains when you're grounded. We'll talk about it after dinner," Jennifer said with a warning in her voice for added measure.

She gestured to Corey and said, "Ellie, this is Corey Rainwater."

Jennifer watched her daughter size up Corey. "Rainwater," Ellie mused aloud. "You an Indian or something?"

As if she realized she'd been rude, Ellie's vibrant eyes widened and she averted her gaze from the stranger's amused expression.

"Ellie, mind your manners," Jennifer scolded.

"That's okay." Corey smiled and charmed them both. "I'm part Apache."

"Wow! Those are great boots! Did you make them?" Ellie moved closer into the room, her eyes on the beautiful moccasins.

"No, my grandmother was good at working leather, and my little...sister beaded them," he responded, his voice subdued.

"So what kind of motorcycle do you have? I could hear it coming up the driveway but I couldn't see it." Ellie went to the window again and looked out.

"A Harley."

"Wow, cool! Wait until I tell Mary Lou! Could you give me a—"

"Ellie, let the man get his coat off, will you?" Jennifer interrupted with a laugh. "She's not used to strangers coming to dinner," she explained to Corey.

Jennifer knew that Ellie's innate curiosity had led her from one question to another and she hadn't noticed the painful catch in his voice when he'd mentioned his little sister.

But Jennifer had. His distance was back and she could almost believe that the passionate kiss they had shared had never happened, if it wasn't for the way he looked at her.

Get a grip, Jennifer. It's for the best. Tomorrow he will be gone. She didn't want to think about how the loneliness would swell around her again. She'd enjoy his company tonight and in the morning get back to her routine of running her ranch and finding a foreman. She'd have to go down to the paper and get them to run that ad again.

"Here, let me take your hat and coat," she said. He handed his hat to her. The band was still warm from his skin. The coat followed. "Can I get you something to drink? I have beer or iced tea."

"A beer will be fine," he replied, his eyes traveling slowly over her face.

That sadness was still with him, she noted, and it seemed to intensify every time he looked at Ellie. Jennifer went to the refrigerator and got him a beer from the six-pack she had bought today with the other groceries. She set it down in front of him and he popped the lid and took a drink.

"So," Ellie began, glancing at her mother anxiously, "can I have a ride on your bike sometime?"

"I don't think so, Ellie. I'll be leaving tomorrow." The disappointment he saw in the child's eyes, eyes so like her mother's, piercing green and filled with a burning intelligence and the innate straightforward curiosity of the young, bothered him.

"Then I suppose you'll have to give me one tonight," Ellie stated firmly. Then she gave him the cutest, most mischievous smile that had him responding with a slow smile of his own. A kindred spirit in a small child? He would have never guessed.

Hell, it would be too easy to let himself slip into this little family, into that woman who chuckled and turned away. But he couldn't because of the dark fear that lurked in his subconscious.

He smiled a very wicked grin and watched the amusement filter out of Jennifer's eyes at his next words. "Only if your Mom agrees to a ride, too." The amusement in Jennifer's eyes was replaced with a longing, a deep hunger that lasted for a split second. It was enough to twist his insides, nevertheless.

"Will you, Mom?" Ellie said with a soft wheedling tone.

Corey could easily see what a monumental task Jennifer had in bringing up this child alone. Once again he thought about Ellie's father and wondered at his absence. Hell, it was none of his damn business. She wore no ring on her finger, but these days that meant absolutely nothing.

"Yeah, come on, Mom," he said, using the same soft wheedling inflection.

Jennifer took a deep breath and looked at him. "As long as it's after dinner."

"What's your favorite subject?" he asked Ellie, her eyes so intent on him it was almost unnerving.

"Lunch. What's yours?" she quipped.

"I'm not in school anymore."

"What? Does it actually end?" Her voice rose in mock surprise.

He looked at Jennifer with upraised eyebrows. "Precocious was putting it mildly."

Ellie leaned forward and cocked her head. "You do look a little bit dangerous. I think it's the five o'clock shadow."

The spoon Jennifer had been stirring the chicken and dumplings with dropped from her suddenly nerveless hand. The loud clattering broke the sudden pregnant silence. She whirled, her hands flying to her hips. "Ellie!" An embarrassed flush swept over Jennifer's face and she could feel the heat of it travel right to the roots of her hair.

Ellie had the intelligence to look abashed and kept her mouth closed.

Smart girl, Corey thought.

Though he would like to thank Ellie for riling her mother up. Jennifer looked beautiful angry. Her eyes flashed and her blush was sweet, unassuming. He liked that. He was beginning to like her and her daughter a lot. He could see the apology on her lips, but he beat her to the punch. "Dangerous good or dangerous bad?"

The husky way he said it had Jennifer's face flaming. "Ellie, please take Two Tone outside and feed him and then finish setting the table."

"Yes, Mother," she said with a world-weary sigh, and rolled her eyes.

"Does 'grounded for the rest of your life' mean anything to you, miss?" Jennifer said in her best mother's voice.

Ellie escaped like a scampering fox being chased by a hound. But before she disappeared into the dining room, she winked at Corey and he couldn't suppress a chuckle. He might as well admit it to himself. He was thoroughly charmed.

Jennifer let her hands fall in exasperation. She walked over to the table and sat down in the chair that Ellie had just vacated. "You see what I'm up against?"

"Don't try to weasel out of an answer by changing the subject, Jennifer."

"Caught that, huh?" He was enjoying himself, she thought suddenly and looked away. "You look like an outlaw."

"So is that good or bad?" he persisted, his dark eyebrows rising.

"Like Ellie said, I think it's the five o'clock shadow."

He rubbed his fingers over the stubble on his face. "You don't like it?"

"No, it's very sexy," she said as reassurance, then clamped her hand over her mouth. Corey smiled, then leaned back in the chair.

"I guess that means dangerous good. It's okay, darlin'. I think you're sexy, too." He leaned forward.

Jennifer had to stop this conversation right now. With a flash of acknowledgment in her eyes for his teasing, she said abruptly, "It's time to eat."

"Coward."

That was okay. She'd be a coward, because he not only looked dangerously desperate but he was dangerous, and she hadn't realized just how desperate she'd become in a few short hours. Desperation for something that couldn't happen. Desperation for a man who couldn't stay.

He exuded a raw sexuality that she would notice even in a crowded, smoky, noisy bar. His flirting would be so easy to reciprocate. "No," she finally replied. "Just smart." She couldn't encourage him. "You're the one leaving, after all." She smiled to lessen the sting of her words.

The barb struck home and Corey sobered. "Yeah, right. *Smart* is the watchword."

She could feel his eyes on her as she dished out the chicken and dumplings, and she quickly changed the subject. "I hope you're hungry. I think I made enough for an army." Turning with the serving dish, she met those hot, thick-lashed eyes and her breath got trapped in her lungs.

He got up quickly and took the bowl out of her hands. Their fingers brushed and Jennifer quickly pulled her hands away. "I'll get the vegetables," she said.

He disappeared into the dining room. His voice drifted out to her as he conversed with Ellie. A fluttering weakness washed through her, draining her will away. She could probably entice him to stay, if only for a short time. Tears pricked the back of her eyes. Why him? Why couldn't it have been someone stable, someone safe?

Realizing she was standing in the middle of the kitchen floor holding two steaming bowls of vegetables, she made her body heel. Taking two deep shuddering breaths to calm herself, she proceeded into the dining room.

"I'm not that fast, but I'm working on it," Ellie was saying.

"Barrel racing is more than just speed, Ellie. It's knowing how to read your horse, how to maneuver, how to handle the pressure."

Jennifer was surprised at the serious tone Corey used. Warmth curled around her heart to know that he was interested in her daughter's passion. "Don't let her get you going on barrel racing. She'll never let you alone."

"Oh, Mom," Ellie said, wrinkling her pert little nose.

"Don't 'Oh Mom' me." Jennifer set the bowls down on the table. Suddenly Corey was there pulling out her chair for her. Jennifer's amazement showed on her face.

"So what do you think of my mom? Want to date her?" Ellie asked the question as if she were asking him if it was raining.

"Ellie!" She looked over her shoulder and met Corey's peacock-green eyes. Her face flushed to the roots of her hair.

"Ellie, a man would have to be a fool not to want to date your mom. And I'm no fool. But I don't think I'm your mom's type."

Jennifer couldn't speak she was so embarrassed.

"Sit down, Jennifer, or the food will get cold," he said with amusement so close to her ear his warm breath feathered the sensitive shell, raising goose bumps on her flesh. Jennifer plopped into the chair. As he scooted the chair forward, he whispered in her ear so softly that Ellie couldn't hear, "You look beautiful tonight, Jennifer." His hand brushed her shoulder before he walked back around the table and sat down.

"He held my chair too, Mom. Isn't that nice?"

"It's surprising, that's for sure." Her voice came out hoarse and she cleared her throat before going on. "I didn't think there were any gentlemen left in the world."

He looked up from dishing out his chicken and dumplings. "It's not every day that a gentleman meets ladies worthy of gentlemanly conduct."

His hot, possessive eyes held hers. The look made her insides turn to honey and her pulse stuttered a beat. It was not a gentlemanly look at all.

Jennifer stared down at her plate and concentrated on the white china. Dear God, it would almost be worth a one-night stand to explore what this man had to offer.

Passion, a little reckless voice whispered. Real live honest-to-God passion. But she wasn't a reckless woman anymore. Somehow she'd lost that verve for life somewhere through the years.

Jennifer remained relatively quiet most of the meal and watched her daughter interact with Corey. Ellie, for all her mischievousness, was not that comfortable around men she didn't know, yet she took to arguing with Corey about the best way to maneuver a horse around barrels as though he was a longtime friend. She laughed with him and teased him and he teased her right back.

Jennifer felt vulnerable for the first time in thirteen years and it frightened her. She didn't know if it was good or bad, but she wouldn't get the chance to find out. She had to accept that he was leaving right after this meal and she would never see him again.

That thought made her want to cry. She should have been smart in town and never invited him. Then she wouldn't have to live with the memory of his loneliness and the knowledge that this little dinner had affected him so much. She still remembered his reaction when she had invited him.

Yet she still got angry because she wanted something that wasn't possible.

Corey turned his attention to Jennifer when Ellie excused herself to go to the bathroom. "You're pretty quiet, Jennifer. Don't you have any questions of your own?"

Jennifer shrugged and toyed with the pie left on her plate. "It seems moot to ask you about anything when you're leaving town." She knew she sounded sullen and petulant and she shifted in her chair hating this feeling inside her.

"You knew I was just passing through, Jenny. I told you, so."

His voice was apologetic and somehow wistful, and she felt shame for her bad behavior. "I'm sorry. It was mean-spirited of me to make that comment. You're a guest and I'm not a very good hostess."

He got up from his chair and went to the window. "You're a fine hostess. I understand exactly where you're coming from, darlin'. Believe me, if I—" He cut off his words as Ellie came back into the room.

"Corey, are you a rodeo rider?" Ellie asked abruptly.

Corey turned from the window at the sudden suspicion

in Ellie's voice as if she'd just discovered something that she hadn't realized before. "I was. I'm not anymore." He was surprised at the bitterness in his voice. He noticed how Ellie seemed a little rigid and wary of him and, to his utter surprise, it hurt.

Ellie glanced at her mother and they both seemed to knot up as if his presence in the room had been somehow offensive.

Damn. To diffuse the tension, he moved from the window and grabbed Ellie's hand. "How about that ride I promised you?"

Ellie looked at her mother, her eyes bruised with the kind of pain that Corey knew so damn well. He sucked in his breath, suddenly wanting to take the little girl in his arms and show her that the world wasn't as cruel and disappointing as her look suggested. He closed his eyes against the rush of memories. His throat constricted. Her father had left her, he realized now. She hadn't just lost him to death. She had never known him, and the sudden burst of pain and sympathy settled in his chest like a time bomb ready to go off later, when he had time for the rage and hopelessness.

At times he wished he'd never known his father.

Jennifer watched Corey's face and wondered all over again if he had been hurt and by whom. She ached because it seemed apparent that not one person in this world had ever shown him kindness. She wanted to be that person. Oh God, if only things could be different.

She shook herself out of her introspection. "That sounds great. Doesn't it, honey?"

Jennifer's too-bright voice had Ellie smiling. "Yeah, let's boogie." Ellie tightened her hand in Corey's.

A few minutes later, Jennifer stood in the driveway watching Corey carefully maneuver the bike so as not to pose a danger to her daughter. Her emotions were raw and unpredictable since this man had stepped into her life this morning.

To be so attracted to a man who was everything she vowed she would never get involved with again was daunting. Yet she couldn't seem to help herself. Her body reacted every time she saw him. And when he got close to her, he was like a magnet and she was the crazily spinning compass wheel.

Trying to will away the thick knot in her throat, she put a smile on her face as they roared from the driveway. Minutes later they returned.

"Your turn, Mom," Ellie said, getting off the bike and going to sit down on the stairs to the kitchen.

Corey waited. She could feel his presence in the pores of her skin, so keen was her awareness. She thought about how close she would have to get to him on that machine and almost made an excuse.

But that wild, reckless part of her that had been her ruler when she was a teen resurged and she was suddenly caught in its devilish grip. Before she could change her mind, she settled on the bike.

"Put your arms around my waist and scoot forward more." Jennifer swallowed at the husky tint to his voice and did as he instructed. Desire grew warm and heavy in her stomach as she snuggled up against his backside, her thighs running along his.

"Tighten your legs, darlin'." His voice was now thicker and insistent.

This was how he would sound when he was making love, she thought. His voice soft and unwavering. She hesitated, then did as he asked. She felt the tautness in his back as she allowed her body to mold to his. Oh God, she thought suddenly, this was a bad idea.

The motorcycle flared to life and surged forward. The velvet night surrounded her, and the roar of the engine thrummed through her with powerful vibrations, charging her blood. She felt like a butterfly being released from its cocoon. A surge of adrenaline made her laugh out loud as the wind whipped his hair against her face. The sensation stung, but was welcome. It seemed that after thirteen years of numbness she was finally beginning to feel. The hot imprint of his powerful male body beneath her breasts was as heady as wine and she had never felt more alive then she did now.

She relished the feel of being close to a man again. It had been so long, so very long. She cursed,the feeling, as well. It reminded her that she was a woman with needs. Needs denied for a long time.

This ride brought back memories of Billy Joe Williams and that wild ride after the prom. Even dressed in a floor-length skirt, she had been more than willing to drive up to Sunset Meadow and neck with him. She'd hiked up her dress and tucked it around her legs and taken off with him on his motorcycle.

Her father had grounded her for a week. He was furious when she came home at three o'clock in the morning, when her curfew had been midnight.

She had tried to explain to her father how she felt. Wild, free, untamed, as if the world were her oyster. Her father hadn't understood. No one but bad boys understood how she felt.

She hadn't given Billy Joe anything that night except her lips. She had saved her virginity for her husband. That thought brought back memories of her crazy attraction to Sonny Braxton.

The summer she had been seventeen the rodeo had come to town and everyone was so excited. Everyone including her. She had gone down to check things out and had fallen head over heels in love with a brash, brave bronc rider named Sonny.

He was at the top then, full of his oats and no boy. He'd taken one look at her and easily wooed her into marriage, then his bed, and finally impregnated her with Ellie.

Six months pregnant and just barely eighteen, Jennifer had walked into their trailer and found him in bed with a trick rider. She had gone home to her parents, had the baby alone and then gone to college.

She'd never seen nor heard from Sonny again.

It had been difficult and painful. And now this man in front of her was from the rodeo, too. Well, she'd learned her lesson, and she would not be seduced by the power of a pair of turquoise eyes. She stiffened and yelled in his ear, "Enough."

Jennifer's nearness made his whole body ache. The feel of her against his back was like heaven and hell. He could feel the softness of her breasts, was acutely aware of her arms around his waist, was branded where her thighs joined his.

When he felt her stiffen, he realized that the ride was over and headed back to the house. A sense of helplessness stole over him. How could he ask her to live with his fear? The constant unrelenting fear that underlay his very actions. His life was defined by that fear. How could he change the path of his life now? How could he become the man she needed and wanted? The simple answer was he couldn't.

Back at the house, they went into the dining room and talked about benign things. Politics, the weather, the ranch—anything personal was avoided. In the midst of the conversation, Ellie dropped off to sleep.

Corey looked at his watch and Jennifer felt a flutter of

panic, realizing he was going to suggest that it was time that he leave.

"It's midnight, Jennifer. I should go." He glanced at Ellie, his face softening. "Want me to take her up for you?"

"Yes. Thanks. She's getting too big for me to carry her." She pushed back her chair and gently smoothed her fingers through Ellie's bangs.

Corey's body tightened. What he would give for her to touch him like that with that look on her face. He rose from his chair and gathered the child in his arms. Her weight was nothing, her body soft in sleep. With a murmur, Ellie turned toward him and slipped her arms around his neck. Emotion tightened his throat and chest. A powerful longing for a life he had denied himself a long time ago surged up in him with a fierceness that had him breathless.

Jennifer led the way and he watched the elegant way she moved, the soft sway of her hips as she climbed the stairs. Corey got a glimpse of the beautiful house decorated in tasteful southwestern designs. Colorful Navajo rugs covered the hardwood floors, and dun-colored pottery adorned oak tables.

Ellie's room was typical for a girl her age. A bedspread decorated with horses lay on a canopy bed; matching curtains hung at the windows. He laid her down on the bed where Jennifer had pulled the top blankets away. She came around him and pulled off Ellie's boots and covered her.

He watched her fuss over her child, removing the elastics from her braids and unplaiting her hair, loosening the shirt the girl wore and tucking the blankets around her. The tightness in his chest changed to an ache so powerful he had to turn away. He made his way back through the house, gathered up his hat and coat, then exited the house, unable to bear seeing what he could never have.

He would leave as he promised himself he would. All alone, he could still feel Ellie's slight body in his arms. Damn, what would it be like to hold a child of his own? What would it be like to have a life he created call him Daddy and look at him with eyes full of love? The thought twisted his gut with pain. He would never know. He would never father a child.

He sensed Jennifer's presence even before she touched his arm. Suddenly there was light and heat, and he jumped from the sizzling contact. She must have felt it, too, because she backed up slightly as if he were some kind of wild animal she must be wary of. And maybe he was.

Chapter 4

He turned around and she gasped audibly. Hunger, heat and loneliness stared back at her. She recalled his hot seeking mouth, so soft and demanding, and she remembered her response. Just as hot, just as demanding. Huskily, his voice full of need, he said, "Darlin', come here."

Panic clutched her heart. If it was a battle of wills then she had an uncomfortable feeling she would lose. He could crook that little finger at her and she would melt into a marshmallow. She wanted to run, she could feel the need to flee inside her. But when his face came into the light, she couldn't. His eyes glowed a pure aching turquoise so full of loneliness and need she felt as if she could cry. She took a step forward and he made no move. None whatsoever. He was so still he could have been a statue. She took another, and when she was close enough to him, she stopped.

Very slowly, as if he knew she was frightened, he reached out and pulled her close against the lean hard length of him. Jennifer began to tremble, and she wanted so desperately for this man to be hers. That thought scared her down to her toes.

His eyes gazed deeply into hers as if he was searching desperately for something there. Something that his life depended on. She could feel the rapid rise and fall of his chest, her breasts crushed against him.

She thought he would kiss her. She was so sure that what he wanted was her body. But instead of taking her mouth in the hungry way he had this morning, he just moaned softly and laid his forehead against her shoulder.

Her chest filled and burned. This tenderness was unexpected. It was easy to say no when she believed that he wanted something physical. The way he held her spoke more clearly than his words could.

For a full minute he held her, just held her in the soft hushed night. It seemed as if the bugs were awed by his magic, for even the chirping grew silent. As awed as she was by his heartbreaking charm. It felt so good to be cradled in his arms, so warm and safe. He smelled so good. So musky, so male.

Softly, almost a whisper of sound against her ear, he said, "Can I touch your hair?"

"M-my hair?"

"Yes, darlin'," he said patiently. "I've wanted to from the moment I saw you."

"Why?"

"It's like fire in the sun and so silky-looking. May I?"

"Oh, God," she whispered on a breath of air. Not meaning to say yes out loud, she did, anyway. "Yes."

Gently he reached up and threaded his fingers through her hair, letting it flow through his hands like cascading streams of burnished liquid.

"Where the hell is your husband?" he asked suddenly,

harshly. He leaned closer, breathing deeply of her scent, and placed soft, warm kisses on her temple.

Jennifer was so surprised by his question, she couldn't speak for a moment. She didn't want to talk about Sonny with this stranger, this man who had come to her rescue out of nowhere. A guardian angel in a rough, dangerous package. Trust came hard where men were concerned. She wasn't just going to open up to him. He was leaving. What could her answer possibly matter to him?

"I don't know you. That's a pretty personal question." She evaded out of necessity. Out of self-preservation.

He nodded, bringing his face closer to hers. Her eyes dropped to his mouth and she couldn't seem to stop the overpowering need to feel him beneath her fingers. Gently she traced the outline of his lips, touched his mouth, and the contact fulfilled something basic and female inside her. The potent need to touch a virile powerful male. Yet, there were other things about him that she liked. His integrity. His gentleness. His honesty.

He closed his eyes, and his voice was thick with desire and longing when he spoke. "Believe me, Jennifer, if it was only hot, mindless sex involved, I wouldn't hesitate for one minute."

Hot, mindless sex. She couldn't breathe. This man stirred feelings in her that she never knew she possessed. Heated thoughts of Corey stripping her, straddling her, taking her, rushed through her mind. The powerful attraction was unwanted, stunning in its potency, and so frightening. And all she had to say was, "Yes."

"I want to get to know you, too," he offered, instinctively answering her unspoken thoughts. Grabbing her hand, he pressed her palm to his mouth then moved it to his face.

She swallowed convulsively and he watched her throat

move, wanting to put his mouth there and feel her swallow against his tongue. "Intimately," he added, his eyes moving from the soft column of her throat to her face. "I want to know what you're thinking behind those deep green eyes. For the first time in my life I want to explore a woman emotionally as well as physically." He felt her stiffen against his body. He was baring a part of himself uncharacteristically, but he was so tired of running.

Was he trying to scare her off? Most likely. He didn't want to explore his feelings for this woman, but already the attraction was so strong he thought seriously of seducing her right here in her driveway, and once a physical tie was established he could then garner an emotional one.

What the hell was he thinking? He could only hurt her. Hadn't he promised himself he would never get involved with a forever kind of woman? Jennifer was the type of woman he'd always steered away from, and with an unreasonableness that astounded him he wanted her. "But you're a conservative little cowgirl, aren't you? You don't sleep around. Certainly not a one-night stand with some drifter moving through town. That would be—" he leaned down and whispered in her ear "—*reckless.*"

A quivering tingle trickled through her whole body, striking a chord deep down. *Reckless.* That was what she'd been with Sonny. Sonny, who'd cared more for the rodeo than for her. Sonny, who'd taken any woman he could seduce into his trailer. Into *their* trailer, into *their* bed where her daughter had been conceived.

Anger hot and burning hardened her heart, and she erected barriers for sheer protection. She couldn't trust him. Ha, she couldn't trust herself.

She raised her chin and met his molten green gaze.

"Why are you doing this?" she challenged, dropping her hand and narrowing her eyes.

"Because I like torturing myself. Or maybe because a sweet, beautiful, rich—" his eyes shifted from her face to look up at the house, where he could see the patio and the pool "—Anglo woman wouldn't be interested in a man like me, so I'm safe."

"Don't put words into my mouth and thoughts into my head. You're only doing this to unnerve me. Why don't you just get on your bike and leave? That's what you want to do, so go ahead. Stop baiting me."

"I'm leaving so you won't get a chance to be reckless." With his fingers buried in her hair he cupped the sides of her face. "I just want to know if he's dead. Only a fool would ever walk away and leave you."

"*You're* leaving," she said more contemptuously than she felt, trying to ignore the distracting movement of his thumbs that left a tingling fire over the skin of her cheekbones. It was frightening, this sense of wanting a man she didn't know. Frightening and powerful. Yet, looking into his tortured eyes, she almost felt closer to him than anyone else.

"I'm a fool," he said simply, with a shrug of his impossibly broad shoulders.

The thought of him leaving brought back the unreasonable panic. God, she didn't want him to go, but she surely wouldn't let him know that. This was crazy, and she thought she'd put her crazy days in the past. Crazy days when she had let Sonny woo her and use her and throw her away.

No matter how much she wanted this man, no one was going to throw her away again.

Her anger at the remembered treatment by her husband lent her the strength to step away from the dark seduction of Corey. "I'm sorry. I just don't know you." She clenched her fists, her nails digging into her flesh. She would not touch him. She would not.

His arms dropped away from her and he smiled without humor in the darkness, his face in shadow beneath the brim of his hat. All she could see was his beautiful mouth, and all she could think was that she wanted it pressed against hers.

He sighed a mournful sound that went through her like a sharp biting arctic wind leaving in its wake a sudden aching emptiness. She tightened her resolve. She couldn't let her heart sway her mind. He was leaving. Yet another man who didn't want to make a commitment. Yet another rodeo rider who would break her heart and she'd only known him for one damn day. You can really pick them, Jen, but good, she chided herself.

His mouth was on hers before she could fend him off. The kiss spoke volumes, the aching sweetness almost unbearable.

Then he hugged her hard and close for a few agonizing minutes.

When he pulled away, his face was ravaged with pain. Without looking at her, he straddled his bike. He sat there for a few moments as she watched him war with himself for composure, for control. It made her feel powerful that he would have to fight himself. Just as she fought herself.

Abruptly he turned and looked at her. "Thanks for the delicious dinner. I haven't had a home-cooked meal in a very long time, and never by a beautiful woman with fiery hair."

His words released the heartache that had just begun to stir, and she bit her lip, tasting the intoxicating essence of him.

She didn't know what to say. She wanted to ask him to

stay, because standing here in her driveway she realized how terribly lonely she was.

But one night with him wouldn't be enough. She would want more and that want would turn into a raging river of want. An insurmountable river that would only swell and grow with time.

She would want a commitment. She had to have someone who would stay around and be a father to Ellie and a husband to her. No, he should leave. Better never to know how much he could make her feel.

Her resolve was hard-won. Thirteen years of fending off amorous advances would not go for naught. She needed to consider everything in the equation. What would one night of lovemaking cost her?

Too much. Too damn much.

Sonny had hurt her, but this man could bring her to her knees. She knew it inherently. One taste of his passion, the feel of his body, the possession of that body and she would be lost. All the independence, all the pain she had endured would go flying out the window and she'd have to fight to get back what she would lose in him.

"You're welcome. Have a safe trip to wherever you're going." Her voice came out bitter and cutting.

He smiled again that sad, heart-wrenching smile. "I'm going nowhere. You take care, darlin'."

Her heart twisted at the tired, defeated bitterness in his voice. Her chest filled until she thought it would burst. *Please, don't look so damn neglected and forlorn.* He looked so lost that it pulled at something deep inside her, stirring all her nurturing and protective instincts. She had the overpowering urge to take him in her arms and hold on to him until that look went away.

He's running.

She must not forget that. But she couldn't help the rush

of tenderness that moved through her or the thought that if he would just stay and let her get to know him, she could get him to stop running. Save the outlaw mentality, Jen, she told herself sternly.

He tightened the bead on his hat and kicked the motorcycle into life. She stepped back out of his way and he had to look over his shoulder at her. His hand raised to his hat and she felt that stab of awareness surge through her again.

And regret. Deep, deep regret. She saw the same emotion in his eyes and her heart ached. She would probably never meet a man who would stir her like this and she'd just lost her chance to explore the attraction. Lost the chance to have a precious memory.

For only one night.

It would not be enough, she thought greedily.

It would be a night that would probably haunt her, a more reasonable voice said. One that she would never get out of her mind. She would unconsciously compare him to every other man she met. She was better off never knowing, she reminded herself.

Then she was watching his red taillight disappear into the darkness. The loneliness seemed to settle on her like a fine blanket of mist. The regret like a lead ball in her stomach.

Walking into the house she didn't feel the least bit sleepy. When Two Tone scratched at the door, she let him in and he happily trotted up the stairs, his hooves clicking against the hardwood. She knew he would curl up with Ellie and fall asleep, the way he did every night. She went into the dining room, picked up the pie plates and silverware, put them in the dishwasher, then turned it on. Upstairs in her bathroom she stripped and got into the shower. She knew she wouldn't be able to sleep. She'd sit in her window seat and look out at the night.

Suddenly, without warning, a small sob shook her. She leaned against the wall, her tears mingling with the spray from the shower. No man had ever touched her so gently. She remembered the way he'd touched her hair when she thought for sure his interest in her was purely sexual. The way he'd looked at her, the barely concealed passion in his eyes. They shared something that went deeper than lust.

She covered her mouth with her hand and turned her face up to the spray to stop the cries issuing from her tight throat, but still the tears fell. She wanted desperately to help, to erase the loneliness from his face and find out why he looked so heart-wrenchingly sad.

She closed her eyes tightly and leaned her face against the cool tiles. It would have been so easy to console him with her body. The thought of enfolding him in her arms and giving him pleasure made her cry harder, her whole body shaking with the effort.

She wasn't looking for a temporary answer, she reminded herself. Sleeping with him would have been reckless and impulsive, and she couldn't afford that kind of behavior now. She couldn't think about herself and her needs. She had to think of Ellie and permanence.

But all those rationalizations did nothing to stem the tide of need that rushed over her.

She thought back to the evening, to the way he'd been with her child. Ellie was just as taken with him as she was. Her daughter had never had a father. After the divorce, Sonny had acted as if he'd never fathered a child. He'd told her she could "keep the brat" and even insinuated that the child probably wasn't his.

That had been the one and only time she'd ever hit a man until this afternoon when she'd hit Jay for taking liberties.

She stood under the water until she was shivering, then

wearily she turned the faucet off, dried herself with quick angry strokes and put on a light cotton nightgown.

She towel-dried her hair, went into her bedroom and sat down on the window seat, feeling sick with despair, marveling that she'd never cried so hard and so long over Sonny.

Tears were precious and she chose who she shed them over. Sonny hadn't deserved them, but Corey did. She guessed that he deserved a lifetime of tears.

She didn't want to close her eyes and sleep, because then she would remember. She would remember his kiss and she would relive it, and all the painful desires and all the things that could never be would rise around her as ghosts.

She looked out the window, but didn't see the night— only a pair of hot aqua eyes and a battered, wounded soul.

He stopped the bike just outside her fence, everything inside clamoring for him to turn around and go back to her. His eyes closed tightly, his hands gripped around the handlebars until they hurt, he fought the urge. He wanted to go back and strip those soft silky pants off her, pull that blouse over her head, run his hands over her body, straddle his motorcycle and have her straddle him. Hot skin against hotter skin. Silk against steel.

He groaned low in his throat thinking about her body moving over his, him deep inside her.

Hormones. Nothing but the long-denied desires of a man. Hell, it had been too damn long since he had a woman. He sat in the darkness, his body pulsing, his blood hot in his veins.

Yeah, hormones. Lust. Need. Want. All of those.

He questioned his motives. In his dreams, where all things were possible, why, when he'd brought her to fulfillment and taken his own, did he want to wrap her around him and sleep with her against his heart? Why did he never want to let her go? Because there was more than lust to his hunger.

But he couldn't explore that hunger, he told himself. He was a man with baggage and Jennifer Horn was a woman he'd only dreamed about and that was where she had to stay—in his dreams.

Corey pulled away from the fence, then opened the throttle when he reached the road, the powerful bike fishtailing in the gravel before it righted itself once it hit the better traction of the blacktop. He fought the bike for control while the wind pulled at his hat and coat and tangled his long ebony hair.

He pushed the throttle higher, wanting the wind to take this feeling away. Believing that if he went fast enough, he could outrun the desire throbbing through his blood. He moaned softly into the wind, his fingers remembering the silky fire of her hair.

Why did it feel as if he'd left half of himself back in her cozy house? Why did it feel as if he'd left his heart in her soft, warm hands? Because there was an emptiness in his chest.

He made it back to the motel in record time. He wouldn't sleep, he thought as he parked the Harley. He knew he wouldn't. He might as well just gather together his stuff and get back on his bike and ride until he couldn't keep his eyes open.

Finally he got off the bike, his mind so preoccupied with his inner struggles that he didn't see the shadows waiting. He didn't hear the scrape of a boot heel against the asphalt. Delving into his pocket for the key to his room, he stiffened and the hair on the back of his neck lifted in warning. But awareness came too late. The white-hot agony of the blow to the back of his head knocked him to his knees. He felt the warm rush of blood over the back of his neck.

The attack was so sudden and vicious that Corey found his quick reflexes and formidable fighting talent couldn't respond in time.

The blow from a baseball bat across his back pushed him down to the ground and he scraped his face painfully against the asphalt of the parking lot. A blow from a booted foot exploded against his side, knocking the breath out of him. He grunted from the pain and tried to pull in enough oxygen to get another breath. Torturous blow after torturous blow rained down on him. He curled into a fetal position to protect himself as best as possible, the nausea from the pain and the suddenness of the attack roiling in his stomach. He felt cold and paralyzed. In his disorientation he wondered if his father had beaten him. He wondered if he was at home lying on the carpet instead of the hard ground. And he wondered, as he did when he was a child, if he'd done something to deserve this. He thought that he should be used to pain by now, but some rational part of his brain was telling him shock was setting in.

Finally they stopped kicking him. He was unable to move, his ears still ringing from the blows, his vision blurred. Sounds came to him as if through water. He could hear the smashing of chrome and metal and the breaking of glass. But he was moving in and out of consciousness at this point and couldn't pinpoint the noise.

He thought he heard someone whoop and say with smugness, "Look what we got ourselves here, boys. A nice little bonus."

Suddenly the commotion stopped, and one more kick landed with excruciating precision against his back where the baseball bat had inflicted pure agony. "Hey, chief. I hope the little bitch was worth it."

He recognized the voice before he gave up the fight and darkness closed in.

The shrill ringing of the phone startled Jennifer out of a light doze. Adrenaline stabbed through her, and she whirled to get the phone so that the ringing wouldn't wake Ellie. "Hello."

"Jennifer."

Corey's voice was so weak she could barely make out her name.

"Corey? Corey! What's the matter?"

"Need you. Motel."

She heard the phone drop, but the line was still open. "Corey! Corey!" she said frantically, but the hum of the open line was her only answer. It was ominous and frightened her to death.

She dropped the receiver in the cradle, picked up her discarded jeans skirt from this morning and struggled into it, stuffing her shirt into the waistband. She ran through the house, grabbed her denim jacket and shrugged into it, and hardly remembered reaching the back door. She slipped out the door closest to the bunkhouse and entered at a run. She tripped in the dark and swore, then got up and grabbed Jimmy, one of her live-in cowhands, and shook him with all the pent-up frustration and fear in her. She explained that she wanted him to stay with Ellie and he agreed immediately. She then asked Tex, another of the hands, to come with her.

Something was wrong, terribly wrong and she was frantic to get to Corey. She took a deep calming breath and tried to push the panic back. But it was like pushing a ball underwater. It kept bobbing to the surface.

She drove like a complete and utter maniac. Tex looked at her with surprise on his face. Once he made a comment about her killing them both, but she just flashed him one of her quelling looks and he clammed up. She was sure he'd never seen her this way because she'd never been this way.

She hit the brakes so hard when she got to the motel that Tex was jerked forward from the sudden stop. Immediately she saw the motorcycle on its side, smashed and dented as if someone had taken a sledgehammer to it. "Oh my God!" she whispered, not enough breath left in her lungs to shout. She threw the truck into park, not even bothering to turn off the engine. She left the truck door open and raced into the only motel room with the door ajar.

He lay on his side, the phone resting on the bed where it had fallen. A high-pitched busy signal was the only noise in the room. A fear she had never felt before in her life arrowed through her. A world without Corey Rainwater in it was an unbearable thought. She flew to the bed and touched him. When he moaned, some of the panic left her.

She felt Tex at her back. "Help me get him to the truck, then go get the doctor and tell him to come to my ranch. Ride there in the doctor's truck." Together, they supported Corey while he stumbled to her truck. His face was ashen and again fear sliced through her, making her voice urgent, "Hurry, Tex."

The drive to the ranch seemed to take an eternity. He didn't stir. She kept one arm around him to steady him and glanced down every few minutes to make sure he was still breathing. Only one man—or rather, group of men—were capable of such utter violence.

Her hand shook on the wheel, and tears coursed down her face. She couldn't even wipe them from her cheeks. She couldn't take her hand from the wheel, and she sure as hell wasn't going to let him go.

Back at the ranch she ran into the house to get Jimmy

to help her move him inside. She told him what had happened at the grocery and feed stores, and he swore softly under his breath.

"I'm responsible for this," she groaned as she helped Jimmy get Corey up the stairs to her room. They laid him down on her bed and she cupped the back of his head to ease him down onto her pillow. He moaned softly in pain, the small distressed sound wrenching at her heart. When she pulled her arm away, she saw blood on her hands and on the sleeve of her jacket where the back of his head had rested while she held him. Fresh tears blurred her eyes and for a moment she looked at the crimson stain on her hand. The anger and hatred that jolted through her surprised her in its intensity. She wanted to see the men responsible hung by their thumbs, whipped, punished. The violence of her thoughts astonished her because she was not a violent woman.

She went into the bathroom and frantically washed the blood off her hands. She removed her denim jacket and threw it on the floor in disgust.

She leaned against the sink, trying to quell the rest of the panic inside her. And the anger that seethed for Jay. She was sure he was responsible for this and with that knowledge came the guilt.

It was her fault that Corey was in this mess, his motorcycle smashed and him injured. Seeing him hurt bothered her the most.

She started to shake and couldn't stop. What if he had been killed? She couldn't bear the thought that her actions two nights ago had caused such danger to him.

She felt consumed with guilt. She felt responsible and she would make it up to him.

Chapter 5

Corey woke to the soft singing of the birds through the open window of the room where he lay. The bed was soft and sweet-smelling, the sheets' scent much better than sunshine and clean air. They smelled like…his brain couldn't seem to function. He shifted restlessly. They smelled like…damn…they smelled like Jennifer.

Memories surfaced. Soft hands shaking him awake countless times. A husky voice asking if he knew his name and other equally silly questions.

His eyes cracked open and he groaned at the stabbing brightness. God, his head hurt. The back of it felt on fire, and he vaguely remembered the doctor saying that he had received a mild concussion and that he'd have to stitch his head up. "Mild, my ass," he croaked.

He turned over and came face-to-face with a tiny black-and-white pig, whose forefeet were resting on the edge of the bed. The curious little eyes studied him, and Corey thought he was the cutest creature he'd ever seen. He smiled, reached out and let the animal smell his hand before he petted him.

"That's Two Tone. He has the run of the house and has to know everything that's going on, I'm afraid."

Corey's eyes raised and connected with Jennifer's. Her voice was husky, as if she'd just woken up. But he knew that she had been up through the night, checking to make sure he was all right. Her concern touched him deeply and made him feel very vulnerable.

"He's cute," he managed to say around the pain in his midriff. Raking his hand through his hair, he grimaced and the action pulled the healing flesh of his face.

"Be careful. He uses that to his advantage."

Corey patted the little pig again and shifted, his face contorting in pain. Jennifer's assisting hands were instantly there, shooing Two Tone away and helping him to sit up.

"What am I doing here?"

"You called me, remember?" She cocked her eyebrows and smiled slightly.

She was pleased that he had called her. He could hear it in her voice, and in his injured state that knowledge pleased him immensely.

"How do you feel?"

"Like I've been hit with a baseball bat and kicked by a bunch of yahoos. Not to mention that little war going on in my head."

Jennifer smiled wryly and settled the pillows to best support him.

Corey closed his eyes and willed away the pain. When he opened them, she was sitting on the edge of the bed. He wasn't stupid. The attraction he felt for this woman was unique. Women had come and gone in his life. Nameless, unfocused faces that jumbled into one big blur. Jennifer stood out like a shining gem, polished to a brightness that hurt his eyes, his heart. Oh God, he wanted her so bad. But he could hurt her so bad and that would destroy him.

She had that small-town charm. Never turn a person away who was in need. She had obviously been watching him while he slept, and something warm curled around his heart. Whether it was because she was afraid for him or because her integrity demanded it, she'd done it. Her sleepy eyes watched him with a hidden hunger burning just at the fringes and it hurt him to look into those eyes and know that she wanted him.

"You must be tired from watching me all night. Why don't you get some rest?" His voice was hoarse, his eyes revealing the vulnerability he felt.

"I will. Later. After Ellie has gone to school. And I'm sure you're going to be okay."

She leaned forward and he watched the material of her shirt tauten over her breasts. She snatched a bottle off the nightstand along with a glass of water. "Here, take these. That should help the war to cool down into a skirmish."

He remembered how sweet she had tasted yesterday and last night. He licked his dry lips, wishing for the coolness of her soft skin against them. "Are you always this kind to strangers?"

His eyes shifted to hers and he could see the banked desire in them, as well as a wariness and loneliness to match his own. He lifted his hand and accepted the aspirin, his fingers brushing hers as he took the water glass.

"No. I don't usually get calls in the middle of the night from men who need my help."

He thought she was lying. He could see that she would help anyone in need. Then he drank thirstily, his throat working as he swallowed the aspirin. He leaned forward to replace the glass and winced at the sharp pain in his ribs and back.

"Here, let me." She took the glass from his hand and set it down. The brush of her hand was an electric sensation against his skin. "Where am I?" he asked.

"Upstairs in my bed."

She tried to answer casually, but he could hear the strain in her voice.

In her bed? He was in her bed! No wonder it smelled so good and felt so good.

"You needed eight stitches. The doctor took care of stitching you up. He said your ribs would be tender for a little while. He also said that your back is bruised. It looks horrible."

"Yeah, that's where they hit me with the bat."

Jennifer covered her mouth and looked away, unable to tolerate the guilt. "I'm really sorry about all this."

He leaned forward slightly and snagged her chin, turning her face up to his. He could barely stand the self-condemnation in her eyes. "Why? Jennifer, you had nothing to do with this. Butler and his boys are nothing but cowards. They couldn't even face me in the light of day, but had to slink around at night to ambush me. Don't blame yourself, darlin'."

"I do and I'll make it up to you." She knew she'd said the wrong thing as soon as the words were out of her mouth. His face shuttered. His eyes turned steely.

"No, you won't."

"I wish you had minded your own business. Jay would have probably lost interest in a day or two."

He sat up very painfully and leaned up against the headboard. He glared at her. "And what would have been the price? A bruise on your pretty face? Who knows where he would have stopped? Bullies only get meaner." He couldn't bear to see her skin marred with bruises. His mother's face swam before his eyes. Bruised, battered, her eyes so tired and old.

No, Jay Butler would have to go through him to get to Jennifer.

But you won't be here to protect her, an inner voice reminded him. You're going to leave her. Leave her here with the demons.

He had to! He didn't have a choice. He would talk to the sheriff before he left and explain what was going on. But that thought did nothing to ease the twisting of his gut.

"At the very least you should press charges," she encouraged as she smoothed down the bedspread.

"It wouldn't do any good, Jennifer. There are no witnesses and I didn't even see them. They attacked me from behind." He closed his eyes wearily as another stricken look crossed her face.

"But your bike and—"

"My bike," he groaned loudly. "What about my bike?"

She bit her lip and looked away, but not before he saw that same guilty look. "I had it hauled over to Martin's garage."

"I don't like the sound of the word *hauled.*"

"He says it's pretty much beyond repair," she said softly.

He closed his eyes, a dark panic welling in his chest. He was trapped? Dear God! There had to be a way out of this town. Surely a bus must run through here. He couldn't stay with her, he thought frantically. God, he wouldn't be able to keep his hands off her.

"What about the saddlebags?"

She got up and walked across the room and turned them out. "The clothing is being washed. The buckles are in this drawer, and your boots are near the bed. There was nothing else in them."

"Great. So what you're telling me is that I'm without transportation and flat broke."

"Broke?" she squeaked.

"I had fifteen hundred dollars in those bags to tide me over for a while."

A thoughtful look came over her face and she said in a rush, "I could use a foreman."

His body stilled. "Jennifer, I don't think my staying here would be a good idea."

Her eyes flashing, she tossed the empty saddlebags back on the chair and placed her hands on her hips. "What do you expect me to do? Let me see, you save my dignity and what can I do in return? I got it! Perhaps I can throw you out in the street bruised and battered. Hell, why don't I throw you in the gutter and let you crawl to wherever you so desperately want to go?" She glared at him, but he looked at her with a defiant, sardonic expression that only pushed her temper higher. "This is all my fault!" she shouted, goaded by his attitude.

Folding her arms over her chest, she stared him down, "You'll stay here until you're well. I don't want to hear anything else from you. You can make a decision about the job then."

"Jennifer, I'm not staying here."

"I'll get you something to eat then. I wouldn't dream of throwing a wounded man into the gutter without offering him something nourishing first," she said tartly. With a flip of her flaming hair, she strode from the room.

The woman was magnificent. Her anger and shame stood out clearly on her face. And her green eyes crackled with suppressed fury. What was he going to do with the bossy, pushy little thing? He couldn't stay here. He couldn't. Jennifer was much too tantalizing. Much too beautiful. And he was much too needful.

He'd wanted her from the moment he'd laid eyes on her, but that had been a physical reaction. Now, now he wanted her with a desperate yearning hunger that had nothing to do with his physical needs.

He couldn't stay here.

He was afraid of the darkness on his soul. His legacy.

He couldn't stay here.

He was too weak.

He couldn't stay here.

His demons would find him and in the process find her. He couldn't allow that.

He couldn't stay here.

He didn't deserve her.

He didn't know who he was, where he was going. He couldn't stop running. If he did, he would have to face his fears and the madness that hovered around them. But, God help him, he wanted to stay. He could brave the madness for her. For Jennifer.

Jennifer came back with soup, crackers and a glass of milk on a tray. She set it in front of him, avoiding his eyes. When she went to pull away, he grabbed her hand and held her, waiting patiently until she finally looked at him with a huffy little sigh.

"You don't owe me anything, darlin'. Not one damn thing," he pleaded.

Her expression was one of misery. He didn't want her to feel this way. Damn, he didn't want her to care.

"Jennifer...please."

"Eat your soup and then let me look at your stitches." She lifted her chin, meeting his hard look straight on.

"I wish you didn't possess so much backbone," he snarled.

Her eyebrows raised and she looked him up and down. "That's like the pot calling the kettle black."

Against his will, he smiled. "Yeah, they shouldn't," he agreed, his smile widening.

Jennifer felt her world shift precariously as she swallowed, trying to dislodge the awe rising in her. She was staring and she knew it, but couldn't seem to help herself.

He leaned forward very slightly and asked, "You have a bunkhouse for this foreman you need to hire?"

"The bunkhouse is for the hired hands. We have a foreman's cottage. The previous foreman had a family, so my father built it for him for privacy," she whispered, her hopes rising as if someone with complete and irrefutable evidence had just proved there really was a Santa Claus.

"I'll stay there until I feel able to travel."

Her hope crashed and she couldn't hide her disappointment. "Corey, you'd be more comfortable here. The mattress in the cottage is lumpy," she argued.

The hell he'd be more comfortable here, he thought. Being around her, seeing her move, knowing he was in her bed would only drive him crazy. Yeah, he would be about as comfortable as a porcupine turned inside out.

But he knew when not to argue. He would just go his own way as he'd done for so long. There was only so much that he could take. Finding the woman of his dreams in this one-horse town was not one of them. Nor was seeing her fiery hair and not being able to touch it. Or being close to those tempting curves and resisting the urge to mold his hands around them. That would be more torturous than sleeping on a lumpy mattress. He just shrugged.

"Let me look at your stitches," she said, rising suddenly, the discussion of where he would be staying obviously settled. He liked that about her. Self-confident without being overbearing. Steady and strong and so very sweet.

She moved around him and tipped his head forward slightly. She smoothed her hand against the nape of his neck and jumped back when he sucked in his breath sharply and moaned softly. His body had tautened like a bowstring, his breathing suddenly harsh and ragged.

"I'm so sorry. I didn't mean to hurt you," she cried.

Corey recoiled, the soft touch to his neck like fire in his loins. The woman was driving him to distraction every time she touched him. Trying to prevent any more mishaps, he shouted, "Don't touch me!"

Jennifer stiffened her shoulders. She caught her bottom lip in her teeth and worried it. Hurt and pain shone in her eyes. "I'm sorry. I won't. Call me if you need me."

"What in hell do you think you're doing?" Jennifer's voice cracked like a whip in the stillness of the hayloft. She had been angry and worried when she checked on Corey hours later and found the bed empty.

"Pitching hay," he drawled.

"You exasperating man." She felt the irritation curl inside her. "I *know* you're pitching hay. You're supposed to be in bed. Now let's go." She struggled not to stare. His hair was braided and the dark wisps at the ends tumbled against his tanned flesh every time he moved. A red bandanna was tied around his forehead to catch the sweat. She lost the fight and openly stared.

In the act of sticking the pitchfork back into the hay, he grunted, clutching his ribs. She jumped forward and wrapped her arms around him, lowering him gently to the unbundled hay. She snatched the pitchfork out of his hands. "Corey, why are you doing this?"

"I don't want your charity, Jennifer," he muttered quietly.

"It's not charity."

"Then what do you call it?" he asked, his voice raised.

"I call it being human, and from what I can tell in the

short time that I've known you, you haven't met many of those."

His mouth tightened, and his breathing seemed labored.

She sat down next to him. "It's not charity. You're going to work for me once you're well. We're just delaying payment. God, Corey, if it wasn't for me, you wouldn't be in this mess."

"So it's guilt."

"Yes, partly."

"What's the other part?"

She wouldn't touch that question with a ten-foot pole.

"Jennifer?"

"What?"

"What's the other part?" he said insistently.

"Oh, do you have to know everything?" she groused loudly. She got up but didn't get far.

He grabbed her wrist and pulled her around. He rose painfully, awkwardly. She ached to help him.

"Yes, I want to know. I want desperately to know," he said, as if her next words could shatter him.

She looked up at him, the need in his eyes almost buckling her knees. Tears pricked the back of her eyes, the pain below the surface. Just a little kindness, she thought. She wouldn't lose herself if she was just a little bit kind. "Because I care what happens to you."

"What did you say?"

She screwed up her courage. Her voice rose with each word. "I said that I care what happens to you."

He turned away, his body so rigid that Jennifer backed up slightly. What had she said that would make him so angry?

He picked up the pitchfork and started to pitch hay with ferocious energy. She was mesmerized by the way his back muscles flexed, the way his arms bulged. The tingling in her body intensified until it was a profound ache. The guilt rose in her too, at the sight of the mottled flesh of his ribs and tight stomach. The huge black and blue bruise that marred his lower back made her want to touch it and make it better.

"Corey, you asked."

"I'm sorry I did!" The tone of his voice was strange, choked, and the steely edge spoke of his need. What did he want her to feel? she thought suddenly. What more did he want from her than her sympathy?

This time she grabbed his arm and made him face her. He winced and she let go. "What the hell is that supposed to mean? I don't understand what's going on here. Maybe you should explain it to me," she demanded.

His eyes blazed into hers and he swore softly, glancing away. "I don't need your pity. I don't need anything."

"It's not pity."

"It's not pity, hell! What else could you feel for me, Jennifer?" He laughed harshly.

"How about compassion, Corey? What's so wrong with old-fashioned compassion? You protected me. You stopped Jay from hitting me in the face. They beat you, stole your money and smashed your motorcycle because of me, because of what you did for me. I'm grateful. I want to thank you."

"Grateful?" he said bitterly.

"That's not a nasty word, Corey. What do you want me to feel?"

The air suddenly stilled in the barn. His body was so taut and immobile that Jennifer felt a slight bit of panic. The tension built slowly, becoming almost tangible. She shivered inside when she looked at him. The shadows cast his tight muscles in relief as though he were a living statue, a magnificent work of art.

His nostrils flared and his eyes darkened with hunger. What had she inadvertently said? She never should have asked him what he wanted her to feel. She could see him fighting himself, warring with the need that had manifested itself the moment she had met those turquoise eyes. It whispered in the still air like the soft voice of seduction.

He moved forward and grabbed her, pulling her body close to his. His eyes darkened further with pain and bitterness, need and a helpless plea. "This, Jennifer! I want you to feel this." His mouth captured hers, his kiss savage and hard. A bruising pressure that Jennifer opened to— unable to deny the passion building inside of her. Passion they both denied.

In the stillness of the loft, every little sound seemed to intensify. She could hear the soft cooing of doves in the rafters, the stomping of horses below her, the gentle play of the wind through the open door. And at the sound of the wind, she panicked. Suddenly she was afraid that she would feel him slip through her fingers and disappear like the elusive wind. She clasped him tighter, never wanting to let him go. It had been so long since she'd held a man.

His breathing was harsh in the silence, telling of a man who had fought himself for days and nights in anguished loneliness. In sheer desperation. His kiss said it all. His hard hands on her upper arms broadcast the unreasonable desire that had sprung between them.

He probably would never believe her, but she knew about that loneliness. She had lived with it for a long time, but she had had Ellie to keep her company. He had no one and the rigid torture in his posture spoke more loudly than his words ever could. The need to soothe and comfort rushed over her with powerful, fierce need. This man had done everything he could not to shatter her peace. He'd reined in his desire so that he wouldn't hurt her when he left. Because she was sure that he wanted her even before now. He'd wanted her that night in her driveway when he had taunted her into anger. Anger that had sent him away.

Lost in her need, she fought the rough hold of his arms, but not for him to release her and step back, but to let her go so that she could hold him closer. She wrapped her arms around his neck, and held him as tight as he was holding her. His ravenous mouth moved from her lips down her neck, gently suckling her skin, making deep masculine noises in the back of his throat that took her control away.

His large hands cupped her breasts, his thumbs rubbing over her engorged nipples. She groaned softly and she felt him shudder and tremble.

His answering groan brought her back to reality with a jolt. What was she doing? She couldn't, wouldn't allow this! With all her might, she pushed against his chest.

Immediately he let her go and stumbled backward, sitting down heavily on a bale of hay.

Her mouth stung and tingled and she wanted that pressure back. She wanted to explore his chest with her hands, but the ravaged look on his face and her own common sense kept her immobile.

In a voice filled with self-loathing, his eyes bruised with unbearable pain, he said, "Don't."

"Don't what?" Her breathing was still ragged.

He clutched his ribs, doubling over. "Don't look at me like that. Don't make me want to stay."

"I need a foreman. That's all, Corey."

"You don't want me."

"You could help me for just a little while. It would help you out and get me through calving." She felt relieved that her heated body was finally cooling down. But her hands still trembled from the force of their passion. "I need a foreman, Corey," she repeated. "The work is too much for me. I can't be in two places at one time. I can't run the ranch and be a mother to Ellie. That is all that is important to me."

"You don't want me," he said again, his breathing equally ragged.

"Why? Why wouldn't I want you?"

He refused to look at her and he refused to answer.

"Corey, what are you running from?"

"Do yourself a favor, don't ask me any questions." He dropped his face into his hands then raked his hair back from his face.

"You're running from something," she said again stubbornly, wanting answers even though she knew they would probably not be what she wanted to hear.

"I'm not running from anything." Except maybe myself, he thought silently. Yeah, that was most definitely it. He was running far and fast from himself, but it was like running in quicksand.

"What was that kiss all about? Why did you do that?"

He wanted to say a thousand things. Because I want you more than I want to breathe. I want you crying out hot and wet into my mouth. I want to connect with you. I want to touch you where no other man has ever touched you.

He looked at her. "Didn't you want me, too, or does my Native American heritage repulse you?"

He said the words as if the whole world were against him and it quite stunningly broke her heart. She wasn't going to admit that she wanted him. Her sanity returned in a rush. She couldn't afford a relationship with him. She should have kept her distance, but how could she when he was hurting so bad? How could she when she couldn't stop thinking about him? But if she admitted her feelings now, it would make them so very real. "Is that it? You think I'm like Jay? That I would discriminate against you because you're Native American? To me, Corey, a man is a man whether he's black, white or green. I wouldn't give a damn if you were striped!''

He was black, all right, but inside where she couldn't see. ''You didn't answer my question. Didn't you want me to kiss you?''

''No, I didn't want you to,'' she lied. ''But it has nothing to do with your heritage,'' she added quickly. ''I was just trying to explain something to you, you stubborn jerk!''

Without warning, he backed her up against the jutting eave support of the sloping roof. She couldn't help admiring the sleek animal grace of him as he moved so fast she barely had time to register the movement. Solid and seductive. ''You know something, Jennifer? You're giving me mixed signals.''

''Wh-what do you mean?'' she stammered, not understanding the sudden explosive change in him.

''You want to know what I think?''

''What?'' she was coerced into asking by the sultry glint in his eyes.

''You are a wild cowgirl with a hidden reckless nature. Your eyes give you away. The way they look at me. The way they caress me. They say one thing. But those lips, those soft, sweet lips are telling me something else. So which is lying, Jennifer, your words or your eyes?''

''I'm not lying! I'm not going to get myself involved with a man who can't commit. I won't do that again, especially to some rodeo jerk who can't even handle compassion and mistakes it for something else. Don't work for me. See if I give a damn. You can leave right now if you want. Go ahead. Leave!''

His lips compressed, and he closed his eyes, backing away from her. His fists clenched at his sides, then he opened his eyes.

Jennifer gasped out loud with a soft heartfelt moan. She was aghast at what she had said and was instantly sorry. She hadn't lost her temper so completely since she'd been a young girl. He'd goaded her, but that was no reason to be vile. She covered her mouth, and through a blur of tears, she whispered, "Don't go." Then she ran from the loft, in such a hurry to get down the ladder that she nearly fell. When her feet hit the ground, she ran out of the barn into the blazing sunlight. Grabbing the reins of her horse, she vaulted into the saddle.

She galloped away from the barn and the tears that had started to build broke loose. It wasn't his words that had her running away. It was the look on his face. A face ravaged by strain, with lines of soul-deep pain etched around his eyes and mouth. But still, that hadn't caused the tears. No, then she had looked into his eyes. Into wells of deep dark agony, pain so raw, torment so deep she thought she could drown in it.

She saw a man on the edge. Keenly on the edge. And she could be the catalyst that sent him over. She saw that so clearly in his eyes. He wanted her and her blood pounded from that knowledge. He was willing to risk everything, including his sanity to have her. She saw that, too. But she still wanted him with an irrational need that was dictated from her heart. She would be willing to take the risk because she knew now that if she didn't, she'd never know what real love was. It had been staring her in the face ever since she'd met him. He was her one chance to know something powerful, something forbidden, something so reckless that she could not only lose him, but herself, as well.

He wasn't anything like her ex-husband. He had integrity. Oh, God, she couldn't use that old excuse about never getting involved with a rodeo rider. He wasn't anything like Sonny at all. He was much, much more.

The fear at that thought sent her leaning over the saddle, urging her mount to a higher, dangerous speed. She leaped walls and fences without thought, letting the wind stream around her. She had to think. She had to come to grips with the knowledge that her safe little haven could become unstable.

After she'd slowed her horse to a walk, she came to the conclusion that she had waited for this man all her life. She knew that a passion and sheer touching of souls was possible, and that promise throbbed with stunning potential so intense she felt her muscles tighten in response.

If she let him go and never knew the touch of his hands, or the beauty of him, she would never have the chance again. Something would be lost to her. Something of herself, something important that she needed to discover again. Something that had been lost when she'd been betrayed. Trust. And if she trusted again, she could become the uninhibited woman she had once been. She was so sure that she gasped, the knowledge becoming like a bright spot in her mind. She slid to the ground, letting go of the horse's reins. He drifted off, but she didn't notice. She was lost and found, bereft and on the edge of joy. And so scared she was spitless. If she let Corey touch her, she would be lost and she had to make sure she was prepared to live with herself once he was gone.

He emerged from the barn long after Jennifer was gone. He clutched his painful ribs and looked out over the meadow, as if he could see her even from a distance, as if she burned like a fire on his heart. He rubbed his temple and swore soft and low. Staying here was not an option, he told himself. But he wanted to. He wanted to be good enough to deserve Jennifer and Ellie.

But he knew he wasn't good enough. His father had told him enough times. He'd failed his mother, he'd failed his sister, and somehow he'd failed his father. He must have. He'd failed at the rodeo. He would fail with Jennifer, too. It was only a matter of time.

His attraction to Jennifer Horn was dangerous. To her. To him. To Ellie.

"Come on, you flea-bitten nag." Ellie's voice drifted to him and he turned to find her trying to get her horse to keep his concentration as he was going around the barrels. He walked painfully to the fence and leaned against one of the posts.

Ellie reined in the horse and slumped dejectedly in the saddle. She looked so pitiful that he couldn't help himself. "Ellie, you're trying too hard."

She looked up, her face breaking into a beautiful grin when she saw him. "You're up! Jeez, that's great, Corey! Are you feeling better?" She nudged the horse over to the fence and dismounted. Tying the rein to the split rail, she ducked under and stood next to him. Her exuberance was going to wear him out. He gestured to the paddock next to her practice ring. "Why aren't you training that little mare? She's got champion written all over her."

Ellie looked over her shoulder and sighed. "Yeah, I know, but no one can get near her. Mom bought her at an auction because the horse was being abused. Unfortunately, we haven't been able to get her to trust us. Mom won't let me even try to ride her."

Corey looked at the animal again. "Would you like to?"

"Yeah, are you kidding? I'll never make time with dog meat here," she said, indicating her mount. "He's just too old. Mom worries too much. I understand, but I really want to compete, Corey. Do you think you could talk Mom into it?"

He pulled on one of her braids. "I don't know, Ellie. I'm not going to be here that long."

Disappointment clouded her eyes, but he could see she tried to hide it. For some reason, that little act of sparing his feelings got to him. His throat clogged. "I'm sorry, Ellie."

In a mimic of his move, she pulled on one of his braids. "That's okay, Corey. Mom said you weren't staying long. Just until you healed. Don't worry, I'll find some other way."

She bent down and picked up a pad of paper that Corey hadn't noticed near the post. "What's that?"

"Just some scribbling."

"Let me see."

"It's not really that good, Corey," Ellie said nervously and bit her lip.

"Come on, darlin', let me see."

She looked up at him with anxiety and trust. Anxiety, he realized, because she was nervous about his opinion. She cared what he thought.

He opened the pad and came face-to-face with one of his demons. He swallowed, his hands shaking. The drawing of Two Tone was good for a thirteen-year-old child. He stared at it so long that Ellie shifted nervously.

Memories flooded over him. Memories of his father explaining art to him exactly as he was about to do with Ellie. Guiding him, taking the time to see that he had done it well. Of course, Corey thought bitterly, those fleeting fond remembrances came before the vicious attack that had changed his father into a self-destructive abuser.

"So what do you think?"

"It looks just like him. It's good, Ellie. With practice it

could be outstanding.'' He looked down at her, noting the pride on her face. He reached out and gently smoothed a strand of hair off her face. ''Do you have any drawing pencils?''

''Sure.'' She stooped down and retrieved a pencil box. She pulled open the worn lid, took out a sharply pointed pencil and handed it to him.

He turned the pad so she could see. ''His eyes aren't quite right. Do you see?'' He used the eraser out of her box. ''Now look.'' He sketched Two Tone's eyes from memory.

''It was the arch. That's what I was missing. Jeez, Corey, that's great.''

''His snout is just a little bit shorter. That's what's throwing his face out of proportion. See?'' She watched as he sketched, hanging on his every word as he described what he was doing.

The phone in the barn began ringing and Ellie's head jerked up. ''That's probably Mary Lou. I'm supposed to be going to her house next week. I'd better get it.''

He smiled and handed her the pad. ''We'll talk later.''

She smiled at him and clutched the pad to her chest as she raced away, disappearing into the barn. Beautiful child. Beautiful mother. Damn stubborn beautiful mother.

What was he going to do? He sauntered over to the fence of the corral that penned in the little mare. He stood staring at her for a few moments. She had an elegant head, and intelligent shining brown eyes that were wary and frightened. His guess would be Arabian mix. Definitely fast, he thought. He clicked his tongue and the animal's head raised and studied him. He said nonsense words in a soft liquid voice and coaxed the sleek animal closer. With the language of his forefathers still streaming from his lips, he ducked under the fence and stood still, his voice soothing.

The mare moved a little closer as if drawn to him against her will. He held out his hand. The horse's nostrils flared and she whinnied. Then she turned and bolted to the other side of the paddock.

There was potential here. She had responded, if only briefly. He could work with her. It would take a couple of weeks, but he bet he could get a saddle on her and have her barrel racing within three weeks. Tops.

But you won't be here for three weeks. You won't be here another minute if you can help it.

There was a low grunt at his feet and he looked down to find the little pig butting his ankles. Gingerly he crouched and scooped him up. Holding him like an infant, he scratched the exposed pink tummy. The little pig grunted again in pleasure and closed his eyes.

Corey's face twisted and he clenched his jaw against the surge of emotion, raw and painful. God, he thought, he wanted to stay here. He wanted to stay here so badly. Sucking in a quick breath, he continued to cradle the pig and headed back to the barn to finish what he'd started.

When his chores were done, he borrowed Jennifer's truck and drove into town. There was unfinished business that he needed to attend to. He trailed the man he was looking for to Jack's Trap, a beer and pool hall on the outskirts of town. He pushed open the swinging doors and walked into the dim interior.

Tables and chairs were scattered around, some patrons sitting at the tables and some at the bar. Corey spied Jay at the bar. He knew he was leaving and he knew that he couldn't possibly walk away and abandon Jennifer and Ellie without some kind of promise from Jay. Corey could feel the animosity in the air, but not one to back down from a challenge he sauntered up to the bar.

When Jay saw him, he swore softly and slipped off the

stool. "What's the matter Butler, scared?" Corey said, sneering.

Jay bristled and backed up. "No."

"You should be," Corey said, his gaze cold and hard as his voice dropped a notch. "I've got a feeling that the only friends you have in this town are your brothers. In fact, I could probably take you outside right now and beat the hell out of you and no one would intervene."

"That's not true." Jay paled and looked around anxiously. "I have a lot of friends."

Corey grabbed the front of Jay's shirt and changed the subject, moving his face a little closer to Jay's, his body taut with overt male aggression. "What would it take for you to leave Jennifer alone?"

"Get the hell out of town, chief. That's what it would take," Jay snarled.

"I've got your promise, Butler?" Corey reinforced his words by tightening his hands in Jay's shirt, shaking him hard once.

Jay swallowed and shifted his eyes from Corey's, his pale complexion turning blotchy red. "Yeah," he growled. "That's what it would take."

"Done. I'm leaving tomorrow on the next bus out of town. Keep your promise, Butler, or all bets are off and you'll have me to deal with. Are we on the same wavelength?"

"Why don't you take your threats and stuff—" Jay stopped short when Corey's expression went dangerously still. Jay's face turned sullen and resigned. "We're on the same wavelength."

"Wise decision," Corey said, and turned away, leaving as quietly as he'd come.

He never saw the murderous look in Jay's eyes, or the evil smile.

Chapter 6

It was dark outside the next day when Corey finally made it back to the foreman's cottage. He'd had two full days of activity, including roping, wrestling and inoculating the new calves. He'd also untangled three bulls that had been caught in some leftover barbed wire some reckless ranch hand had left lying about. All in all, he'd used muscles he'd forgotten he had.

Jennifer had been right, it was like a small house. The three spacious bedrooms and one bath were on the upper level, while another bath, kitchen, den, living room, dining room and laundry room were downstairs. He couldn't spend another night in her warm cozy house in her sweet-smelling bed imagining Jennifer wrapped around him. They had fought about it, but he wouldn't budge. He'd picked up his clean wash and exited to the bunkhouse. Jennifer had given up.

Painfully, he pulled off his boots and dropped them to the floor, then he went into the bathroom and washed the dirt off his face, gingerly cleaning around the almost-healed scrape on his face.

He raised his head and looked up, trying to avoid his own eyes in the mirror, something he'd been doing for weeks now. Ever since he had gotten out of the hospital the vague anxiety had plagued him. Followed by the paralyzing fear when he'd even tried to go near a rodeo again. His outlet for his pain was gone. Now all he could do to assuage his torment was to keep moving. Never to stop or it would swallow him whole.

How could he go on with his life if he couldn't even look at himself in the mirror? What would he have to offer Jennifer? Hell, where had that thought come from? He couldn't stay. He wasn't a fool. He knew what he saw in her eyes. He couldn't be that man.

He had thought when he was a child, if only he could be good enough, his father would love him again. Show him how to draw and sketch. Put his big hand on his head to ruffle his hair as he used to do instead of drawing those hands into fists to hurt him. He wanted to be whatever Jennifer needed because she was all he would ever need.

Walking from the small bathroom to his saddlebags, he searched around for the aspirin he thought he had packed before he'd left the house. But he couldn't seem to find the tablets. His hip was aching so bad he didn't think he could sleep.

He wasn't used to the activity he'd gotten today. His whole body ached and throbbed, but the exquisite pain to block out all the other pain was coming from his battered soul.

He went to the open door of the cottage, looked up at the house and saw a light on in the kitchen. "Damn," he whispered to himself. Was she awake?

Before he could even think that what he was doing

wasn't smart, he was at her back door knocking softly. He needed to apologize for his actions in the barn yesterday. He'd acted like a complete idiot. And he needed to find out when the next bus left town.

Jennifer was in the kitchen making coffee because she couldn't sleep. The kiss in the barn still haunted her. That wild ride brought back memories of how excited she had been about life and it reminded her now how bitter she had become. Where had the joy gone? The pure sweet magic of just being alive. Had Sonny taken that away from her? Had her responsibilities so paralyzed her that she couldn't enjoy just being alive? Those revelations had shaken her. She didn't know she had such a depth of feeling inside her. Never knew she could respond so forcefully to a man the way she had responded to Corey. Never knew she could hurt this bad. Shouldn't she reach out and grab that bit of intensity? Was she a fool? She'd be a fool to let him walk out of her life without once knowing his touch. She shivered in the flimsy robe she wore, her nipples puckering against the fabric. Her body felt intensely alive and throbbing.

She closed her eyes to better concentrate on how his hard, demanding mouth had felt against hers, the almost desperate way he'd held her, as if he needed something from her. Something more than the pressing of lips and bodies. Something more than physical, something elusive and tantalizingly close.

Reckless magic.

She could almost reach out and touch it. She couldn't stop thinking about Corey. How he had looked, the pain in his voice when he believed she had rejected him.

The knock on the door jolted her out of her thoughts. She'd been staring into space while the water overflowed the glass pot she'd been filling. She turned off the tap, disgusted with herself.

Setting the carafe down, she went to the door, holding her breath, praying it was him. Her prayer was answered. His broad shoulders filled her doorway. She could only think of how those thick muscles had felt beneath her hands, the warmth of his skin against her sensitive palms. "Corey," she breathed, unable to keep the need she felt out of her voice.

"I was wondering if you had some aspirin. I'm a little achy. I haven't been on a horse since I got out of the hospital."

Out of the hospital? She repeated the words to herself as she turned her body so that he could get past. Why had he been in the hospital? "Just another reason you shouldn't be on a horse. So don't expect any sympathy from me. Well, why don't you come in?" Regardless of his pain, she couldn't get it out of her head how he had looked straddling that big bay while he roped calves. He'd handled him gracefully, making hard grueling work look like artistry.

He raised his eyebrows. "Are you sure you want me to come in?"

"Don't be silly. Of course you can come in. I'm making coffee, if you're interested."

"That sounds good."

He brushed past her, his chest sliding along hers, and she heard her own quick intake of breath. She quickly moved away from the door and him, hastily making the coffee while he settled himself down stiffly at the table.

"I'll go get the aspirin," she said breathlessly. "Be right back."

Jennifer found the bottle of aspirin and quickly returned to the kitchen. Unscrewing the top, she shook out two tablets.

"Better make it four," he said.

"Are you sure you're okay?" Her hand reached out, but she drew it back. He had said not to touch him.

"Yeah, I'm great," he answered, the bitterness breaking through his words. "Just great."

She dropped the tablets into his hand, trying not to touch him. But still the awareness was there. It crackled between them like heat lightning trapped in a jar.

She wiped her palms on the soft silk of her robe, then went to the stove and poured two cups of coffee. "Black, right?" Her palms were perspiring so badly she was afraid she'd drop the mugs.

"Right." He must have heard the tremor in her voice because with a pained expression on his face he said, "Maybe I should go."

"No. Please!" She put her hand on his shoulder, but instantly pulled it back. "Please stay."

He stood up abruptly. The chair fell back and hit the floor with a bang. "Damn it, Jennifer. Don't act this way around me. I promise I won't touch you again unless you want me to. I'm not some lustful savage who will drag you under me and sate my wild desire!"

She looked up at him, her mouth suddenly going dry. Somehow she had hurt him. Only now did she realize that his actions were not because he didn't want to be touched, but because he craved it.

She knew what she wanted. She wanted to explore what was in her heart, even though her head told her she was being a bigger fool than when she had fallen in love with Sonny Braxton. Ten times a bigger fool because the love she felt for her outlaw was ten times bigger.

She didn't even have to think about her response. In the day since they'd almost made love in the barn, she had thought of nothing else. He would leave. She knew that and suddenly that didn't matter to her. She wanted him, even for one night. For one glorious night of reckless abandon that would remain with her for the rest of her life. "Corey, what if I want you to touch me?"

He groaned softly, gathering her into his arms and pulling her against his hot, muscular body. "Jennifer, this is craziness. I didn't want this to happen. I fought against it."

"What about now, Corey? Are you still going to fight it?"

"Right now, Jennifer," he growled roughly, "I feel if I don't have you, I'm going to die. But I don't want to hurt you when I leave."

"I can accept that you have to leave," she lied. When the time came she wouldn't cling to him, she wouldn't plead and she wouldn't beg. She would just let him go. "I understand that you have to leave. I'll take tonight, Corey."

She could do this. She could make love with him and let him go. It would come with a high price, but it was one she was willing to pay.

She could never give herself to a man without giving him her whole self. She couldn't give herself to a man she didn't love. It was true she did love him. She'd fallen into his needful turquoise eyes and lost her heart. She couldn't tell him that she loved him, because she knew that he didn't want to hear it.

Whatever he was running from was interfering, and the only way she knew to fight it was to touch him physically, show him in the most fundamental way how she felt about him.

It would mean that she would have to stop playing it safe, but for Corey, she would do it, even if he left. She would endure the almost unbearable pain. She would let him go. A brief affair with him was better than never knowing a passion beyond any other. A passion that would burn long after physical desire was met, if only she could break through his noble attitude.

"I was just passing through. How the hell did this happen? I'm alone for a reason. I'm not fit to be with anyone, but I still want you. I really want you."

"I want you, too. I want you to touch me," Jennifer encouraged.

"I want to. God, you don't know how much I want to. But I can't."

"Why? Don't you want to make love to me?"

"Of course I do. I feel it every time I'm near you. But it wouldn't work. You're like the tree, rooted, stable, and I'm like the wind, restless, constantly moving." He stepped back.

"Corey, the wind does blow through the tree and the tree does bend and spring back."

"I don't have anything to give you," he moaned. "I'll be leaving tomorrow on the first available bus. You said you would lend me bus fare."

"I did say I would, but don't go yet, please stay for just a little while and talk to me. If you don't want me, I understand."

He turned around, but she persisted. "You said you were in the hospital. What for?"

He stopped and looked over his shoulder.

"Please, Corey, I'm a really good listener." She put all the pleading and beseeching she could muster into her voice, into her eyes, into the very air around them.

He released a ragged breath and sat down.

She sat across from him and curled her hands around her mug to keep from touching him. "You said you were in the hospital," she prompted.

He surprised her by smiling that sweet boyish smile she

liked so much, but then there wasn't much about this man she disliked.

"I...I was a rodeo rider. A damn good one. I was...at the top, winning just about every rodeo for about ten years. Then I drew Widowmaker."

Widowmaker. The blood seemed to stop flowing in her veins. A cold icy dread filled her. She knew about Widowmaker. He was one of the meanest, orneriest bulls to ever hit the circuit. "I heard they were going to remove him from the circuit."

"They haven't. Anyway, I drew him. I've ridden him before to the buzzer, except this time...my hand slipped. He moved to the left unexpectedly and I found myself eating dirt." His eyes dropped to the table and he refused to look at her.

"And...what happened?"

"At first I was dazed from the wild dizzying ride. I expected the rodeo clown to take care of the bull, but he didn't. Widowmaker just ignored him. He came after me instead."

"Oh my God!"

"I scrambled out of the way. He charged and caught me along the ribs. It was just a scratch, but then he whirled and stood there pushing up dirt with his foreleg. I think everyone in that arena stopped breathing the silence was so absolute, like the calm before the storm. It was surreal, like something out of a movie. I didn't know what to do. I knew if I ran he would catch me before I could make it to the fence. The clown tried to get the bull's attention off me, but Widowmaker was focused on me. It was almost as if he wanted me and only me. He charged again and I barely managed to get out of the way. He gored me...in the hip so close to my...groin. Anyway, he tossed me up in the air like I was a rag doll. The clown opened the gate and he finally went through. I ended up in the hospital.''

"And what else?"

"You want it all, don't you?"

"I want to know what you're running from."

"You wouldn't understand."

"Try me."

"I break out in a cold sweat even thinking about the rodeo. It's not an option anymore."

"Bull riding is not the only competition."

"I can't even be in the ring again without losing it, Jennifer. The first few times I tried bronc riding, I fell off because I couldn't concentrate. I couldn't find my rhythm. Something happened to me. I lost something that I can't get back." He was shocked that he was telling her this shameful story that he had never told anyone. "I've got to go," he said abruptly.

"Corey, please don't. Stay and tell me more."

She got up and came around the table, unable to stand the pain and fear on his face. She put her arms around him and he closed his eyes, pressing his face into the hollow between her breasts. She knew that in that arena, in front of all those people he'd lost himself. His pride, his sense of worth. He'd lost his nerve. But she felt that there was something else driving him besides the loss of his pride. Something she wasn't even sure he was aware of. It was, she was certain, a temporary thing if only he could stop long enough to face his fear.

He struggled out of her hold and stood up, readying himself to leave. "I haven't got anything to give you."

Her eyes searched his deeply before she looked down, following the smooth, lean, muscular line of his body all the way to his groin where evidence of his arousal pressed solidly against his jeans. Her gaze lingered there. "Looks like you have more than enough."

His groan was deep and long as his head dropped back. "You do know how to play with fire, but even a woman with backbone and sass can still get burned."

He dropped back into the chair and leaned his elbows on the table, letting his head fall forward. A black silky curtain of hair covered his ravaged face.

Tenderness and the need to console him rose in her. She leaned forward, bracing herself on the edge of the chair. The nape of his neck was partially exposed and she brushed the rest of the black silky hair away and placed her mouth on his sensitive skin. He smelled so good, male, musky. A heady virile scent that made her dizzy.

He moaned softly and twisted his head and Jennifer suspected he was going to tell her to stop.

But she didn't stop. Her tongue came out and flicked against his hot skin like a lick of flame, and with a growl deep in his throat, he grabbed her around the waist and pulled her across his lap.

She protested with a soft sound of objection. She wanted to taste his salty skin again. She craved him like some women craved chocolate. An all-encompassing need for which there was no substitute.

The fierceness with which his mouth claimed hers took Jennifer's breath away and quieted her complaint. His mouth and lips were a different taste altogether. It was a wild, savage kiss, telling of a man who'd been alone for all his life. A man who desperately needed her. She felt consumed, overpowered, safe.

"Ellie?" he whispered against her mouth.

"She's sleeping," she whispered back. He wasn't going to pull away this time. She was primed for him, had been primed for a long time.

"Ah, hell." He pulled away from her and sat up.

"Corey?"

"I don't...damn...I don't have any protection."

Jennifer swallowed hard, gathering her courage. "I do."

He looked at her then. The shock on his face would have made her laugh if she dared.

"What did you say?"

"I bought...some...a little while ago. I thought I was getting serious with this one man, but he was just interested in my assets."

Corey laughed softly and leaned his head on her shoulder. "Jennifer, I'm interested in your assets, too."

"Yeah, but you're interested in getting into my jeans and I'm interested in letting you."

"Where is it?"

"What?"

His laughter sputtered again. "The protection."

"Oh." She laughed, the humor diffusing her tension. "Upstairs in my bedroom."

He rose in one powerful push of his thighs, cradling her in his arms. "Well, want to go get it?"

"Yes." She licked her lips. "I want to get it real bad."

He climbed the stairs effortlessly and walked into her room. He dropped her onto the bed and looked down at her. "I can't sleep because I want you. I have a hard time working knowing you're in this house. Every time you come near me I get hard."

"Corey," she breathed, excited beyond words, aching to join with this lonely, stubborn man. "Then don't wait another minute. Why don't you get rid of your clothes first?"

"That's what I like. A woman who speaks her mind." He leaned down, placing both hands on either side of her shoulders and without preamble took her mouth in a searing brand of heated flesh, burning his delicious taste and compelling scent into her senses until her world was filled with him, until it encompassed only him. She reached up, sliding her hands into the hot silk of his hair, tangling around the smooth strands.

He moved his mouth from hers, and his turquoise eyes burned with a seductive smoldering desire that spoke volumes. He searched her eyes. "Say you want me, Jennifer. Tell me, darlin'." His voice was a raw whisper edged with a need that vibrated in the still room, vibrated through her, making her skin hum, her flesh burn, her heart melt like molten gold.

She had never even had a chance.

With all honesty her voice hushed out, "I want you, Corey. I fought it, but it was too much for me."

He sighed. "Ah, Jennifer," he said, lowering his mouth to the soft skin of her neck and nuzzling her gently. "I know. God, how I know. It's like trying to shoulder a mountain."

"Speaking of shoulders, I'd like to see yours. Now."

"Pushy little thing, aren't you?"

"When I'm after something I want very desperately, yes."

He stood up and unbuttoned his shirt much too slowly for her. Unable to wait another minute, wanting to touch him with a fierce longing, she rose onto her knees and grabbed the shirt, slapping his hands out of the way. She unbuttoned the material, soft and worn against her fumbling fingers. Finally, the garment fell open and she eagerly grasped the edges, pulling the fabric away from his chest and pushing it off his shoulders to land on the carpet.

"Oh my God," she breathed. "You are as beautiful as I remembered." She placed her palms flat on his chest, testing his muscles, running her palms over his smooth warm skin, over his nipples, rubbing a little harder when he groaned, the flat disks pebbling under her ministrations.

"You're so sensitive."

He opened heavy-lidded eyes to peer at her. "I thought women liked sensitive men." He gave her a slow, knee-melting smile.

"Oh, we do. We do." She responded by leaning forward and flicking her tongue across one nipple. His hands came up to cup her head just as her mouth closed over the hard peak.

He trembled and jerked. She could feel his reaction against her mouth and in his hands where they rested in her hair, against her scalp. The rush of power and feeling came all at once, almost too much for her to bear. The soft, surrendering groan made her need burn hotter. This strong, brave man trembled because her mouth was on him. That thought and his reaction made her weak and warm.

As she drew lazy circles around his puckered flesh, his breathing grew harsher, his muscles flexing beneath her hands where they were braced against his arms.

Before she could even begin to get her fill, he jerked her head away. His eyes were glazed with desire, his face stark and hard, the passion for her etched deeply in his expression. His eyes bored hotly into hers and she got a glimpse of the wildness in him.

She saw something else there, as well. She saw his fear, real, so very real, burning with the desire. He closed his eyes briefly as if he was in great pain.

"Corey," she said fiercely, raising to her knees so that she was level with him. "Just one night. I understand. You're leaving in the morning. I'll drive you to the bus depot. Don't think about it now. Don't let it intrude on the time we have together. Please."

He tilted her head up. His eyes traveled over every inch

of her face as though if he looked long enough, hard enough, he could burn her visage into his brain. He swallowed and leaned close, so close his mouth was almost touching hers. "Tell me one more time. Tell me you're sure about this. God, Jennifer, don't let me hurt you. I don't want to hurt you, but I'm a bastard. I still want you. I don't give a damn about anything else."

She touched his face softly, gently, and slowly he sank to the bed, wrapping her in his arms.

"Yes, you care or you wouldn't ask me again. I'm sure, Corey. I've never been surer. You're not a bastard, just a bad boy and you understand. Bad boys always understood me, but you, your insight is astounding. You were right. I'm a wild reckless woman inside wanting to get out... wanting—"

His mouth cut off her words, sucking her into a vortex of pure feeling and touching. Their clothes disappeared without conscious thought. He took his time touching her everywhere, claiming her as his and his alone.

Pushing her onto her back he whispered, "Where's the protection, darlin'?"

She looked up at him with unfocused eyes.

"Jennifer...?"

She blinked as if coming out of a dream. He smiled seductively at her expression and she smiled back a little sheepishly. "Oh, in...the drawer by the bedside."

He found what he needed and took no time slipping the sheath on. And then he entered her, his lips parting on her name.

His baby-soft whisper rang in Jennifer's ears like a shrill whistle. Her own cry of pleasure mingled with the sound of her name as he slid into her.

He cupped her face and stared down into her eyes. "I want you to know that this is no one-night stand. I want you to know that this means a great deal to me. Shh,'' he said when he saw her get ready to speak. ''Don't talk. Don't ask me for promises and I won't have to break any. Just know that I'll never forget you.''

She closed her eyes, trying to think around the excruciating pleasure that was running in intense waves through her body. But the thoughts whirled away and the words remained. Later, when she was coherent, she would sort through them. Take them out like shiny pieces of glittering glass to look at and savor the beauty.

She sighed softly. This was what she wanted. And as she knew when she'd made the decision to take what she wanted, she knew the aching pain of letting him go.

But tonight was hers.

Holding him here would be wrong. It would be like holding a wild animal that was trying desperately to find freedom. Corey was tortured and unwilling to tell her why. As much as she wanted him to stay, she wanted him to make that decision himself.

He moved then, slowly, by degrees, and every thought fractured and spun away. There was no yesterday, no tomorrow. Just now, just this man, just Corey.

She felt as if she were trying to breathe in a sauna, the air was so thick with sensuality and the heat of their passion. It had never been like this. She hadn't had much to compare lovemaking to, but she knew deep down that it would never be like this with anyone else. ''Only you, Corey,'' she murmured, her voice filling with a sob from the sheer intensity of their joining.

''God, Jennifer, you're so damn beautiful. Touch me, darlin','' he whispered.

Jennifer was almost unconscious from the intense pleasure that rocketed through her each time he glided into her, holding her breath so that she wouldn't miss a minute, finding each delicious sensation even better than the last. She clutched at him, molding her hands over strong and muscled flesh. His slow deep thrusts were torturous, bringing her closer and closer to peaking splendor only to withdraw and intensify the next wave of pleasure.

She moved with him in the slow dance of the ages as if she were irrevocably mated with him, reunited from some time long past, sweet perfect searing rhythm, the pleasure beyond her comprehension. Surely this kind of bliss could only exist in heaven. How lovely to find a small piece on earth in this man's arms.

He slipped his forearm under her hips and lifted her so that he was deeper inside her. He slowed his thrusts even more and with her hands she urged him faster.

"Come on, pretty darlin', let go."

She tensed, the need in her coiling tighter.

"Stop…moving…so slow. Please, Corey, have mercy. It's been…so…long."

"Not until you give me what I want." Sweat poured off his body with the intense concentration that it required not to lose command of himself. He was close to breaking, his control hanging by a thread. He thrust slowly, his whole body taut with the devastating need inside him.

"Corey, please. Harder, faster."

He leaned down and took her lips, pushing himself as deep as he could go, rocking slightly. A flash of exquisite sensation shattered through her, and she cried out, "Corey, you're so bad."

His body jerked as she spasmed around him and he whispered on the quiet air, "Bad, yeah, so bad."

He rolled to his side pulling her against his chest and she nestled against him. It felt so right.

"You're leaving tomorrow?" she finally asked.

"Yes." He lifted himself onto his elbow and looked

down into her flushed face. He pushed a wisp of hair off her forehead and leaned down to kiss her lips. "I can't accept a job with you."

"Why?"

"Because, Jennifer, I'm not ready to commit or settle down." He seemed to know those words would hurt her, but they were the ones she expected to hear. He sighed when the disappointment clouded her eyes and she closed them briefly as if to keep back tears. "You're sorry, Jen darlin'?"

She reached up and pulled his head down, cupping the back of his head, kissing him with warmth and tenderness. When the kiss ended, she smiled at him. "No. I'm not sorry. I'll never be sorry. It's what I wanted."

He eased away from her, slipping out of bed. "Where are you going?" she said, her words laced with uneasiness.

"To the bathroom. Any objections?" His mouth quirked with amusement.

She watched him walk across the floor and disappear into the bathroom. He moved beautifully, with a graceful prowling stride. A loose-hipped swagger with no self-consciousness at all. The man had more sex appeal in his little finger than most men had in their whole bodies.

How was she ever going to let him go?

He came back to bed and stretched out alongside her. Gently he reached out and drew the covers away from her body. "Beautiful," he breathed, gazing at her breasts. His dark head bent and he took a suddenly puckering bud into his mouth.

She cried out his name in wonder and delight, her hand caressing the back of his neck.

He pushed her back and she couldn't believe it when she felt the hard heat of his arousal against her thigh. "Corey? Already?"

His head lifted, that savage heat in his hot turquoise eyes. "I'm always ready for you, darlin'. I hurt for you, Jennifer."

Her skin grew damp everywhere and tingled. Her heart tripped into a faster beat.

"I'm hurting, Jenny," he said again. His mouth hovered over hers, then dipped down to rain her with little biting kisses.

She ran her hand down his taut abdomen until she reached the hardest part of his body. The part that made him so intriguingly male. "Is this where you're hurting?"

He growled deep in his throat as she stroked him. "Thank God we have all night," he managed to say, his breath ragged, his words hoarse. "I just might get enough of you."

He kissed her feverishly then fumbled for protection with trembling hands. And when he entered her with force and need, his raspy voice close to her ear, he said, "But I doubt it."

The sun was hot, too hot on his skin, the sand of the ring beneath his bare feet grainy and burning. The absence of sound was deafening and he raised his head suddenly, the instinctive fear clutching around his heart. He came face-to-face with the pitch-black bull, his eyes red glowing embers of hatred. His father stood next to the animal, feeding him fire with his bare hands. Corey swallowed, his throat dry with terror. The sun beat down on his bare skin and he looked down to find himself naked and vulnerable. He wanted to cover himself and cower, but he knew if he did he would die. Death breathed down the back of his neck, trickled over his skin, brushed cold fingers down his spine. The black monster moved and his shadow enveloped

*Corey as the sun was blotted from the sky and an unnatural
darkness covered everything.*

*She stood beyond the shadow in blazing white, her fiery
hair loose and blowing free around her face. She reached
out to him but he couldn't seem to move and then she, too,
was swallowed by the blackness, fading slowly until finally
disappearing as if she had never existed.*

*Pain ripped into his side like a white-hot brand, piercing
his body. He gasped and cried out, falling into the dirt.
Blood splashed darkly against the ground and he felt the
life seeping out of him...*

He jerked awake, half sitting up in bed. Jennifer sighed
next to him. That small sound was oddly comforting. He
slipped out of bed and stood at the window, trying to get
control of his breathing. His body shook. The nightmare
lingered in the shadowed corners of his mind, taunting and
tormenting him. He braced his hands on either side of the
window and leaned forward. Cold sweat slipped from his
hairline, running down his cheeks like tears.

Would he ever be free of this damn unrelenting fear? His
heart felt crushed. For the first time in his adult life, he
knew what it was to be close to what he had yearned for
as a child. He turned and looked down at the sleeping
woman he'd been snuggled up to only moments before and
he marveled at her courage.

She'd been hurt before by a husband who didn't want
her. He was sure her husband had abandoned both wife and
daughter. It was inconceivable to him that someone would
actually leave Jennifer.

"Corey?" Her eyes opened, her voice husky with sleep.
Just the sound was enough to send his heart racing.

Her arms were around him before he could move away.
Immediately her body jerked and she released a heartfelt

sigh. "Oh, Corey," she said softly, pressing harder into him. "Nightmare?"

He trembled and took another shuddering breath, squeezing his eyes tightly closed. He nodded once quickly.

"About the bull?" He nodded again, not willing to burden Jennifer with his past and the horror he lived with when he closed his eyes.

She dipped down and picked up the silk robe she'd been wearing when he brought her upstairs earlier. Gently, she grasped his arm and pulled him away from the window. With tenderness she wiped his face and dragged the cloth down his chest. The soft silk flowed over his nipples and his sex responded with immediate evident need.

She dropped the robe and cupped his straining manhood, molding her fingers over the swelling flesh.

He was a fool to let her seduce him into bed. He was falling fast. He was falling hard. He felt as if he were falling without any support. The nightmare had left him feeling alone and terrified. The demon attacked his unconscious mind, but Jennifer's hands eased away the dread.

His body bucked with each stroke of her hand. He moaned with each touch, each gentle exploration. "Jennifer, I'm hurting." His voice was raspy with the heightening pleasure of her touch and the fading panic.

He was hurting, all right, both from her touch and from the pain in his heart. He reached for protection and reminded himself he had one night. Well, if that was all he had he was damn well going to build enough memories to last a lifetime. He grasped her upper arms and eased her against the bedroom wall. He dipped his head and clamped his mouth over one nipple. She cried out from the ardent pull each time he suckled her nipple against the roof of his mouth.

His deep masculine moans were mingled with hers as he

switched to her other breast. "Corey." His name was only a whisper of sound, a wisp of breath, but he heard her.

He responded by crushing her against the wall, drawing her leg up his scarred hip. He probed her expertly, knowing just how much of him to insert into her to make her frantic for more. His body was tense with need, and slowly he slipped inside her.

Stardust gathered around them like glittering pieces of white fire as frantically they both moved in perfect harmony, reaching not for the bright, swirling bits, but for the very white-hot stars themselves, to then clasp the heat and invite it inside where it burned and broke into quivering fiery supernovas.

Minutes later he unbuckled his knees and picked her up in his arms, holding her tight and close. He moved to the bed, gently laying her down. He knelt on the floor and leaned against the bed. He knew if he got in bed with her, he would never want to get out.

"Corey, tell me about the nightmares."

He had always believed that he would never be able to tell anyone his innermost feelings. He had always believed that he could never trust anyone or feel close to anyone. Never feel close enough to let someone touch him. Yet he had already told Jennifer more than he'd ever told anyone in his life. It gave him a warm, soft feeling inside, one he had never experienced before and suddenly leaving became much more difficult. He could see in her eyes that she genuinely wanted to know and he again lost the battle against his own inner will. The one that always told him never to tell because of the shame.

"The bull doesn't gore me in the hip in my dreams. Sometimes it's my groin, sometimes my chest, my stomach." He swallowed the bile in his throat as he remembered other terror-filled nightmares where his battered body lay in the dusty ring and his father stood over him, laughing.

She reached for him and wrapped her arms around him. "There are people who can help you with this. I know…"

He jerked away. "No. No shrinks. I don't need anyone telling me how I feel." He pulled away and began to dress.

"Jennifer, the sun is beginning to rise. I should go before Ellie wakes. It wouldn't do for her to find me in here with you."

"You're right." Gently she touched his face, caressing his cheek with her questing fingers. Then abruptly she pulled her hand away and let him go.

He closed his eyes because no matter how much she tried to cover it up, he heard the slight tremor in her voice. He was so attuned to her he could hear her need, could feel it prickle where she'd touched him, sinking bone-deep into his body with aching clarity.

He wished this had been simple sex. It would have been so much easier. He jerked on his jeans and threw on his shirt, not even bothering to button it. He gathered up his boots and stopped briefly at the door. "Let me know when you're ready to take me into town."

Chapter 7

Jennifer forced back the surging pain in her heart. All the way to town she denied what she already knew to be true. She couldn't love him. She just couldn't. She'd only known him for three days. Then why did it hurt so much that he was leaving, she asked herself. Why?

Last night was a wonderful dream that had to end. She had to accept that.

"One ticket to—" She turned to Corey who stood with his saddlebags hanging over his shoulder. He looked strained and tired. She wondered if his head was hurting. Damn, why should she care? Why should she care for a man who had protected her, kissed her with so much emotion and need, touched her with such tenderness that it brought tears to her eyes? A man who looked as if he didn't have a friend in the world.

"Where do you want to go?" she asked.

He shrugged and her chest ached with that little gesture. It said he had nowhere to go and that he didn't care.

"What's the end of the line?" Jennifer asked, turning back to the teller.

The woman glared at Corey and said in a waspish voice, "San Antonio, mister. You want to go?"

Jennifer saw Corey's jaw clench as he struggled for control. "Yeah, that's fine. As long as it's far away from here."

Her heart twisted with fresh pain and she turned away. Ellie stood next to her, solemnly waiting for her mother to buy the ticket. At Corey's words, she saw Ellie flinch and swallow convulsively.

"San Antonio. One ticket, please," Jennifer asked.

The woman quoted her the price and Jennifer paid for the ticket. She turned from the counter and walked the few paces to where Corey stood.

"I'll send you the money for the ticket when I get where I'm going and get a job, okay?"

"No."

"Jennifer, I'm not going to argue with you about this again."

"Then don't. Just take it and go. You don't owe me a thing."

He was about to protest again, but she pleaded, "Please, Corey, let me do this. I *owe* you. This doesn't even cover the cost of the motorcycle. *Take it!*"

"All right, Jennifer," he said with resignation. His intention was to send her the money, anyway. She could do whatever she wanted with it.

He refused to look directly at her. It was too painful. She needed him. Her eyes spoke it in volumes. The need for a foreman, the need for him to stay, the need for *him*.

Apprehension was growing inside of him at the thought of leaving Jennifer and Ellie here with those vicious cowboys. There was the bargain with Jay, yet how could he trust the man? How could he leave her? God, what kind of a man was he?

A coward.

Maybe that was what he was running from. He didn't like feeling this way. His whole world had been shattered. The goring, the deaths and for the first time he was feeling...what? Whole? As if for just a little while he was getting some of himself back. Or was he losing himself to her. Her and Ellie.

She reached up and lightly touched his cheek with the back of her hand. "You're going to send me the money, anyway, aren't you?"

He shrugged and looked away, her soft touch almost breaking him.

"Maybe," she said, whisper soft, "you'll deliver it in person." Very deliberately she got up on tiptoe and kissed his mouth softly. He could taste her regret.

Then she was gone, brushing past him. Ellie turned around and smiled. He saw in her expression a child who knew about abandonment. He saw her cover up her pain and smile, once again to spare his feelings. It was as if the child recognized the lost little boy in him who didn't know where to turn to or who to trust. The tears flooded his eyes and blurred the vision of her sweet smile.

Then she broke away from her mother and hugged him around the waist with tight affection. "Bye, Corey, and good luck. I'll miss you." Then she was gone out the door, clasping her mother's hand.

Her gesture almost broke him in half. It almost sent him to his knees. But with years of hard control he fought that weakness and endured. As he did when he'd been a child. Happiness was always followed by pain. A sick feeling of apprehension stirred inside him as he watched them cross the street and go into the diner. And with the apprehension came the shame. He clenched his fist, crushing the ticket, and with a swift jab hit the wall. The pain of split knuckles barely registered.

He loved her. Loved *them*. But it didn't change a damn thing. He was heartsick with the knowledge. Despair wrapped around him. To hell with it all, he silently screamed. He was leaving because he had no choice. All those years he'd avoided it, ducked it, hid and ran from it, but now, in a few short days, he'd succumbed to the delicious feel of family, home, a normal life. God, a sweet normal life.

Yet, the fear was always there. It was there now torturing him, tormenting him with the sureness of what would happen if he ever let himself take what he wanted. If the black rage lurked inside him, he didn't want to discover it with Jennifer and make all his nightmares into reality. That fear, dark and terrifying, was what made him push the tears away—and let him turn his back on a woman who needed his help and a little girl who obviously worshiped the ground he walked on.

He went outside and sat down on the bench to wait for the bus, ignoring the ache in his heart and the clenching in his gut. The printed time on the ticket was ten forty-five and it was ten-forty now. He looked across the street and watched Jennifer and Ellie sit down in a booth near the window. Ellie waved, but Jennifer refused to look.

He was leaving.

He watched them for a while and felt the apprehension intensify. His body craved Jennifer's touch as he watched her push Ellie's hair out of her face. He wanted her hands on him. He tore his eyes away from them. The grief was a heavy pressure in his chest. He rocked forward, trying to ignore the force of his need to get up and cross the street. Where the hell was that damn bus!

He was leaving.

He closed his eyes to block them out, trying desperately to hold on to his composure. He was so close to breaking down right here in a bus terminal. So close to tears his throat ached with holding them back. Closing his eyes didn't help. It intensified the feeling, bringing back the memory of her hands on him urging him faster. The feel of her spasming around him, crying out her release into his mouth. Those soft, hot, moist lips. Oh, Jennifer!

His breath caught with the agony of wanting.

He was leaving.

He knew he could help Ellie win competition after competition. He could train that mare and together the girl and that horse would make an unbeatable team. He would get such pleasure in watching her win. Watching her with that sweet determination on her young face. So fresh, so innocent, and he would fight hard to let her keep that innocence, that verve for life. He would if he had deserved the chance.

If it wasn't for the violence he feared was hidden inside him.

He looked down the street and saw the bus making its way slowly toward him like a fat silver bug. He rose in anticipation of those doors opening. He saw himself climbing aboard, felt the soft cushion of the seat against his back....

He *was* leaving.

Jennifer didn't hear the bell on the door ring. She didn't even notice how quiet the diner had gotten. Her thoughts were in chaos. She had the urge to run out the door and beg Corey to stay. But that was foolish. He wouldn't. He'd told her time and time again that he wouldn't. It was for the better.

Then why did it hurt so bad? Why was it every time she

closed her eyes she could feel his hands, see him flash that devilish teasing smile, smell the warm clean scent of him?

She had just decided to beg him to stay, when the bus pulled up and obscured him from view.

She rose in a panic, then turned and walked right into Jay Butler and his brothers.

"Where's your pretty-boy half-breed? Don't tell me it was wham-bam-thank-you-right-kindly-ma'am."

"He ain't so pretty now." Emmett snickered.

Jennifer didn't want to admit it, but the words stung. In the next instant she knew that wasn't fair. Corey had warned her from the very beginning. He had never lied to her, never let her believe anything except that he was leaving. In fact, if she wanted to be completely honest, she'd thrown herself at him. She'd kissed his neck and said outrageous things to him for one purpose only. To get him into her bed. She would cherish their lovemaking for a very long time. She would not let Jay sully her precious memories.

"Jay, you must have him mixed up with yourself. I know what you're after, and you're not going to get it. So back off and leave me the hell alone." Jennifer distastefully removed his hand from her arm as if it were a live snake.

"You started this the other night, you little bitch, and I'm going to finish it. You're going to be my woman and my woman only."

The bell rang on the door and Jay turned around, his lip curling into a sneer. Tucker Garrison stepped into the diner, his eyes narrowing on his father. "What a surprise, *Dad,* you bullying people again?"

Ellie felt that persistent little flutter in her heart when she looked at Tucker. Quiet and serious, the sixteen-year-old had been her friend for as long as she could remember. He didn't smile often, but when he did it was all that more

devastating in its rarity. It was only now that she seemed
to be having a problem breathing whenever he was around.
He kept his distance from all the other kids at school, but
there had always been something about him that drew her.

"Jay, why don't you leave her alone?" Tucker persisted,
and Ellie got the impression that he was deliberately avoiding her eyes.

"Shut up, you little bastard, and don't get in my way,"
Jay snarled without taking his eyes off Jennifer. "So come
on, Jennifer, give me what you owe me."

"There's only one thing larger than your overinflated
ego," she said. "The Goodyear Blimp. I have no interest
in a relationship with you now or ever! Leave me alone!
Ellie, let's go."

Jay grabbed Jennifer's upper arms, his mean eyes narrowing in threatening malice. "You're not going anywhere
until I get the kiss you owe me."

There were low murmurings in the diner, but no one
intervened. No one wanted to draw Jay's viciousness to
them.

"Let go of my mom, you bully," Ellie demanded, jumping out of her seat, her dark green eyes flashing.

"Ellie, go out and sit in the truck and wait for me."

"Yes, Mom," Ellie said.

Ellie went to leave the booth, and Stuart, Jay's youngest
brother, blocked her way.

Ellie's little chin lifted and her eyes narrowed. "You're
blocking my way, Mr. Butler. Would you kindly move?"
There was steel in Ellie's voice and Jennifer couldn't keep
the half smile from her lips. God, was she her mother's
child!

Stuart pulled on her braid and Ellie lifted her foot and
stomped on his booted one. When he didn't move, Ellie

said, "Even a dumb animal knows to move when he's prodded."

Stuart stepped back in surprise. Ellie continued with acid sweetness, "Didn't your mother ever teach you guys any manners?"

Tucker tried to muscle his uncle out of the way. "Leave her alone, Stuart. She's just a kid."

His voice was different, deeper, protective. Ellie had never heard him use that tone before. He'd always been so quiet, so polite.

Stuart raised his arm and backhanded Tucker across the mouth. Ellie gasped and gave Stuart a venomous look. "You mean bully," she cried as she slipped out of the booth, squeezing by him.

Tucker lay on the floor cupping his face. She touched his shoulder gently and he flinched, but his eyes reached for hers. They were darker and deeper than she expected full of mystery and magic, and her young heart gave another little lurch. She pressed a napkin to his bleeding lip, and smiling softly, she said, "Are you okay?"

"Smart-mouthed kid. Smart-mouthed mother," Jay drawled. "The two of you are peas in a pod."

"I think you've got it wrong, Butler. You're the one with the smart mouth. Too bad those smarts don't extend to your brain."

Corey's unnerving turquoise gaze captured Stuart's attention. "Don't touch the boy again, cowboy."

Jennifer caught her breath and her eyes went immediately to the source of that deep, compelling voice. He stood with his hip thrown out in mock relaxation, one thumb hooked in the loop of his jeans, and the other lying against the smooth leather of the saddlebags draped over his shoulder. His hat was pulled low over his remarkable eyes, his smile was lazy, but edged with cold steel. His stance did nothing to alleviate the threat radiating off him like shock waves moving soundlessly through the still air. He looked as if he was chastising four children instead of facing down four hostile men who had already beaten him once.

Jay stiffened, then turned around to face Corey. "You still in town, chief? I thought you would be long gone by now," he mocked snidely.

Corey heard the gloating tone in the man's voice, saw the smug smile crawl across his florid beefy face. Bullies. He hated them and he knew why. His father had been one, and Jay wasn't any different. Jay was afraid of him. He could see it in his eyes. And from experience, he knew that bullies were afraid of the people who could defend themselves and cruel to the ones who couldn't.

"No, I'm stuck here for a while at least. My motorcycle was vandalized and I was mugged."

"Well, now, ain't that a crying shame." Jay smiled and his brothers all laughed. "Yeah, a crying shame, indeed. Me and my brothers were out honky-tonking a couple nights ago and we were real near the motel, but we didn't see no one."

"No, I reckon you didn't. You were too busy beating the hell out of me." Corey's eyes narrowed and a thin smile appeared on his lips when Jay stepped back involuntarily.

"You've got two good legs...still," Jay said threateningly, but with less heat. "Why don't you walk out of town?"

"Well, I'd like to oblige you, Butler, but I've got myself a commitment." The grim warning in Corey's tone made Jay pale.

"What commitment?" he sneered with an insinuating tone. "The lovely Jennifer's *body*guard?"

Corey's anger rose when he heard the snickering. Jay

and his brothers circled him like coyotes surrounding a sleek black panther.

"No. Her foreman. She hired me. We had a bargain, Jay, but you didn't keep up your end, so I'll be sticking around."

He heard Jennifer's quick intake of breath, but didn't dare take his eyes off Jay and his brothers. Jennifer had pointed out each one, by name, on one of their trips into town. Now he noticed that Jay was the smallest of the four. The others were bigger, and they certainly outnumbered him.

Well, he'd been in tougher fixes. He was in one now with a gorgeous redhead.

When he'd been rodeoing he learned a good offense was better than a good defense. Corey charged before they even realized what he intended. He caught Clovis in the chin and the man sunk like a ton of bricks. He whirled, taking a hard punch to the chin that rocked him back, but he deftly ducked the next swing coming up with a punch to the soft flesh of Jackson's underarm. The man sucked in his breath sharply, the pain etched on his face.

Emmett grabbed him around the neck, his forearm cutting off his wind while Jay hit him in the stomach. Corey's ribs protested violently, but he ignored the excruciating pain. Suddenly the pressure on his throat loosened and Corey was able to block the next punch.

He looked over to see Jennifer still holding the napkin dispenser that she'd used to hit Emmett. Her face showed her surprise and a sudden wild look sprang to her eyes, followed by a smile. Corey returned her grin, then looked over at Ellie who was covering her mouth in surprise after she'd deliberately tripped Stuart. He laughed out loud, suddenly feeling very light and airy.

Jay helped his brothers up and they regrouped, arguing

with one another. The bell on the door jingled and the sheriff strode in. "Problem, boys?" He touched his hand to his holster and gave them all a penetrating gaze.

Jay responded in the negative and all four Butlers exited the diner.

Corey wiped the blood off his lip. The throbbing ache in his ribs traveled in slow waves all through his body.

Suddenly a burst of clapping started in the corner of the room until the whole diner joined in. Still feeling as light as a cloud, he ignored the clapping, smiling people. He was annoyed at them for not stepping in and helping two children and a beautiful woman, so that he could have gotten on that bus and already been away from here. Away from these painful wants and needs. Hell, who was he kidding? These painful wants and needs would have just followed him.

Corey walked painfully over to the boy and helped him up, giving Ellie a smile of encouragement. "You okay, kid?"

Tucker flushed and nodded then brushed past Corey and exited the diner.

Ellie ran after Tucker. She caught him by the arm, and when he refused to turn around, she walked around him. "Are you okay?"

"No. I have a mean-spirited bastard for a father who likes to pick on women and children because that's all he can intimidate. God, they're like a pack of rabid wolves."

"Tucker, you came to help me. I appreciate that."

He flushed. "Fat lot of good I was."

"You were wonderful." She took the bloody napkin out of his hand and dabbed at his split lip. "Want me to kiss it and make it better?" Ellie didn't know where the words had come from, but suddenly she felt awkward as Tucker stepped back, obviously uncomfortable, as well.

He flushed again and jammed his hands into his pockets. "Um, so are you going with me tonight to dig night crawlers, or what?" he said testily.

Ellie was so relieved to have the topic changed that she quickly nodded. "For sure. I wouldn't miss it."

"Great," Tucker mumbled and brushed past her, calling out gruffly, "See you around, kid."

Corey had Jennifer by the arm and was leading her out of the diner when Ellie entered. "Ellie, who was he?" Corey asked.

"People say that Jay fathered him, but I heard he raped Tucker's mother."

"What do you know about rape, Ellie? You're only thirteen years old."

"Yeah, but I know about sex, Corey."

He looked over at Jennifer who only shrugged her shoulders. "She would have found out about it from less reliable sources. I just thought she should hear it from her mother."

Corey shook his head in resignation and his attention shifted back to Ellie. Gravely, he said, "Rape is not about sex, Ellie."

Ellie slowly nodded her head as if she'd known all along.

"Corey..." Jennifer started but never got to finish.

"Don't say a word. Just get in the truck." He moved through the booths as people reached out to clasp his hand and give him the thumbs-up.

With Jennifer on one arm, he grabbed Ellie by the hand, then dipped down quickly to pick up the saddlebags he'd dropped just before attacking the Butlers.

Ellie looked up at him with deep respect in her eyes. "You don't even fight dirty."

He looked down at her. "How would you know about that?"

"Hey, I watch Clint Eastwood movies," Ellie said indignantly.

When they reached the truck, Corey swung Ellie up into the seat and gently pulled on one of her braids. "You, little darlin', are watching too many movies. I only fight when I'm provoked. Violence never solves anything."

"Yeah, I know, but you sure didn't like Mr. Butler saying those mean things about Mom."

Corey looked at Jennifer over the high seat, with a wry look on his face.

"Don't look at me. It isn't my fault she's so intuitive," Jennifer defended herself.

His eyes shifted back to Ellie who gave him an angelic smile. He tweaked her nose. "Little darlin', I'm feeling real sorry for the man who's gonna have to tame you."

"Tame me? I don't reckon anyone will tame me." She matched his drawl perfectly.

He laughed, shaking his head. "Lord help us all."

When he didn't immediately get in the truck, Jennifer asked, "Did you mean what you said in there? Have you accepted my offer of becoming my foreman?" She couldn't keep the hope from her voice as she watched him. Watched his face tighten in remembered pain.

"Yeah, I guess I did. I said it, didn't I?" He growled his answer, angry for being a fool and not getting on that bus.

"Good then, Mr. Rainwater, get your backside in this truck. We've got a lot of work to do," she ordered solemnly.

"Yes, ma'am," he replied. Another smile spread across his face, and he settled himself next to Ellie on the passenger side. The apprehension was gone, replaced by the unexpected feeling of going home.

They rode in silence for a few miles, over terrain that was dusty and dull brown.

"Jennifer?" Corey broke the silence.

"Yes."

"What's with that mare you have corralled? I never see her doing anything but lounge around. Are you going to breed her?" he asked casually, not looking at Ellie.

"No. I hadn't planned on it. I was at an auction and the man who was auctioning her was beating her. Had been for a while. I bought her on the spot. I can't abide the beating of animals. It's too bad she's wild. She looks like she would be a sensitive little thing."

"Would you mind if I try to gentle her?" He felt Ellie stiffen next to him. She lifted her face to him, and he would have gladly pulled down the moon, the sun and the stars to get her to look at him like that again. Hero worship, pure and simple.

"Why?" Jennifer asked, interrupting his thoughts.

He cleared his throat and gave Ellie a conspiratorial wink that brought the foxy look back to her face, a shrewd gleam to her eye. He chuckled a little and Jennifer gave him a sidelong glance.

"Well, I think she'd make a champion barrel racer."

"Oh, you do?" Jennifer said knowingly, glancing at Ellie, who was staring out the windshield as if she wasn't hanging on every word.

"Yeah. I'm really good with horses. At least you'll have a working animal instead of one not pulling its weight. The mare has potential, Jennifer. A lot of potential," he said softly.

The softness of his words was like a gentle caress against her body. God, the man didn't even have to raise his voice to make a point. She couldn't seem to refuse him anything. "I guess it couldn't hurt. But, Miss Eleanor Jean Horn, before you try to get on her back, I want Corey's word that it's safe.''

Ellie seemed to burst at the seams. "I promise, Mom. I'll wait until Corey says so." She looked at Corey and smiled and Corey was lost.

"That brings up another problem. I'll need a horse," Corey said.

"Take your pick in the stables."

When the truck pulled up to the house, Corey let Ellie out. To Jennifer, he said quietly, "Can I talk with you for a minute?"

"Sure." She turned to her daughter. "Ellie, go ahead up. I'll be there in a minute."

Corey came around to the driver's side and leaned his forearms on the edge of her door. Glancing down, he scuffed his boot on the ground. Then he looked up and pinned her with a look that could freeze fire.

"I think it would be best if we...if we weren't intimate again."

Jennifer's hands tightened on the wheel. "Oh. It was that bad?"

He reacted on instinct, jerking open the truck door and pinning Jennifer between his body and the rigid steel of the truck. When his face was inches from hers, he said, "I'm going to say this just once. You were amazing. Responsive, hot, wonderful." He couldn't resist, his mouth brushed hers. "I just can't give you false hope that I'll stay on very long, and to be frank, Jennifer, the thought of making love with you, then walking away makes my stomach knot up."

"Then—"

He never let her finish. "No, Jennifer, I can't stay. I can't be what you want me to be, ever. It wouldn't be fair to you."

"Corey, are you running because of the goring? Are you ashamed?"

He stiffened, then met her eyes squarely. "That doesn't even begin to touch how I feel. I don't want to discuss this with you, Jennifer."

"But what if I want you? What if I don't care about what's going to happen in the future?"

"I care, darlin'." He caressed her face with the tips of his fingers. "I care very much. You aren't a one-night stand woman, and you broke a rule for me, didn't you?"

She looked down. "Yes."

"I rest my case." He turned then and walked away from her.

Chapter 8

Jennifer felt the anger build within her with every loose-hipped step he took. What the hell was going on with this guy? She took a monumental risk in sleeping with him and he acted as though he'd taken advantage of her. Well, she didn't sleep with just anyone. She'd *chosen* to make love to *him*. Hell, she'd waited thirteen years. *Thirteen years!*

It had been worth the wait.

She stomped after him and grabbed his arm, turning him to face her. She saw the pain in his eyes and the distressed look on his face. A man on the edge, she thought again. She wanted so much to pull him back from the chasm. "That wasn't a one-night stand and you know it!"

His eyes pinned her with their intensity. She saw his fear, need and, God help her, his vulnerability.

"Okay. How about a once-in-a-lifetime encounter?" he quipped, his emotional distance obviously back in place.

She took a deep fortifying breath at his shuttered expression. The vulnerability disappeared as if it had never been. But she'd seen it. It had been real. Her heart spasmed because of it. "Corey, you weren't the only consenting adult in that bed last night."

He looked down and toed a rock with the tip of his dusty boot. "You're right!" He ground the rock beneath his boot as if he were trying to crush something inside himself. "I was just as consenting as you. I let you seduce me, because like I said last night I'm a bastard."

"You let me!" Her voice rose with each word.

"Jennifer, keep your voice down."

"Keep my voice down? I will not! I'm not ashamed of anything. Corey, what's so wrong with what we did? It was beautiful and I won't have you making it into some kind of shameful act on your behalf. I wanted you, so stop with this nonsense about being a bastard." She swallowed convulsively so that she could get the next words out of her mouth without stumbling over them. "It was wonderful, but I know the score. I'm a big girl. You walk away in the end. I know that. There's no reason we can't—"

"No!" he said vehemently. With an exasperated flick of his thumb, he pushed the hat off his head.

"Corey, look—"

"No, Jennifer, you look. I made a mistake last night that I don't intend to make again. I'll turn around right now and walk off this ranch if you push me on this, I swear it." He turned away, his body rigid.

"What are you afraid of?"

"You," he said harshly. He looked toward the house where Ellie had disappeared. "And her."

"Why?"

"You make me want to stay." The anguished words burst from his mouth as he grabbed her upper arms and shook her. "I can't. I can't be what you want me to be. And she...God, she makes me want to be a father in the worst way, but that's another impossibility. I won't have kids."

He shifted uncomfortably, shying away from the hand she lifted to touch his face. "And you deserve kids, lots and lots of kids. She deserves a normal father." He faced her, his turquoise eyes tortured and shielded at the same time. He raked his hands through his long hair. "I'm a drifter who's wasted his years on the circuit. I have no future, Jen. Accept that. It was true what I said last night. I have nothing to give you except maybe heartache." Abruptly he turned to go.

Again she stopped him. "It isn't easy for me to ask."

"It isn't easy for me to say no."

She watched him saunter toward the bunkhouse with his saddlebags draped over his shoulder, and her emptiness and sorrow was almost too much for her to bear. Too late, she thought. The heartache was already there.

How could she get through that thick skull of his that he was all she needed, all she wanted? She'd been waiting for him all her life. She hadn't realized it until now. He'd set her free, yet he didn't know how to set himself free.

She wanted to know about those shadows in his eyes and she wanted the knowledge she needed to banish them back into the darkness. He hadn't said he *couldn't* have children, he said *wouldn't*. Why? What could he possibly fear? The need to know ate at her.

She'd let him inside her heart too deep to dig him out. This man who was tortured, yet protected her as if he was her own appointed guardian angel. This man who was obviously running from something painful and deep, yet had stopped for her. He'd fought for her, been beaten senseless, his personal property ruined. Didn't he know that he had himself to give? All the passion she'd experienced last night couldn't have been just show.

She had taken greedily and she wanted more. "The fight has only begun. You're going to lose and you're damn well going to like it!" she murmured under her breath as she watched him disappear into the foreman's cottage. She kicked at the dirt determinedly before she turned and walked into the house.

The next morning she found the first slashed canvas. The frame was broken and splintered with jagged pieces of wood sticking up like bleached broken bones. The tattered canvas had held some kind of painting, but it was unrecognizable now. An undercurrent of uneasiness spread through her as she fingered the ruined edge of the material. She'd asked Corey to dinner last night and he had refused right through the cottage door. He wouldn't even open it to talk to her face-to-face. She had been so angry she'd told him to go ahead and starve.

She looked down at the canvas and a slow-moving pain traveled into every part of her heart. Corey. It had to have been Corey. Why? Why would he take the time to paint something and then destroy it?

She let go of the cloth and went around to the barn. Just then, her neighbor, Stanley Martin, drove up and belatedly she remembered she had made an appointment to show him the new litter of pigs. He wanted one for his daughter Lilly.

"Damn," she muttered under her breath as she looked at the barn. She was sure Corey was picking out a mount. She wanted to talk to him about the ruined canvas. She wanted to know what was going on in that gorgeous head of his.

She sighed and walked away from the barn, forcing a smile at Stan when he got out of his truck.

"I'll take this one, Tex."
Corey had been moving down the stalls looking at all

the animals. Tex had been talking a blue streak about all their attributes, but Corey knew which horse he wanted. He'd been watching the big stallion since he'd first stepped into the barn.

He couldn't concentrate on Tex's words. All he could think about was how Jennifer had looked yesterday afternoon. How she had stood up to him and challenged him. The woman was on a mission. He could see that. He wasn't blind. She thought she could save him. And she didn't want to take no for an answer. Well, to keep his sanity, he could not touch her again.

He had to walk away. It was frightening knowing that even as he said it to himself, he still wanted her. Wanted her beneath him, moving with him. He wanted to wake to touch her fiery hair in the morning, more beautiful than the blazing glory of the rising sun. He wanted to see those sleepy green eyes open and feel those lips soften beneath his.

"Oh no, you idiot, he's a monster. You don't want him."

Tex broke into Corey's wicked thoughts and he snapped back to attention. He stepped closer and spoke the words that came from deep inside him, from the part that was Native American. It was a phenomenon he'd never questioned. The big gray lifted his head just as Corey knew he would. Large, liquid brown eyes watched him. The pointed ears flicked forward.

Tired from the night before because he'd stayed up painting, using canvases and supplies he'd borrowed from Ellie, Corey didn't worry about the animal biting him. He reached out his hand.

"No! He bites," Tex said, the danger vibrating in his voice.

But it was too late. Corey reached out and felt the warm breath of the animal as it snuffled his hand. He stepped even closer, his voice lowering and softening even more. He touched the velvet nose and stroked the animal's sleek neck.

"How many of these unruly animals does she own?"

"Five, not including him and the mare you're training. She's a mite softhearted when it comes to abused animals."

Corey winced at that comment. "Tex, get me some tack."

Tex stood still, his mouth gaping open in surprise. "But, son, he's a monster. Jennifer won't be happy to see you eating dirt or, God forbid, with broken bones. She'd skin me alive."

"Jennifer doesn't own me, Tex, she's just hired me. I'm my own responsibility. Don't worry. I'll let her skin me."

Tex hesitated then a grin flashed across his craggy face.

"Tex—" Corey pinned him, his gaze direct and focused "—just do it."

"Yes, boss, you're the crazy one."

"Stan, I think this little one will do for Lilly. She'll love him." Jennifer kept her concentration on what she was doing. But she wanted to talk with Corey so badly it was like a pressure in her chest.

"Yeah, the child wants a pig in the worst way. I think the little sow will do fine," Stan replied, holding the little black-and-white-speckled pig gently.

Jennifer hadn't planned on the breeding business, she'd just fallen into it after she got Two Tone for Ellie on her ninth birthday.

"Who's the big Indian in the black Mexican hat? I haven't seen him around here before."

Jennifer closed the gate and dusted her hands on her jeans. "He's my new foreman."

"I thought you said that big gray stallion was too mean

to train. I didn't want to sell him to you, Jennifer." Stan sounded miffed.

"He is. I tried to train him, I really did, but he tried to bite me a dozen times. I was thinking about selling him as stock. It's such a shame, though, because he's such an intelligent and beautiful animal."

"Your new foreman seems to think so, too."

Jennifer whirled and her eyes went to the corral like radar. "Oh, hell, I don't have the patience or the time to hire another foreman. He's barely healed. That horse will kill him."

She took off at a run, but it was too late. By the time she got to the corral gate, he was already astride the gray. The animal quivered and sidestepped. She watched as Corey jammed his hat tighter on his head and tightened the string.

She could only mutter, "Oh my God!" as the horse erupted into motion. But he didn't buck straight up in the air in that twisting-bronc motion. Instead she saw horse and rider charge across the corral and cut a young bull from the herd with expertise. Then she noticed the branding fires and two of her ranch hands waiting with the red-hot iron.

It was something to see. A pure cowboy in action. Corey's big thighs bunched and clung and she noticed how the gray knew what to do without being directed. Corey already had his rope out and was swinging the lariat over his head with quick easy flicks of the wrist. He handled the rope and the bull with skill and grace that startled a gasp out of her and the many ranch hands who'd gathered and now stood transfixed. There was a compelling magnificence about Corey that awed her. A powerful, radiant force that affected her down to her toes. A respect that insinuated itself around her. She watched him take an animal that she'd considered hopeless and bring out the promise, the sheer beauty in him. Monster, as she fondly nicknamed the stallion, stuck to the bull like glue, so precisely and beautifully in tune with it that she found herself gaping along with the rest of the hands. Both man and animal moved as one in perfect harmony. They did ten bulls quickly and efficiently.

And she couldn't help noticing the new spring to the gray's step, the arrogant way the horse swished his tail and strutted.

She'd tried time and again to get That Big Gray Monster to obey. She'd cajoled him, bribed him, even trained him over and over and still nothing had worked. Leave it to Corey to choose himself a rogue horse.

Whoops greeted Corey as he dismounted and patted the horse with pleasure. She saw his mouth moving and the horse's ears swivel to catch what he was saying. He tipped his hat and his voice rose clear and full of authority, "Let's get the rest of these bulls branded." No matter how much she wanted to talk to Corey, branding was a hot, sweaty, dirty job and these guys would be hungry by lunchtime. She figured she had better talk to Tex to make sure everything was okay in the mess hall.

Before she could turn away, Corey's gaze captured hers. His eyes were blazing with triumph and a hardness she hadn't seen before, as well as a desperation that made her stomach knot. Very slowly he raised his hand to his hat and just touched the brim before he whirled. She watched in awe as the horse took off, and Corey, with the agile grace of an acrobat, mounted the animal on the gallop.

Her heart fluttered in her chest. She felt a sudden and unexplainable urge to call him back and have a showdown with him. Tell him that her heart couldn't withstand his indifference.

She bit her lip as she approached the mess hall, her mood

bleak. The demolished canvas was still uppermost in her mind. What had he seen in that painting that had made him destroy it?

A shiver of apprehension wrenched through her. She was in for a battle if she wanted to win him. She thought about their night of lovemaking and yearned for the warmth, the sweet contentment and the startling passion that had swept over both of them when their lips had met. She wanted it all with him. Everything. Happily ever after. She wanted it for herself. She wanted it for him. And she wanted him for Ellie.

Ellie deserved a father like him. One who gave a damn. It was obvious that Corey enjoyed Ellie and she had such a huge dose of hero worship that Jennifer's throat knotted thinking about how Ellie would feel when Corey left.

Jennifer found Tex in the mess hall, muttering and cursing to himself, and without a word she plunged in and helped him prepare the huge lunch.

Hours later the hands began to file in one by one and Tex made sure all of them had washed their hands before he let them sit down to eat steaming mashed potatoes, large thick steaks and fresh green beans. Jennifer searched the many faces, but could not find the one she sought.

Heading for the barn, she ducked inside the cool interior, a balm to the heat outside. Corey was brushing down Monster, preparing him for the afternoon workout.

"That was the most amazing horsemanship I've seen in a very long time." Corey seemed to fill the barn with his presence, his sheer sensuality and strength permeating the very air. His short-sleeved black T-shirt was stuck to his chest, outlining every gloriously hard muscle. Jennifer felt a thrill in the tips of her fingers, the base of her scalp, along her exposed skin, like a slow warm tingling.

"It's not so amazing, darlin'. He's a cow horse and your

neighbor had him riding fences. He was confused and didn't understand. I just put him to work with what he enjoyed doing. He settled down because now he's happy.''

She sensed that he was annoyed she was here bothering him. Or was he nervous?

She watched him continue to brush the horse with strong quick movements. His forearms, darkly tanned and powerful drew her attention. He'd used those arms to handle hundreds of live beef on the hoof, stopping them literally in their tracks. He was easily the most devastating man she'd ever met and he didn't even have a clue.

''Want something in particular, darlin'?'' He turned and scowled at her, his voice edgy. He still wore his hat and it was pulled low over his face so that all she caught was a glimpse of hot aqua and a glittering flash of warning. He still wanted her and that thought sent little frissons of heat down her back.

She smiled at him, a wicked, nasty little smile that brought dancing lights to her eyes. A smile her father would have immediately recognized and sent her right to her room. It felt good. It felt too good to be her old self again to play it safe. She didn't want to play safe anymore. She wanted Corey, hot, out-of-control and hers. ''You nervous, cowboy?''

His eyes narrowed and flashed beneath the ominous brim of his hat. He looked every inch the outlaw she'd named him. He straightened from brushing the horse and faced her. With his legs spread, he dropped his hands to his hips, which bunched the strong, flexible muscles across his chest. Her eyes were automatically drawn to him, totally caught off guard as need rocketed through her. It wouldn't be so hard if she hadn't felt those sleek muscles with her own fingertips. Heard his indrawn breath catch when she'd touched his nipple with her tongue.

Her eyes raised to his face. She could see him swallow convulsively. "Jennifer," he warned.

"Are you going to draw on me? That's fine with me. I like the weapon you use." Her voice purred, like a contented cat. "It's so deliciously...*deadly*." She spoke slowly, letting the words come out soft and husky.

"Jennifer, don't push me."

"You won't leave me, Corey. I need you."

He swore so viciously that Jennifer stepped back. "Go back to the house and take care of business. Stop this right now."

She bit her lip, suddenly contrite. Taking the few steps that brought her up to the stall, she picked up Monster's bridle. "You're right. I'm sorry. I just don't want you to think that what happened last night was all one-sided. I wanted—"

He held up the hand with the brush in it. "You've made your point and I've made mine. Don't say any more. Not another word." He turned to finish brushing the horse.

Jennifer decided to ask him about the canvas when he was in a less volatile mood. She shouldn't have pushed him so soon. But she wasn't about to give up.

"Didn't your parents ever discipline you?" he asked caustically, brushing harder than necessary. But Monster didn't seem to mind. He snorted and leaned into each powerful stroke.

"Yes, but usually it didn't do any good," she said. "I was heading for a big fall, but I'm thankful to my parents. And they helped me pick up the pieces. They died knowing that I could handle the ranch. And I'll die before I let Jay Butler think he can use me to take it over. That's what he wants, you know. His ranch is adjacent to mine. He thinks that now that my parents are dead, he can move in and take over my land. That's what all this two-stepping stuff is all about. He doesn't like to lose, Corey, and he doesn't like interference.''

"Don't worry, darlin', I can take care of myself. Butler's a mean-spirited bastard, but he better think twice about hurting you.''

The threat in his voice made Jennifer smile. "You're such a big bad hombre, huh?''

He looked up at her, his face impassive until he realized that she was teasing him. Unexpectedly his face broke into a grin.

"How long have your parents been dead?'' he asked as he picked up each of Monster's hooves to examine and clean out the dirt and debris.

"A year. They died in a plane accident. My father liked to fly. They were on their way to Vegas.'' She laughed. "My dad loved craps and Mom loved the slots. They always had a budget. When they lost what they had set aside, they came home as happy as clams.''

He saw the fond memories in her eyes and winced. He envied her her memories. "My parents are dead, too, and my little sister.'' He picked up the brush again, unable to stop the flash of emotion that sliced into him.

"I'm sorry.''

His chest filled and he didn't trust his voice. Two little words and they meant so much to him. Silence lengthened and thickened in the barn as once again Corey's curiosity about Jennifer's husband surfaced. Could that fall she had mentioned been her breakup with her husband? Had this man hurt her? The thought made him angry. Without examining the reason that he wanted to know, he asked the question that had been plaguing him since he'd met her. "So where's your husband, Jennifer?''

The unsuppressed anger in his voice had her eyes lifting from the buckle she was fiddling with on Monster's bridle.

"Gone. I found him in bed with a trick rider. Our bed, where Ellie was conceived. It did something to me, changed me." She let out a quick breath. "I guess that would change anyone. I haven't trusted a man since."

Corey stopped brushing and walked over to the stall door. "He cheated on you?" His face showed his disbelief and confusion. "He had a woman like you and he wasn't satisfied? He wasn't happy with the little life he'd created inside of you? He threw it all away? The stupid bastard." Corey couldn't believe what he was hearing. The man must have been a moron. He had all that Corey had ever wanted. He *had* it in his hands. "He threw away this—" he caressed her cheek with his fingertip feeling the response in her as she shivered "—for one night of lust?"

Jennifer's throat tightened. "Not one night, Corey. Many, many nights. Trick riders, barmaids, barrel racers, anyone who was willing."

"The fool. The monumental fool."

He forced himself to move away from her, thanking God that there was a stall door in the way. He felt that fierce yearning build in his chest, churning in his gut, and Corey cursed the man who was stupid enough to throw away what was so infinitely precious to his own self. A family. A beautiful family. "And what about Ellie?"

"He's never seen her. He even insinuated that she wasn't his."

Corey wanted desperately to hit something. The deepening pressure in his chest built. He wished the man was here right now so that he could take him apart. "He wasn't worthy of you, Jennifer. You'll find someone." Why did that hurt? Why did those words stab into his gut like knives? He walked back to the big gray and continued grooming.

"Yeah," she agreed.

"Yeah," he echoed, his tone changing.

"Enough about me. What about your parents? You must have gotten that amazing talent with horses from your father," she offered, not put off by his short, irritable tone.

"What makes you say that?" he said scathingly, shame and the old fear bubbling up in his throat. He'd gotten a talent from his father, all right, but it wasn't his way with horses.

"Your last name is Rainwater, not a traditional Anglo name. I assume that the Indian blood you have came from your father's side of the family."

"Naturally." He gritted his teeth. Half the blood that flowed in his veins came from his father. He held the brush tighter, the seething anger making its way closer to the surface.

"So I assumed that he was the one who taught you how to handle horses."

He straightened slowly, the anger vibrating through his body exploding in ringing force. It wasn't anger directed at her, but the power of it swept through him like a brush-fire out of control. He threw the brush across the barn, a devastating fury crossing his face. His anger was even more fearful because it was so sudden. "The only thing I learned from my father was how to hate." He stepped out of the stall, causing Jennifer to back up quickly. He cringed inside even though he hoped the violence he had inside of him would be contained. He didn't like the frightened look on her face. He latched the gate angrily, his movements choppy.

"Ms. Horn?"

At the sound of Jimmy's subdued voice, she turned around. "What is it?" she said sharply.

"I was checking the fences on the north pasture and,

well, someone shot Sidewinder and Happy-Go-Lucky.''
His young eyes were stricken at the brutality.

She covered her mouth and tears filled her eyes. "The
vet?''

"I already called him, and the sheriff, too."

"I'll come right away. My horse?''

"Saddled and waiting, Ms. Horn.''

"Jennifer, do you want me to come with you?'' Corey
was filled with concern for her, his anger banked.

"No. That's all right. You eat and work on the branding.
I need you here. That's why I hired you. You're doing a
good job. Thanks.'' She avoided his eyes and he didn't
blame her.

She didn't look back as she rushed out of the barn, and
instinctively Corey knew that Jay Butler was involved.

He did as she'd asked. He ate and then returned to the
branding. When the day was complete, he once again took
careful care of his mount. When his chores were completed,
the stallion bedded down and watered, he shucked his
T-shirt and loosened his jeans. Leaning back against the
stall he was surprised to find that the scent of her lingered
in the air. He closed his eyes and remembered how the soft
delicate perfume of Jennifer's body had smelled their one
enchanted night together. Remembered how her skin had
tasted.

She wanted him to stay, maybe even wanted something
more, but his mind closed down on that idea. He couldn't
let himself even contemplate becoming part of their lives,
but he couldn't help wishing for things that could never be.
He groaned softly and raked his hand through his sweat-
soaked hair. He wanted to wake up beside Jennifer every
day, to face Ellie every morning over the breakfast table
and watch her animated face as she talked about things that

interested her in the fast way children did, jumping from one subject to the next. He wanted Jennifer to support him, love him. He wanted to make a child with her, to watch her stomach grow with his seed, to hold his child in his hands and look into those young, innocent eyes and know that this little life he created was his responsibility.

But how could he be sure the secret fear he carried with him wouldn't turn into a horrible reality?

He couldn't. In that second, the dream he'd just created and built died and with it went more of himself.

He exited the dim barn and walked to the outside hose. Turning on the tap, he raised it over his head, sighing as the cool water brought him some physical relief.

Jennifer was lost in thought as she came around the corner of the barn, heading for the tack room to deposit her saddle and bridle. She would have to talk to Jimmy about mending her bridle. It was getting frayed.

Surprisingly, she wasn't thinking of how she'd arrived at the pasture to find her bulls, Happy-Go-Lucky and Sidewinder, down in the field, lowing in pain. They'd had to put down Happy-Go-Lucky. The bullet had shattered his leg and the vet had said there was no other choice. She had done it herself. Destroyed thousands of dollars of prime stock that her father had carefully and dutifully bred and nurtured. It had made her fighting mad. Her insurance would cover the loss, but the genetics and sheer promise of Happy-Go-Lucky were lost forever. He had been in his prime with a lot of young yet to be conceived. Thank God, Sidewinder's wound had been superficial. She had told Jimmy to post a guard on the pastures where her breeding stock grazed. She had also told her suspicions to the sheriff. Fat lot that would do.

Instead she was thinking of how dark Corey's eyes had

turned when she'd asked him about his father. She thought about how much she wanted to soothe him and take away the pain and fear in his eyes. What was he afraid of? She now discounted the goring. At one time she was ready to believe that he was drifting because he couldn't face his failure.

She'd had all afternoon to think about why he would hate his father, and she could only come away with one conclusion. Abuse. She'd recognized his pain when he first kissed her. And she knew there was something embedded deep down inside him that made him do what he did. Some reason that he wouldn't allow himself to have children.

The sound of running water brought her thoughts back to the present. She looked up and stopped dead in her tracks. Corey was using the outside hose to cool off. He was rinsing off the worst of the day's grit, she thought distractedly.

He faced her, his eyes closed, the water sluicing through his hair and over his smooth chest. Her eyes dropped down his powerful body, heat curling in the pit of her stomach. The water was soaking into the waistband of his unsnapped and low-slung jeans. He was breathtaking—even dirty, sweaty and wet.

As if he felt her presence, he stiffened and his eyes opened. His jawline tightened and his wonderful eyes flashed with the innate stubbornness that she had come to know so well.

"I thought you were down at the north pasture."

"I…was…I   came…finished…with…the…sheriff…" Her words trailed off and she was unable to pull her eyes away from him. She knew she sounded like an imbecile and she felt like an idiot.

"What happened?" he said tightly, the concern evident in his voice.

She couldn't draw her eyes from his chest if her life depended on it. "I had to put down Happy-Go-Lucky."

"I'm sorry, Jennifer." There was true sadness in his words. "Do you think it was Butler? Just give me a reason, darlin', and I'll take care of him."

"Yes, I think it was Jay, but I have no proof, and violence only begets more violence, Corey."

"I know that. But, Jennifer, it's the only thing *he* understands."

Her dazed eyes traveled from his face down his body and she licked her lips slowly.

Corey took a deep breath. "Jennifer, turn around and get the hell out of here. For God's sake, for my own sanity, stop looking at me like that."

With an embarrassed groan, she wrenched her eyes away from his magnificence and turned away, but she didn't move. She couldn't seem to get her legs to move.

She heard Corey swear again and she heard him approach, her throat going dry. She could hear his raspy breathing and the sexy jingle of his spurs. She closed her eyes tightly. The sun had set and the darkness was complete except for the wan light from the barn and the quarter moon. She could feel his presence behind her, engulfing her, protecting her. His hands were like red-hot brands when they dropped to her waist, and without any urging, she dropped her tack and turned in his arms.

"Jennifer, didn't we agree that we weren't going to complicate matters?" His voice was a tortured rasp that sent heat and sensation skittering across her skin.

"No, you gave me an ultimatum. I don't take threats well, and I can't forget the way you made me feel. I don't want to forget the most wonderful night of my life." Her eyes focused on his lips, and to save her soul she couldn't look away.

The stark look of pain flashed across his tanned face and for a moment she felt as if the ground had been wrenched from beneath her feet. "Jen," he breathed, "you're driving me crazy. I couldn't sleep last night. I need you. I'm hurting so bad."

She couldn't help herself. Her finger came up and touched his mouth and he took it inside his own, suckling her with delicious sweeps of his warm, moist tongue. Closing her eyes against the powerful sensation of his wet velvet tongue against her skin, she groaned when his mouth left her finger and came down on her lips, hard, demanding, masterful. Jennifer made a low sound, surrendering to the urgency clamoring within her, her mouth softening beneath his seeking lips.

With a moan deep in his chest, he pressed her body against the wet heat of his, and her clothes soaked up the moisture on his skin. An urgent stirring sizzled in her blood, pumping through her body when he roughly clasped her hips and pulled her against his hardness. She moaned again when Corey's hand moved up her body, cupping the back of her head, deepening their kiss, his mouth frenzied and wet.

With a force that knocked the breath from her lungs, he backed her right against the warm heated wood of the barn. Abruptly the kiss ended, and unable to let her go, he commanded hoarsely, "Run."

"Corey," she started to say between thoroughly kissed lips. But her words stopped when she saw the look in his eyes. She could push him into it. She saw that he was hanging by a thread, but suddenly she couldn't do it. The power she held over him would be corrupted if she forced him to break a promise. She could see that she was forcing him. His jaw was clenched, his eyes hard with something besides passion, and his body tense with his need and the inability to help himself.

A man at war with himself. It was breathtaking.

He closed his eyes as if in agony. "I don't want to break my word, but if you don't go now I'm going to lose it and take you right here in the dust and mud. Run. Now!"

An hour later, when a knock sounded at the cottage door, he expected to open it and find Jennifer standing there. Instead he found Ellie, breathless, clutching a sketch pad to her chest, her eyes bright with mischief.

"Shouldn't you be in bed, little darlin'?"

"Yes. I should, but I'm not. I snuck out to see you. I haven't seen you all day and I wanted to show you something." She gave him a coy smile, which slowly disappeared from her face. "Is this a bad time?"

"No. Come on in and show me."

She walked in with Two Tone on her heels. He just trotted in as if he owned the place and sat down near Corey's feet, looking up at him with those dark, intelligent eyes. Corey reached down and petted him, smiling at the pig's pleasure-filled grunt.

Ellie sat down in one of the brown leather chairs and opened the sketch pad. "I've been working on this since you showed me what I was doing wrong. I wanted to know what you think."

He came around and sat on the arm of the chair. "Ellie, this is beautiful. That little mare never looked so good."

"I watched her a lot before I tried sketching her." Her voice was filled with pride.

"Have you ever tried to add any color?"

"Once, but it came out awful. So I've stuck to pencil. Besides," she said, laughing, "you can erase when it turns out wrong."

He smiled and smoothed his hand over her soft hair. It was loose, lying on her narrow shoulders. A feeling came over him, one that was tender and painful at the same time. And to think her father hadn't even seen her. "Ellie, I think it's time for us to begin gentling that mare. What do you think?"

She caught her breath and looked up at him, the expression on her face rapt and full of joy. "You really mean it? You're going to train me to barrel race?"

"Sure I am, darlin'. When I promise something, I don't take it back." He took her little hand in his and squeezed. "Start by taking care of her tomorrow. Feed her and groom her. Spend as much time around her as possible. Let her get used to you. Talk to her, feed her treats."

She nodded knowingly. "You can catch more flies with honey than with vinegar, huh?"

"Yeah, something like that. Now scoot before your mother finds you gone and panics."

"That would never happen."

"What? She never looks in on you?"

"No, silly, she never panics." Ellie picked up her sketch pad and walked to the door. "Corey?"

He smiled at her tentative tone. "What now?"

"I want to tell you something, but I don't want you to take it the wrong way."

"I can take it. Shoot." He got a subtle warning, a tiny shiver up his spine, a shattering pain in his chest before she spoke. Not fully prepared for the words, they gouged into him with stiff fingers.

"Well, I've never had a dad to compare anyone to, but you sure would make a great one." In her young heart, Ellie knew it was true and she also knew that Corey Rainwater would not stay. She wasn't blind, and although she was thirteen years old, she understood about adult love. She guessed that her mother was in love with this guy and Ellie knew how easy it was to fall in love. She knew how easy it would be to love a dad. She'd wished a long time for a dad and if she had her choice, she'd choose Corey.

A long time ago she had found out what her father looked like. She knew his name was Sonny Braxton and she'd decided that when she was on the circuit she was going to find him. She hadn't decided what she would say to him, but she was determined to tell him how much he had let her down, and her mother, too.

"I mean that you're so understanding and willing to help me," she said. "Even some of the cowhands older than you don't have the time of day for the boss's kid. I guess what I'm trying to say is, thank you."

With a satisfied smile Ellie innocently opened the door to leave, unaware of the blow she'd just dealt him.

His throat constricted and he suddenly found things blurring in the room.

He couldn't answer, so he nodded. He didn't raise his head until the door clicked shut. He didn't know how much more he could take before he was broken completely in half. Maybe he had been wrong to come here and stir up her feelings for a father she'd never had. He was going to hurt her when he left and suddenly he couldn't bear that.

Raw gut-clenching pain racked him and he rose from the chair and went to the easel near the window. He'd painted the forbidden picture again. He removed the white cloth he'd draped over it last night. Some of the paint had rubbed off onto it. He hadn't slept, just painted at a frantic pace. Just looking at it was as painful as Ellie's words. It was his fondest wish brought to life. Deliberately he picked up the knife lying on the table and made the first cut. It hurt physically. Each stroke burned in his heart, scarred his soul. But he didn't stop until the destruction was complete. The destruction of himself. The destruction of his dream. And without dreams there could be no hope.

Chapter 9

Lying here in the dark, hungering for Jennifer, wasn't doing him a damn bit of good. He threw back the covers and got out of bed. He should have gotten on that bus. He would have been in San Antonio now—doing what, he didn't know. Wandering aimlessly, hungering for Jennifer. He didn't have money or transportation. He needed this job as much as she needed him.

He picked up the picture of his mother and sister that he kept near his bed wherever he went. He looked into their faces and saw the haunted eyes of his mother and the wise old eyes of his sister. If only his mother had listened to him and left his father. *If only.* He put down the picture and pulled on his jeans. Barefoot, he exited his room, padded across the living room and opened the door. Stepping outside, he took in the crisp night air.

Ellie's words seemed to hush around him like the soft promise of beauty in a woman's sweet smile, the sudden laughter of children and the sharp sound of a baby's first cry. He wanted to reach out and take what she had so innocently offered him. To be her father would be a privilege, an honor, a blessing, but he couldn't do it. He had failed too many people already.

His inability to save his mother and sister was just another failure in a long line of failures. Why was loving so difficult? he wondered. He stepped off the porch and headed toward the barn. The pungent scent of horses and hay greeted him as he stepped inside. He walked down the row of stalls until he got to the one where the mare, Limelight, was bedded down for the night. He draped his arms over the stall and spoke a soft word of beckoning. He'd made some progress with her. She was used to his voice and his scent. Even so, she approached cautiously and he knew how she felt.

He'd learned it was always better in any type of relationship to be cautious. Letting someone touch was risky because touch was the first sensation he remembered hating. Touching hurt.

He closed his eyes, the silence of the barn ringing with his father's vile curses and accusations—and the sound of a hand hitting already bruised and stinging flesh.

Without warning, warm soft hands traveled over his back and wrapped around his waist. He jerked from the gentleness of the caress. Jennifer's touch was like a salve to his soul, cooling the stinging pain of things that could never be. She was teaching him that touch could feel so good. Good enough to die for.

"So did Ellie show you her picture?"

"Yes," he whispered, not wanting to destroy the fragile peace that she had just woven around him, a buffer to the destruction that had him leaving his bed in the middle of the night.

"She's drawing beautifully. Whatever you told her seems to have sunk in," she said.

"I should have known you would know where she was."

"I guess I'm too overprotective."

"No, you're not. Children are precious and need to be watched every second. It pays to be cautious."

"Tell me why you hated your father," Jennifer said after a few moments of silence, her arms still wrapped around his waist, her face against his back.

He'd never talked to anyone about his abusive father. His typical reaction had been to deny. He could remember the lies he'd told friends, doctors and teachers. *I fell.* Or *I tripped.* He used to break out in a cold sweat at the thought that anyone would find out he wasn't from a normal family. Even now, as an adult whose father couldn't hurt him anymore, he hesitated and agonized, still trapped in the dark nightmare.

As if sensing his distress, she kissed his back and her hands moved, stroking his ribs. He sighed, marveling at how soft her touch was, how good it felt to be caressed and held. The hunger that ate at him every day seemed to abruptly abate. He soaked up the essence of her, craving for more of her touch. "I don't want to talk about him tonight, Jennifer."

"I'll help you to sleep then if you want."

"Jennifer, please," he said in a begging tone that told her how close he was to the end of his endurance.

"I promise, Corey. I'll just help you to sleep."

He turned around and met her thickly lashed, tormented eyes. Sincere eyes, loving eyes, knowing eyes. Something broke within him, but instead of substance rushing out, something beautiful and strong rushed in and filled him up. His voice was hoarse and wry when he finally spoke, "No funny business."

She smiled, a look coming over her face that was very much like Ellie's sly expression. "Even if I promise to respect you in the morning?"

He laughed, a great wonderful bubbling inside of him. She returned his smile and wrapped her arms around his neck, holding him close in the warm, pungent barn. The heat of her seeped into his body, warming cold and lonely places—places he thought were out of reach from any human touch.

"I need that tonight, Jennifer. I need you," he offered sincerely. "No pretenses or complications. I just need your touch." He pulled away from her and looked into her face, the dim light throwing shadows across her delicate features. He never realized how much pleasure a human being could derive from a simple touch. He needed to feel her in his arms, to wrap her close and tight. The thought released the tension in him, diffused the bitter anger always seething below the surface, dissipated the restless energy that had him pacing in confusion.

She held such power in her small, delicate hands. He reached down and captured one, bringing it up into the light. He turned it over, studying the elegant fingers and soft skin. Gently he traced her life line and felt her shudder beneath his hands. He wanted to howl at the moon, so intense was the feeling her response evoked in him.

Jennifer looked into his face, noting the signs of strain even the laughter couldn't melt away. "Well, isn't that a coincidence? I need to touch you," she said. She smiled, warmed by the grin that flashed across his face.

Run. The word echoed in her head and she remembered only hours ago she'd heeded his words and run back to the house. When she had reached the bright lights of home she had locked herself in her bathroom until her ragged breathing stilled. She had been up against the barn and if he had stripped her naked and taken her there, she would have let him. She had shaken from the memory of the amazing passion that sprang between them every time they were together. It was unnerving and just a little scary.

No. It was too late for her to run. Much too late.

She was on the verge of falling for him harder than she would have ever dreamed. She was committed, whether or not he wanted her to be, and sadly she couldn't go back. She knew he was going to hurt her by leaving and she still couldn't stop the need to give him all that she had to give. She wasn't sure she wanted to.

She led the way back to the cottage. "Do you want me to touch you on the couch or the bed."

His eyebrows rose and she laughed. "Now who's being naughty?" she asked playfully.

"The bed will be fine." He smiled, leading her up the stairs to his bedroom.

"So accommodating," she teased as she went into his bathroom and got moisturizing cream out of the medicine cabinet. When she returned, she noticed the cloth-covered canvas and her heart contracted. She walked over to it. "Corey?" He glanced up, his eyes narrowing.

"No, Jennifer. It's not ready for you to see yet."

Was that panic in his voice? she thought suddenly. "Will it ever be?" she asked matter-of-factly.

He shrugged, clearly uncomfortable. "I don't know. It's a very special painting."

"Corey, I noticed the destroyed painting in the trash. Are you trying to make this one perfect?"

He shifted from one foot to the other, clearly uncomfortable with her question. "This one is infinitely different than that one. I just wasn't happy with the way the other one turned out."

"Do you always slash them like that? It looks as if you did it in anger."

She'd never seen his expression so closed, so remote and emotionless. "Do you want me to drop this?"

"Yes. I need you, Jennifer. I don't want to talk. I want to feel your hands on me, touching me." He turned so that he was in profile.

The deep blue-black of his hair gleamed from the overhead light in the room. It was one of his most beautiful features, like warm black silk heated from the inside out. Through the opening of his unbuttoned shirt, she could see the hard planes of his chest. She couldn't stop her gaze from traveling down to his navel and to the dark hair that disappeared into his tight jeans.

His voice deepened. "I like it when you touch me."

Abruptly he turned to face her, his expression stark with truth. "I enjoy talking to you and listening to your velvet voice. I love watching your face in passion and anger. You are one of the most honest people I know. I admire the way you've raised your daughter alone. And you've done a damn good job. Putting your life back together after the way you were betrayed couldn't have been easy. The courage it must have took amazes me. I wish I had that kind of strength." He put his hands on his hips and bowed his head. "Ah God, Jenny darlin', I've been alone a long, long time. I never realized it until now. Until I met you."

He sounded so weary, yet not defeated. Pride still burned in his eyes. He was a man who took charge and dammed all consequences. He was a maverick. A loner.

An outlaw.

Her outlaw.

His heartfelt declaration jarred something loose in her chest, and she realized all of a sudden that she didn't even know the meaning of the word *lonely*. She couldn't fathom what it was like to have absolutely no one to turn to. A huge wave of despair rolled over her. She understood how much it had taken for him to utter those words. She locked her jaw, the tenderness welling in her chest for this proud battered man. It was all she could do not to cry.

She stood awkwardly, fiddling with the top to the cream. "Do you want me to take your shirt off?"

For a full minute he stared at her, his eyes burning brightly in the darkness. His body language said loud and clear that he wanted her. His expression also spoke volumes of how much he appreciated her not voicing the tender emotions flittering across her expressive face. "No, I'll do it," he said gruffly. He took off his shirt and laid it over a chair. "Just one thing before you start."

"What?"

"Don't touch the back of my neck. I'm very…sensitive there."

"You mean it turns you on?" The knowledge that the back of his neck was one of his erogenous zones explained the way he'd acted that day she was looking at his stitches. She'd aroused him with only a touch. The knowledge sang through her blood with fiery notes of passion.

He looked down and she could see the effort it took him to fight his need for her. His fists clenched and he took a deep breath. "I love it when you touch me there." Taking deep breaths, he swung away from her.

"Corey, maybe I should go."

"No." He whirled and jumped forward, grabbing her arms as if she was going to flee. His response was immediate and heartfelt. "Don't go, Jennifer. I need this."

She smoothed her hand over his face. "Okay," she said softly. "Whatever you want. You're in total control of this. Just tell me." She watched the taut look fade from his face.

He swallowed in relief. "Okay. I'm so tired, Jennifer."

"Of course you are," she murmured gently. "You've been on a horse all day manhandling bulls. Why don't you lie down on your stomach?"

He sank onto the bed, releasing the death grip he'd had on her arms.

She straddled his lean hips, settling herself to give him the most comfort.

"Okay?"

"Okay," he answered, his voice muffled.

When she'd gotten enough lotion on her hands, she stroked his back until he sighed deeply and relaxed into the mattress. She worked his muscles slowly until she was sure they were thoroughly released of tension. She took her time to touch him and let him know that touch didn't have to be painful or cruel.

She knew why he hated his father. She'd thought long and hard about it while she sat on the window seat of her bedroom looking down at where he slept. Her chest had ached when she came to the conclusion that he must have been physically abused. Although she couldn't be sure, it seemed the logical answer. He avoided relationships, was a complete loner and he was running from a painful past. It made her wonder about the deaths of his sister and mother and how that must eat at him, too. So much, she thought. So much to deal with. The tears built slowly behind her lids as she gloried in touching him, easing his soreness and bringing him comfort.

"Jennifer, you make me feel so safe." His voice was relaxed and told her he was close to sleep.

Those words finally released the hot tears caught in her throat. They rolled down her cheeks and every so often she wiped at her face so he wouldn't know.

When he'd fallen asleep, she left quietly so as not to disturb him. At the cottage door she stopped and her heart twisted painfully in her chest. Another ruined and ravaged painting sat in the trash.

"Oh, Corey," she whispered into the darkness.

Chapter 10

The days passed and Corey kept a polite distance, but he watched her with his hot devastating eyes. She watched him, too, while he trained the mare, taking time after a long hard day to work with both Ellie and the horse. He was so patient, so kind. There were days when Corey and Ellie would have tickling contests that Jennifer could hear from the house. And she watched each day as Ellie fell more in love with him and she ached for him and her daughter.

It was obvious that he enjoyed Ellie's company. She'd find them on the cottage porch hunched over while Corey explained the intricacies of drawing and painting. The sheer stunning power with which he rode a horse and muscled bulls was magnificent, but this gentle, warm teaching was seductive in the way he glowed. There were times when she had to look away from them, finding herself wishing that this was real. That at night he would join them at the dinner table and he and Ellie would banter like father and daughter. She had dreamed that he would help her clear the table as he teased her. Then when all the chores were done and the lights were out, she could snuggle up in his sleek warmth and sleep with him until dawn.

On that big gray horse he looked every inch the outlaw, but when he was instructing Ellie, the outlaw dissolved into an approachable, gentle, truly special man. But this special man would go soon, leave their lives.

Torn between keeping her daughter from experiencing the pain of his departure and the joy of knowing what it was like to have a father, she simply watched and agonized.

Three weeks after he first started training the mare, Ellie was on the mare's back racing around the barrels as if they were made for each other. Jennifer would stand at the window each day and watch. She could see Ellie bloom from Corey's praise, and watched her work harder for him and for herself. With each passing day she watched a championship team emerge, as Ellie either won or placed in the competitions she entered.

Jennifer missed Corey terribly. The scent of him, the feel of his arms around her. She wanted to hold him, wanted to kick some sense into him. His eyes were so dark, still so full of pain and fear. She wished for the right words to touch all those bruised and battered places in him so that he wouldn't feel he had to suffer with his secret alone.

But she didn't want to say the wrong thing. She had no idea how long he'd been living in the shadow of silence. She kept her distance because the need in both of them was too volatile, a constant unrelenting ache, and even though she hadn't said the words to him, she'd promised with body language that she wouldn't make him compromise himself no matter how much she wanted him.

She'd found other canvases, broken, ripped and demolished. Her heart ached with the discovery of each one, because she believed that he was truly trying to work out something very personal and important, yet he was failing, torturing himself over and over again.

And painfully she didn't know what to do or how to approach him. She felt so helpless wanting to protect him and understand.

She knew he felt trapped and she didn't like that hunted look in his eyes. So finally she got in her truck and drove downtown to talk to Gus Waverly. She begged him to try to fix Corey's motorcycle. She knew that Corey might just get on it and never come back, but she decided that was all right. She didn't want him trapped. She wanted him free to go if he wanted to. It hurt just to think about a day without him, let alone the rest of her life.

This day wasn't any different from other days. She stood at the window watching Corey entertain Ellie with rope tricks. She heard her daughter's clear bubbling laughter when he swung the whirling rope around and jumped through it, his dark silky hair jumping around his shoulders, the genuine flash of his grin intoxicating.

When she heard the heavy-stock truck come up the driveway, she noticed the way he immediately put down the rope, transforming into that steely-eyed man who her ranch hands quietly respected.

She saw him rub his hip absently as he watched the truck maneuver into place. He took the reins of the big gray horse and vaulted into the saddle. She would never get enough of watching him move—all sleek muscle and sinew over a breathtaking body, a warm caring heart inside. Suddenly she hurt more intensely than she could ever remember.

She glanced away from the window and picked up a book from the window ledge, the one she'd been reading before she'd heard Ellie's laughter. She brushed her hand over the title and sighed, tears coming to her eyes. *Adult Children of Abusive Parents: The Long Journey Back.*

While she had been in town to plead with Gus, she'd gone to the library, meager as it was, but was unable to find the book she needed. Desperate to understand, desperate to make him understand that it meant a great deal to her what he had gone through, she'd contacted a friend in Houston who had purchased the book and sent it to her. Jennifer had spent evening after evening going through each word. She now thought she knew what had replaced the absent love and security in Corey's life. The rodeo.

She swallowed the tears and once again looked out the window. Corey was rounding up the stock she had sold. She watched him herd the bulls competently, but she saw the tension in his body, the stiff way he held himself. The need to flee was written all over him.

Heartsick and hurting for the small boy he had been, Jennifer gritted her teeth together, her vision blurring again. She reached up and wiped away the tears.

When he had been gored, when he had lost his pride and his livelihood, he had once again lost his base, the foundation from which he dictated his life. And to top it all off, his mother and sister had died shortly after he'd been injured. God, no wonder he was running. Floundering in confusion and chaos, everything must have crumbled for him. He'd had to deal with the fear of the bulls and the guilt of his family's deaths. No wonder he'd wanted to get away from her and Ellie.

And with a chill she knew that she was tempting fate by bringing that motorcycle back within his reach. At the first sign of how much she needed him, she knew instinctively that he would run.

She put the book in the chest under the window, hiding it under some colorful Navajo blankets. She decided to play it by ear for now. No confrontations about his abuse. He would have to be the one to tell her and until she did she wouldn't push for a physical relationship unless he approached her. His silence bound her as tightly as it did him.

When she stepped onto the porch, she saw they had finished loading the truck. Ellie was playing fetch with Two Tone, one of his favorite games. She smiled at the way the little thing trotted after the stick Ellie threw him. With love filling her up, she looked at her daughter and was so thankful for her. Ellie, in her innocent way, was teaching Corey as sure as he was teaching her.

Her gaze moved from her vivacious daughter to seek out the man who had become as important to her as breathing. He was pulling down the handle of the truck to lock the stock inside for transport. She saw him lean his head against the doors, breathing heavily. He rubbed his hip again with anger and agitation, his posture rigid. Jennifer hurt all the way down to her soul. God, how hard this must be for him.

He turned and slid down and sat on the bumper, his hands shaking as he folded them together to stem the tremors.

After a few minutes he finally got up and headed for the cottage. When he reached the porch, he leaned against the pole still breathing hard, his eyes closed, fists clenched.

She stepped down off the porch with every intention of soothing him.

Corey was just getting his breathing under control when he heard the tread on the steps. His eyes flashed open and Jennifer filled his vision. He swallowed hard thinking about dreams coming to life. He had avoided her so much these past three weeks that his hands itched to touch her to make sure she was real.

"You're something else," she said.

"How's that?" he asked, hating the way his voice came out hoarse with longing.

She stepped closer to him. "You're terrified of them, aren't you? That's what you meant when you were telling me about Widowmaker. You aren't terrified of riding them and falling off. You're terrified of them."

He ducked his head, a flush staining his face when he heard a small sound escape from her lips. She took his hat off and threw it on a nearby chair. Cupping his face in her hands, she made him look at her. "There is nothing to be ashamed of. Corey, look at me," she demanded when he wouldn't meet her eyes. "Look at me." When his eyes shifted to hers, he knew they were full of the anguished shame he felt.

She spoke carefully. "You went through a traumatic, life-threatening event. You'd expect some of that fear to linger. There's nothing wrong with that, Corey."

In a voice hushed with anxiety, he said, "I hate this fear, Jennifer. It makes me feel powerless."

"Listen to me, you're not powerless. Look at what you've just done. You loaded those animals. You overcame your fear enough to actually be in the same vicinity."

He looked deeply into her eyes and smiled. He pulled her close and whispered in her ear. "Thank you, darlin'."

She pulled away from him and stepped back. "There is something I want to ask you. It's very important to me."

"What is it, Jen?"

"I promised I would take Ellie to the junior championships next week, but unfortunately I have to make a trip to Phoenix on business."

"Can't you postpone it? Jennifer, this will devastate her. You can't do this to her. She's worked so hard. That buckle is practically hers."

"I know that. I want you to take her. You've been so

good with her, and you've been with us on all the other competitions. Please."

Her words hit him like a physical blow. He flinched, his eyes widening and he was struck totally speechless. Emotions darted through him—shock, fear, vulnerability and, finally, joy. Hoarsely, he said, "You would trust me with your daughter? Damn it, Jennifer, you don't know me."

"I know you, Corey. I know you would die before you harmed a hair on her head or let anyone else harm her. I know that and for me that's enough."

He twisted away from her and went to sit down in a chair, sinking into it as the strength left his legs.

After a moment he looked at her. "You trust me?"

"Yes, I trust you. Will you do it for her? For me?" When he didn't answer right away, she averted her gaze and stammered, "I—I guess I could ask someone else—"

"No! I'll take her. It would be my pleasure to see her ride and win." Who was he kidding? he thought. He would be so puffed up with pride that he would most likely explode. She had no idea what a monumental gift she had just given him.

He stood up and went to her. He had resolved not to touch her, but the compulsion was a force beyond his control. Something sweet and wonderful washed through him and that incredible feeling remained, filling up black, empty places, washing away his darkness and despair.

His fingers brushed her face and she gasped. "Your trust is a precious gift beyond imagination."

"Mr. Rainwater? We need you, sir," a voice interrupted.

"I'm coming." He never took his eyes off her when he spoke. "When I come back, would it be okay with you if I break my vow?"

For another second, he held her gaze, the shocked pleasure in her eyes twisting his heart, increasing his breathing.

Happiness wasn't something he took for granted. He was thankful for every little tidbit that came his way. He was thankful for Jennifer and her beautiful heart. Unfortunately, he could see no way to stop from breaking her heart. Or, for that matter, his own.

Chapter 11

"Ellie, what are you afraid of?"

They stood outside the ring where she was getting ready for her first ride of the day. They'd arrived late last night and she immediately went to sleep. This morning she'd been silent and hardly ate anything at breakfast. The big green eyes so like her mother's pulled at his heartstrings.

"Failing."

"Are you afraid of what your mom will say? She'll love you no matter what happens," Corey said softly.

Her serious little face twisted with a powerful emotion and Corey leaned closer to her. "What is it, Ellie?"

"I'm not afraid of failing Mom. I'm afraid of failing you. My dad didn't want me. He…just left. I never got the chance—" Ellie's anguished voice broke off.

"Ellie, I just want you to do your best, darlin'. You won't fail me. I'm so damn proud of you right now that if my chest puffs up any more it's going to explode."

"Corey?"

"What?"

"I think I'm afraid of failing myself the most."

He pulled the girl into his arms and held her as tight as he could without crushing her. "Ellie, all you have to do is try. Just that. If you don't try, you'll never know whether or not you can do it."

Limelight shifted next to her and Ellie patted the animal's neck. Turning back to Corey, she touched his arm gently and said, "I'll never forget this day." Then she climbed into the saddle.

The loudspeaker's voice boomed. "Well, Molly Duncan hasn't disappointed us today. She has the best time. But there's one more rider, folks, to challenge Molly. She hails from Silver Creek, Texas. Let's see what this little lady can do."

Corey grabbed her booted leg. "Show 'em what you can do, little darlin'."

Ellie settled herself deeper into the saddle and gave Limelight barely a nudge. With the grace and beauty that Corey knew was in the mare, the horse pranced into the ring as if bred for display. Ellie sat erect, her black Stetson pulled low over her eyes, her slim jaw tight with determination. She was dressed in a dark green shirt with white fringe that brought out the red highlights in her tightly bound auburn braids.

Strapped to her jeans was a pair of dyed-green leather shotgun chaps with silver conchos threaded down the legs, an early birthday present from her mother.

Corey climbed the railing, his body tensing when Ellie reached the center of the ring and the horse burst into action, jumping forward with an eagerness that raced in Corey's blood. The eagerness to beat time. Corey watched with a knot in his throat as all the grueling training he'd put her through coalesced into a breathtaking display of pure horsemanship. He watched her guide the horse with skill beyond her years. She was a natural-born barrel racer.

And he wished for the umpteenth time that she was his.

His breath caught while the crowd surged to its feet as she took a precariously close turn, nicking a barrel and causing it to sway. The mare careened skillfully out of the cloverleaf turn, her flying hooves kicking up clods of dirt. Ellie urged her on as they headed for the finish line.

The excited voice of the loudspeaker boomed over the ring. People were applauding and cheering so loud it was hard for Corey to hear. "She's done it! She's beat Molly's time! I can't wait to see this little lady in action tomorrow. Keep your eyes on this one. She's going places."

It all happened so fast that Corey barely had time to respond. Out of the corner of his eye he'd noticed a man having a hard time handling a big black stallion. The horse broke loose with a sharp whinny and charged into the ring. Limelight pulled up sharply to avoid the big black, twisting her body around, but it was too late. Both animals collided and Corey watched in horror as Ellie flew from the saddle. Limelight and the black also went down in a tangle of flashing hooves and sharp piercing cries. Corey hit the ground running, reaching Ellie's still form first. His heart was in his throat as he turned her over.

Her sweet face was twisted in agony. Between gasps of pain she managed to say, "How about that for a dismount?" She tried for levity and failed miserably. He could see her fighting her tears and his heart almost broke for the brave front she was trying to erect.

"Ellie, where does it hurt?"

"My wrist." She tried to crane her neck. "Limelight?"

"I don't give a damn about the horse," he snapped as he cradled her against him and reached for her arm, soothing her as she bit her lip against the pain.

"I hope she's okay." She tried to sit up, but Corey held her too tightly.

"Hold still and I'll check." He looked over his shoulder, his stomach muscles knotting when he realized that one horse had not gotten up. Then he saw Limelight standing on trembling legs, a man—most likely the vet—checking her over. "She's okay, darlin', the vet's with her."

Ellie sighed against him as he heard the wailing sirens of the ambulance now making its way into the ring. "Well, it looks like you're going to ride to the hospital in style."

"You won't leave me?"

"Hell, no. Wild horses couldn't drag me away from you," he promised.

"Corey?" Buck McDonald hunkered down, his face full of concern. "How is she?"

Buck was a longtime friend from his rodeo days. He'd been opening the gate for Ellie's return when the black broke loose. "She'll be okay, Buck. I think it's just a broken wrist. I would appreciate it if you could take care of Limelight, though, then meet us at the hospital so we'll have a ride back to the rodeo."

"Sure, no problem, partner." Buck smiled at Ellie and headed for the mare.

During the ride to the hospital the paramedics immobilized Ellie's wrist and thoroughly checked her over from head to foot. She had a few bruises, but a broken wrist was most likely the extent of her injuries.

Ellie, looking as pale as the sheet she lay on, turned her head and gave Corey a weak smile. "I beat her time. Can you believe it?"

"Yes. Ellie, you were magnificent. I've never seen a child as young as you handle a horse the way you did. You even amazed me."

"It was the most exhilarating feeling I've ever experienced,'' she agreed. "I felt as if Limelight had grown wings and we were flying around those barrels. I felt as close to her as a human being possibly can. It was like we both knew what the other was thinking."

"So that's your secret, you can talk to animals. Nice trick," Corey teased. He was rewarded with a giggle.

"Thank God she's okay," Ellie said.

"Yeah. I know Buck. He'll take good care of her."

When they reached the hospital, Corey walked alongside the stretcher right into the examining room. He had no intention of letting Ellie out of his sight. He stayed through the painful ordeal of x-raying the wrist, keeping out of the way.

When they took her back to the examining room, he again went with her.

A white-coated doctor came into the room. He slipped some X rays up on a lighted screen and studied them for a moment, then turned to Corey and cleared his throat.

Ellie's face screwed up in pain, just briefly, as she tried to be brave.

"Are you her father?" the doctor asked.

"No, but I'm responsible for her." His heart lurched at his own words and how deeply he meant them.

"The wrist is fractured in two places." He gestured toward an X ray. "We'll put a cast on her now, and since she has no other problems you can take her home."

"Corey, I don't want to go home." Ellie's jaw was firm and deep determination swam in her eyes.

"Ellie, we'll talk about that later."

A nurse bustled in. "Sir, I'm afraid you'll have to leave."

"Corey, please don't go," Ellie pleaded.

He looked down to see the bravado totally gone, tears shining in her eyes, and he realized in an instant that she had been trying to be brave for him. "Darlin', I'm not going anywhere." He gently caressed her face with the palm of his hand.

"You have to leave," the nurse insisted.

"Who's going to make me? You?" Corey challenged, thrusting out his hip and narrowing his eyes.

"Are you her kin?" the nurse asked with challenge.

"Close enough. You have some kind of argument?"

The nurse backed down and they began to put a cast on Ellie's wrist.

Twenty minutes later they were in the back seat of Buck's car. Ellie's face was set and determined and Corey felt as if he were being attacked by a full army.

"I don't want to go home. If I don't compete tomorrow, I won't have a chance at the buckle." She stuck out her bottom lip, the sly look in her eye replaced by belligerence.

"Ellie, you've got a broken wrist." He tried to reason with her, but knew that he was already losing the battle inside where it counted.

"I can still ride. I have to, Corey. I'm no quitter," she said intensely.

"Ellie, I know you're not a quitter, but you're injured. It's too dangerous," he said, but even he could hear the doubt in his voice.

"It isn't. I can handle a horse with one arm," she said defiantly.

"Corey, I think the little lady deserves a chance." Buck's voice floated to them from the front seat.

Corey sighed. "Buck, I'm drowning here. I don't need you pushing me under," he said gruffly.

"Sorry," the old cowboy said, but there wasn't an ounce of remorse in his voice.

"Ellie, look at it from my point of view. I'm responsible

for you. I couldn't bear it if I let you get up on that horse and you hurt yourself even worse.''

"You had nothing to do with me getting a broken wrist. It was a freak accident. Corey, I've trained so *hard*, please." Tears welled up in her eyes and slipped out to run down her face. "It's important to me."

Her tears tore through him like little barbed arrows. He knew what it cost her to cry. He could see the effort it had taken earlier to keep herself from bawling. Through the worst of it she'd never let even one tear fall. Courageous and tough, his little darlin'. He couldn't say no.

"All right, but stop that blubbering," he said gruffly, with more compassion than irritation.

Ellie smiled and wiped at her tears.

"How about an ice-cream cone on me?" he offered, chucking her under the chin.

Ellie's grin widened. "Mom says that ice cream can just about cure anything."

"Your mom may be on to something there."

Later that night he sat on the motel bed, watching Ellie sleep, worrying about tomorrow and hoping he had made the right decision. He thought about calling Jennifer, had just about dialed all the numbers when he heard Ellie's voice.

"Don't call her. She'll make me come home," Ellie pleaded.

"Ellie, you're my responsibility. Your mother has a right to know if something happened to you."

She sat up in bed. "I agree, but I'm not seriously injured. In fact, my wrist doesn't even hurt at all. So I'll have a cast for a few weeks. Big deal."

"Ellie, your mom will want to know."

"She's probably still in Phoenix conducting business.

You don't want to upset her when she needs all her negotiating skills.''

"Ellie..." He stopped, at a loss for words.

"Please, Corey. I'll just die if she makes me go home. I don't want to give up."

The fresh tears were more than he could stand. "Ellie, I don't like this."

"Please," she said brokenly as she shifted to sit next to him. "I promise I'll tell her it was my idea not to call her. *Please, please, please. I'm begging you.*"

Some father he would make, Corey thought. A little pleading and a lot of tears and he was considering doing something totally against his conscience. But he knew that it was right to call Jennifer.

"I have to call her and explain things. If she says you have to come home, then that's it." He dialed the number of her hotel room in Phoenix and was told that she had checked out. When he tried the house, Jimmy told him that she hadn't returned home yet. He left a message for Jennifer to call when she got home.

"Well, your mom's not home, yet. I left her a message. You get some sleep now."

Ellie nodded and lay back against the pillows again. It didn't take long before he heard her even breathing.

Her red hair was tousled, thick and rich on the pillow, her dark lashes like half moons on her delicate cheeks. He knew without having to think about it that he loved her. He wanted to be there for her when she needed him. He wanted to soothe her tears when a stupid adolescent boy broke her heart. He wanted to nurture and teach her. He wanted the responsibility of her life in his hands. A life he would cherish and hold right up against his heart.

And the painful realization that he couldn't tore his heart to shreds. The fear he had lived with since he became an adult was too real, too near, always waiting to grab him unaware. What did he have to offer to either of these delicate souls? Jennifer with her full giving heart and Ellie with her innocence and trust.

Unable to answer his own question, he slept out of necessity, because he needed to be fresh and alert for Ellie. He would be driving her home tomorrow and he needed his wits about him. Home to Jennifer. He couldn't help it, he moaned out loud thinking about Jennifer, recalling the way her hands had kneaded his back. The softness of her mouth, the way she gasped and cried out when she found her release.

He hugged his pillow to him and pretended it was her and finally dropped into slumber.

The next thing he knew it was morning and Ellie was shaking him and telling him she was hungry. They got dressed and started out for the motel diner. He still hadn't heard from Jennifer, so he checked Ellie's cast and made the decision to let her ride. He couldn't resist her puppy-dog eyes.

Unlike yesterday morning, Ellie ate a hearty breakfast and even managed to chatter all the way through it. He enjoyed every minute of her breathless questions, smiled at the serious way she listened to his every word.

They got to the rodeo in plenty of time. As they walked over to the booth to get Ellie's number, his arm loosely around her shoulders, he heard a voice from the past.

"Rainwater, is that you? I heard you turned yellow, so did you decide to ride in the baby rodeo?"

He turned around and faced the man, not noticing Ellie's gasp and stiff posture.

Sonny Braxton. Once he had been great and on top, but now he was a drunken lout that didn't have the manners of a goat. He had once been handsome, but excess living had put pounds on his body and carved deep grooves in his face. Pale blue eyes, glazed by alcohol, challenged Corey.

"Braxton, don't you have anything better to do than hang around the junior championships?"

"My girl has a kid riding in this baby's circus," he said, his gaze shifting to Ellie. "Picking them up kinda young, Rainwater. You must be hard-up."

Before Sonny could say another hateful word, Corey's fist connected with his jaw and laid him out on the ground. With clenched teeth, Corey snapped, "Shut your filthy mouth, you poor excuse for a man. And stay out of my way."

Corey turned around, grabbed Ellie by the arm and dragged her after him. When they reached the check-in booth he finally noticed how pale she was. She looked as if she'd seen a ghost. He let his anger go and crouched until he was eye level with her. "What is it, honey? I'm sorry you had to see that."

To his utter horror, she broke into sobbing tears. Her chest heaved with them, her eyes full of horror from something Corey couldn't pinpoint.

He scooped her up and found a quiet spot near the fence where he cradled her against him, her number still in his hand. "Ellie, what's wrong? Please tell me, little darlin'. The fighting upset you. Do you want me to take you home?"

"N-no," she stammered, crying as if her world had suddenly caved in on her.

"Ellie, please," he begged, "tell me."

"H-he's my father," she said in barely a whisper.

"Braxton?"

"Yes. I saw a picture of him a long time ago before Mom destroyed them all. She never told me his name, but

I heard her and Grandpa talking about him one time. His name was in the paper so I cut out the clipping and saved it. I wanted to meet him one day. I wanted to tell him exactly what I thought of him. I never…I feel… Oh God, he's repulsive. He's awful. I hate him.'' She cried harder and Corey didn't know what to do. He just held her and rocked her.

He knew how she felt. He'd seen a dream die before. He'd hated as she hated right now. He knew what it meant to be disillusioned by a father. He knew what it was like to hate a father.

''What did you want to tell him?''

She swallowed and wiped at her face. Taking the handkerchief he offered, she blew her red swollen nose. ''I wanted to tell him that he was a fool to leave us. That we were the best things to ever happen to him and he threw us away like garbage. I wanted to show him how wonderful I turned out. I wanted him to know what he was missing.''

And she wanted to know why he'd left. She wanted his love.

He pulled her tighter. ''He is a fool, Ellie. A big, sorry fool.''

That started her crying again and his words were thick with understanding. ''I know how you feel. He's not worthy of your precious tears, but somehow you can't help caring. Can you, little darlin'?''

At those words, her jaw hardened and anger blazed in her eyes. ''Yes, I care, but you're right. He isn't worthy. And I have a championship to win.''

Corey smiled. ''That's right. Let's go get Limelight saddled up and make Molly Duncan really anxious.''

Corey was relieved to see that sly look back on her face, even though beneath it he knew she still reeled from the shock of finding out what a bastard her father was.

''Let's,'' she agreed.

* * *

Hours later, he drove up the long winding driveway of the Triple X. He could feel Ellie's nervousness.

"What do you think Mom will say?" she asked as she searched out the first sight of the house. Pleasure was on her face and Corey envied her the sheer joy of knowing what it felt like to come home. But then her expression turned serious. "Corey, I would appreciate it if you didn't mention that run-in with my father. I'll tell Mom in my own way."

"Sure, little darlin'," he replied.

He could almost pretend that this was real. That he and Ellie were returning to Jennifer as a family. He could see his life spread before him.

But it was a dream. Jennifer could never be his wife, Ellie could never be his daughter, and this wonderful place full of warmth and love could never be his home.

"She'll be concerned, but you told me yourself how cool she is," he said with soothing tones.

"Yeah. I can't wait to see Two Tone. I bet he missed me. Do you think Mom missed us?"

Corey felt his body tighten and heat. He knew that he'd missed her. He wanted his mouth on hers, her whimpering cries like sustenance for his soul. The woman had gotten under his skin, into his soul, embedded in his heart.

He looked over at Ellie, watching the pleasure on her face flare and blossom as she caught the first glimpse of her home. This little girl had gotten to him, too. He reached out and pulled on her braid.

"Corey?" she asked, her big serious eyes turning to him, her hand landing on his forearm. He clenched the wheel tighter knowing that what was coming was going to be painful for him.

"Yeah, sweetheart," he said, his voice gruff with emotion.

"Thanks for, you know, being there at the hospital, for not leaving me alone with those people." A tremor touched her smooth pink lips.

"I promised your mom I'd look out for you. No one was going to make me leave when you wanted me to stay."

"I was scared and it hurt," she said, keeping her features deceptively composed, but her eyes said all he needed to know.

"You were so brave, I was wondering when you were going to admit that." He chucked her under the chin and smiled warmly again.

"I want to thank you for agreeing not to tell Mom about seeing my father and how it made me feel." She bit her lip, looking as if she might start crying again.

"I think that's something you should tell her. You know your mom's pretty smart. She might see it for herself. She always seems to know what's wrong with you before you do."

Ellie studied him for a moment, her young eyes seeing more than her years dictated. "I know," she said thoughtfully.

As soon as the truck came to a stop, Ellie gave a whoop and climbed out of the cab and ran toward the house.

As he opened his door and followed her, he thought sadly that he had never been this enthusiastic about coming home.

Jennifer heard the truck and pleasure detonated inside her moments before her daughter came bursting through the door. "I won, Mom! Thanks to Corey, I won."

She ran into her mother's arms and it wasn't until Jennifer finished hugging her bundle of energy that she noticed the cast.

"Ellie! What happened?"

"I fell and broke my wrist. Corey was wonderful. He took me to the hospital and wouldn't leave even though the doctors tried to make him. Don't blame Corey. It was all my idea to stay," Ellie said in a rush. "I'll tell you everything later. I need to find Two Tone and Tex and Jimmy."

Jennifer could feel Corey's presence in the doorway and her palms began to sweat. She faced him and her heart began its familiar tattoo. God, the sight of him was enough to make her swoon. His hat was hanging down his back by the cord, his hip cocked in sexy male aggression and his turquoise eyes were doing a slow burn. The message he sent her had her breasts tight and tingling, the nipples contracting in painful need for his hot, wet mouth. He looked so damn good it was all she could do not to go over and throw her arms around him.

Ellie, totally unaware of the sexual tension in the room, said, "I'm going to show Jimmy and Tex my trophy and my broken wrist."

But before she left, she threw her arms around Corey's waist and hugged him hard. She reached up, tugged on his hair, and when he crouched and his face was close enough, she kissed his cheek and whispered in his ear, "Thanks a lot for taking me. You're just as cool as Mom."

Even after she bolted out the door with the ease of adolescence, Corey stayed crouched. Emotion choked him, so that when he looked into Jennifer's soft eyes he knew that they both had him wrapped around their little fingers.

The kitchen smelled just as good as he imagined it would. She was making a roast. He watched as she picked up the oven mitts and shoved the roast back in the oven.

"How did she break her wrist?" Jennifer sounded nervous and anxious and she looked so good. She always looked good. She was dressed in an old red cotton shirt with the sleeves rolled up exposing her elegant arms. Her hair was curling around her face from the heat of the oven. She wiped her hands down her jeans in a nervous manner.

"There was some idiot who didn't know how to handle his own stallion. The black bolted into the ring and collided with Limelight."

"Oh my God! Is Limelight okay?"

"Yeah, she's fine," he answered tightly. "A bruised foreleg and a gash along her ribs, but amazingly, she's okay."

"Thank God. Thanks for taking care of Ellie," Jennifer said softly. "In the hospital, I mean."

"Hell, Jennifer, I should have been paying more attention." The self-condemnation was evident in his words.

"Was Ellie riding at the time?" Jennifer watched him closely and she saw an easing of his expression, and the tenderness that stole over his features took more of her heart.

"Yes."

"Were you watching her?"

"Yes."

"Corey, that's what I would have expected you to do. As much as I would like it, I wish I could wrap her in foam rubber and keep her safe. Accidents happen. You can't be everywhere, every minute."

He shrugged.

"Right?" she pressed. "It's just part and parcel of being a parent."

He stiffened. "I'm not Ellie's parent."

"I know, but—"

"Jennifer, don't go down that road, please."

She stared at him for a moment, regret coursing through her, then she changed the subject. "Are you hungry?"

"Yes," he said tightly, but food seemed to be the furthest thing from his mind.

"The roast will be another forty minutes or so. I hope you'll stay."

He didn't speak but nodded his acceptance.

"How did your business go in Phoenix?" he asked quietly after a momentary pause, his voice sending shivers of delight through her.

"Very well. I negotiated three new contracts and renewed two others." She gripped the sink to keep her body in place, the need to greet him with a kiss so overwhelming that she almost couldn't fight it.

She gasped a little moan of pleasure as he came to her, sliding his hands around her waist and jerking her body against the lean length of his, roughly, almost violently.

"Jennifer," he whispered against her ear, causing quivers of excitement to race from the top of her head to the tips of her toes. He captured her mouth, his tongue thrusting, exploring, desperately seeking her response.

She moaned again, unable to help herself.

As he pressed her back against the counter, he ravaged her mouth in a way she came to recognize as his loss of control.

She moved her mouth away so she could speak. Breathless with a wanting that scared and exhilarated her, she managed to say, "Ellie..."

Corey's voice sounded strained, "She'll be busy for at least an hour, chasing all over looking for those cowhands and Two Tone." He pressed his arousal against her hips.

"The bedroom," she suggested breathlessly. A sense of urgency drove her.

"I won't make it, darlin'," he answered in a voice that was hoarse with out-of-control desire.

Her heart jolted and her pulse pounded. "The pantry," she suggested, her insides jangling with excitement. The area was small, but two bodies could fit and with his body blocking the door no one could walk in on them. It was also a helluva lot closer than the bedroom.

The heat came fast and overwhelmed them. In the aftermath of the awesome passion, they held on to each other tightly, only now realizing what it was like to be apart even if it had been for only two days. Still, it was enough to make them both panic inside, thinking about the inevitable future. One neither wanted to face.

"After the bulk of the branding and calving is done. I'll be leaving," he said dispassionately.

She nodded her head, knowing he was trying to diffuse the intense emotions between them. She chose to ignore the pain that swamped her and, changing the subject, asked, "Besides the broken wrist, how did it go?"

"You're one lucky woman. Your daughter is wonderful, curious, energetic and beautiful. Your husband was a complete and utter fool to give all this up."

"Well, his brains were always in his pants. I can sure pick them."

"Just so you understand that I'm a tumbleweed, too, Jennifer. I didn't mean to get intimate with you." He smoothed his hands over her hair. "Things just got out of hand."

"I know. I'm not saying this was all one-sided, Corey. I wanted you as much as you wanted me."

He closed his eyes and touched his mouth to hers, still deep inside her. "How are things going here?" When her body stilled, he opened his eyes to look at her. "Jennifer?"

"Why don't we get dressed and discuss it over a glass of iced tea?"

"Who says we're finished?"

She gasped as he lowered his head and took her nipple into his mouth, gasping again as she felt him harden once again, inside her.

"It can wait," she groaned as she gave herself up to the spiraling sensation only he could arouse in her.

Heated minutes later, her whole body tingling from his thorough lovemaking, she sat across the table from him. "I lost two bulls when the fence was cut. They were hit by a semi that took out hundreds of yards of fence and gouged up the ground. Thank God the driver was okay."

He swore softly, his eyes heating and narrowing. "This vandalism has got to stop. It think it's time to have a nice chat with Jay Butler."

"We don't have any proof, Corey."

"He cuts your fences, shoots your bulls and we can't prove a damn thing!"

"Look, I don't want to argue about Jay. I want you to help me plan Ellie's birthday party. She's going to turn fourteen. God, I can hardly believe it."

"Of course I'll help. What were you thinking?"

"A good old-fashioned hoedown with a fiddle and country band. What do you think?" she asked enthusiastically.

Corey smiled, his teeth flashing brightly against his dark face. "I think that you're the most beautiful woman I have ever seen."

Jennifer took a deep breath, got up from the table and settled onto his lap, circling her arms around his shoulders and burying her face in the hollow of his neck. He was slipping away from her. She could feel it. Soon he would be gone and no matter how much she told herself she would let him go, she just didn't know if she could.

God help her. She closed her eyes tightly against a wealth of emotions. She just didn't know.

Chapter 12

Ellie's birthday party was in full swing. They had just finished eating cake and opening presents. A group of Ellie's friends were dancing and having a good time and it gave Jennifer a moment to settle back and relax. She closed her eyes and let the music take her away. The fast country beat wrapped around her and she relaxed against the barn wall, sinking a little deeper into the bale of hay on which she sat.

Corey had spent so much time helping her that he had neglected his duties, but now he stood near the door watching Ellie and Tucker dance, a reflective look on his face.

She saw Corey stiffen and draw away from the doorway and then she saw why. Jay Butler stood at the barn entrance searching out the crowd. When he saw Tucker and Ellie, he headed in the same direction. Corey pushed away from the wall with a murderous look on his face. Jennifer jumped up and tried to intercept Corey.

She got to Corey just before he got to Jay. She looked

up into his eyes, pleading with him not to make a scene. With her hand against his chest, she could feel the tension in him.

She turned to face Jay, Corey a large warm shadow behind her.

"Jay, what do you want here?" he said in a steely voice.

"I came to pick up Tucker. Isn't that right, boy?" he said with smug confidence.

Jennifer could see that Tucker hadn't expected Jay and was just as angry as Corey that he was here. Tucker's eyes flicked to Jennifer's and she saw the realization in them that if he said he didn't want to leave, there would be a fight.

Tucker turned to Ellie and jammed his hands into his pockets. "I've got to go, Ellie. I'll see you around, kid, okay?"

Ellie took in the scene and her mouth tightened. She began to reach out to Tucker, but he sidestepped her touch and turned toward his father. "Let's go," he said between clenched teeth, and Jay gave them all a self-satisfied grin as he followed his son out.

Ellie watched Tucker walk away and Jennifer felt her heart constrict when she realized what Ellie didn't even know yet. She had her first crush on a boy. Jennifer's heart ached for her little girl.

Ellie then looked at her as two silver tears tracked down her face and Jennifer heard Corey swear low and vicious.

Jennifer approached her daughter and took her into her arms. "I'm sorry, honey."

"He's mean and horrid, Mom. Just like Dad, just like Sonny."

Shock held Jennifer immobile. How had Ellie found out her father's name?

Ellie supplied the answer. "I heard you and Grandpa

talking about him, and since it was easy to follow him on the circuit I collected every clipping and every article until his retirement.''

Ellie looked at Corey and he nodded his encouragement, then very quietly left. ''I saw him at the junior championships. He wasn't very nice and Corey punched him out. Oh God, I hate him and I hate Mr. Butler. I wish he would die and leave Tucker alone!'' With tears running down her cheeks, she ran out of the barn.

She sighed deeply, calling Sonny every vile name she could think of. Jennifer had a feeling she'd find Ellie with Corey. They had gotten so close in such a short time. It warmed her heart to know that Corey would be there for her daughter. When she got to the horse barn, she stopped in the doorway so her eyes could adjust. She heard Ellie's voice clear and trembling.

''I know it was stupid and that I should have stopped wishing for him to come and visit me, but there were times I just wished...''

''I know, darlin','' Corey encouraged her with his tone of voice.

''Do you know what I wish now? I wish my father was just like you.'' She gently kissed him on the cheek. ''Corey, you're the best.''

Ellie then saw her mother at the entrance to the barn and went to her, wrapping her arms around her waist. ''I love you, Mom.''

Jennifer hugged her daughter.

Ellie said very firmly, ''I'm going back to enjoy my birthday party.''

Jennifer's daughter looked up at her, the pain in her eyes gone and she smiled impishly when she saw where her mother's soft gaze searched. ''You like him a lot, huh, Mom?''

Jennifer's eyes searched for Corey's shadowed form in the barn and the feeling inside her swelled. "Yes, sweetheart. I like him so very much. Now scoot."

Jennifer went to where Corey still knelt in the barn. She lowered herself down and gently took his face in her hands. "Thank you. Ellie's been wrestling with the absence of a father every birthday. I think she just came to terms with it, thanks to you."

His voice hoarse with suppressed tears, he uttered, "Touch me, hold me, Jennifer."

Her eyes widened, realizing that this was the first time in their relationship that he wasn't taking command. The first time he was relinquishing control. The knowledge flashed through her mind, and she loved him all the more. She loved him for his open giving, his tenderness, and even his fears and doubts. She realized how stupid she'd been when she was young. When she thought she loved Sonny. This feeling she felt now didn't even come close.

She pulled him down with her into the hay and very simply touched him by rubbing his back and holding him in her arms.

Corey was coming around the mess hall, thinking about the day before, remembering how he had immersed himself in the feel of Jennifer's hands on him, when he stopped dead, his eyes resting on the gleaming black bike sitting in front of Jennifer's house. She'd had it fixed. Corey was the kind of man who took care of his own debts. He didn't want to be beholden to anyone, especially Jennifer. He didn't want to owe her anything. The fury built and he changed direction and headed instead for the house.

He burst into the kitchen without knocking. Ellie was just getting her lunch out of the fridge. Her eyes widened when she saw his face.

"Is something wrong?"

"No." For Ellie's sake, he tried to rein in his anger. "I just need to talk to your mom."

"She's upstairs changing her bed, I think. I've got to go catch my bus. I'll see you tonight."

He wasn't sure he would be here tonight, he thought as he watched Ellie slip out the door. He charged for the stairs and took them two at a time. "What do you think you're doing?" he snarled when he entered her bedroom.

"Changing the bed. It's something I do every week," she replied flippantly.

He swore under his breath and stalked across the room. Grabbing her arm, he steered her to the window. "*That* is what I'm talking about."

"It's yours, isn't it?"

"Yes, it's mine. I don't want you footing my bills."

"It was smashed because of me, Corey. It was my responsibility to get it fixed."

He heard someone clear her throat. "If you guys can stop arguing long enough, I'm afraid I've missed my bus."

"Ellie," Corey said between gritted teeth. "Go downstairs and wait by my bike. I'll take you to school."

"Cool. Oh, by the way, you guys don't have to sneak around at night. Corey spends enough time in your room, Mom. He should just sleep here. It's okay with me."

Both of them stared at her with their jaws hanging open. Ellie smiled and retreated from the room. "See you downstairs, Corey."

"Damn," he swore, feeling as if his life was splintering into little bits. He felt pushed from too many sides. Ellie and Jennifer. Everyone wanting something that he couldn't give. Wanting him to stay, when he couldn't. He turned to Jennifer, whose shock seemed to have worn off, and he saw the determined slant to her chin, the mulish set of her mouth.

"Jennifer, I told you before. You don't owe me anything."

"Can't you just accept a gift?" she asked in exasperation.

"No. All I've ever wanted from the beginning was to leave."

Her expression changed then from determined to panicked and that was when he saw it. The certainty that if she gave him an opportunity to flee, he would take it. He'd just confirmed her doubts that when she had his motorcycle fixed, he would leave. That realization finally broke him, the knowledge that she knew and had still brought the motorcycle within his reach. He had to get out of here. The pain in his chest was cresting like a huge wave. He would collapse into a heap on the floor like a child and cry if he didn't leave right away. The humiliation of breaking down in front of Jennifer had him backing up, shaking his head.

"No," he growled hoarsely. "No!" He tried to get out of the bedroom, but she stopped the door. His arm slipped, his elbow hitting her in the nose. She backed up, clutching her nose and Corey spun in horror. When he saw the blood, a relentless fist closed around his heart.

You're just like me, son.

He could hear his father's gleeful, accusing voice in his head. "Jennifer. God. I'm sorry. I'm so sorry. I didn't mean to hurt you. Oh, God."

"Don't just stand there, get me a cold cloth."

He bolted for the bathroom, his stomach in knots, his hands shaking so badly he could barely turn on the faucet. He brought the cloth to her and pressed it gently against her face as they both sat on the edge of the bed.

"Well, we can look on the bright side," she quipped.

"At least you didn't pop me in the eye and give me a shiner. Then everyone would wonder what kind of guy I got myself tangled up with."

Her voice was light and teasing, but Corey only heard her words and to him they were an accusation. This was what he'd feared forever. This was why he avoided relationships.

Before Jennifer could say another word, he surged up off the bed, terror gripping him. "You have no idea. No idea at all!" he cried, his voice breaking. Then he left the room, slamming the door behind him.

He sat on his bike for another five minutes, letting the solitude of the immense ranch wash over him. God, it felt so good to be here. After he'd dropped Ellie off at school and let all her friends ooh and aah over his bike, he had kept riding. Almost tried to reach the horizon.

But he remembered Jennifer's face when he'd left, remembered Ellie's quick hug and kiss before she'd bounded off to school and he knew he couldn't leave them that way, without a word, so he'd turned around.

He looked up at the house, up at her room. A light burned in the window and he could see her silhouette. He dropped his head back, the emotion clogging his throat so full, he thought he might finally break down. But the tears seemed stuck in the back of his throat. The horror washed through him again. He'd hit her, hurt her. Something he swore he would never do. His stomach tightened until he felt as if he was going to be sick again.

He swung off the bike, went to the bunkhouse and got the key to the house. He made his way silently through the darkened house, feeling detached, as if he had lost his right to be here, yet she pulled and tugged at him like a magnet and he couldn't stay away from her.

She didn't understand. He saw that in her eyes, before he had acted like a bastard and run off like a scared rabbit. She didn't understand how that little slip of his elbow could hurt him so much. Hurt him deep inside where he kept all the pain from his childhood. All his failure, his powerlessness. Jennifer had no idea how many times his father had broken his mother's nose and Corey had had to watch.

He pushed open the door to her bedroom and stepped in. She sat on the window seat. He knew from being around her that it was a haven, a source of comfort. She went there when she was upset or needed to sort out her thoughts.

His throat cramped up again and he bit his lower lip. God, but she was beautiful in the moonlight, the pale light catching the fiery glints in her hair, turning her skin into cream, her slightly parted lips a flush of gleaming coral.

He stepped closer, stopping abruptly when he saw what she was wearing. He closed his eyes, his chest so full of raw emotion that he didn't know how his body could contain it. She was wearing his blue chamois shirt. The first one she'd seen him in. She must have gone all the way down to the bunkhouse to get it after he'd left.

Tenderness wrapped warm, soft hands around his heart. His pulse beat slow and thick and he wanted to gather her close and never let her go.

He moved closer to the window, reaching out with a trembling hand to touch her soft hair. She stirred and her eyes opened and, quick as a wink, she was off the window seat, throwing her arms around his neck.

"That hold would rival a wrestler's." He tried to keep his voice light, but it cracked under the emotional strain.

"Corey. Oh God, I didn't think you were coming back. What did I do? Please tell me." Her voice broke on a sob and she clutched him tighter.

"Nothing, Jen darlin'. You did nothing. I'm sorry. I'm so sorry. I was angry at myself for hurting you."

"But I want—"

"Shh, darlin', shh. I just need to hold you."

"I want to understand. I want so desperately to understand. You look okay on the outside, Corey. But you're bruised and battered inside, aren't you? Do you think I'm too fragile to hear what you have to say?"

"Not now, darlin'." He sidestepped the issue, stayed in the safety of the silence. "I owe you an apology."

She raised her face without releasing her hold on him. "It was an accident. You can't even tell I was hit. A little nosebleed."

He kissed her nose then her lids as they fluttered closed. He tried to move and she clung.

"Please don't leave me tonight. Please, Corey. I want you to stay with me all night. There aren't very many left, are there?"

"No." He buried his face in her neck, his voice ragged and tormented. "Jennifer, wild horses couldn't drag me from this room."

She muscled him around, hooked one leg around his and with part of his support gone she pushed on his chest and he tumbled onto the bed.

"The Worldwide Wrestling Federation would probably sign you up in no time, Jen. You've taken me down to the mat, now what are you going to do with me?"

"Take you out for the count, cowboy. I've got you just where I want you."

"How's that?"

"Flat on your back."

"Jennifer Horn! You're a mother."

"And don't you forget it."

His eyes roamed over her face then down her body intimately hugging his. "That's quite a fashion statement you're making there. Am I going to have to buy new shirts?"

"No. Just one. You can't have this one back."

"I think it looks better on you than on me, anyway, darlin'." He sat up and pushed his hands through his hair. Jennifer settled behind him and picked up the brush on the nightstand.

"Your hair is all windblown. Let me brush out the tangles," she said softly, urging him to lean against her. Very gently she pulled the bristles through his hair and with every stroke, he could smell the scent of her clinging to the brush.

"Your life hasn't been an easy one," she said. "How long have you been on the road?"

"Not that long."

"All those gold buckles. The ones in your saddlebags. You were a champion. It looks to me like you were making a pretty good living on the circuit."

"I was."

"Is all your money really gone?"

"No. I have a lot of investments and a huge house in Austin."

"Then why…?"

That money and house belonged to someone else, someone he didn't know and couldn't remember. It didn't seem right to use that money. "I don't want to touch that money, Jennifer. It belongs to someone else. That person I used to be. It's hard to explain. I need to do this…what I've been doing."

"Running?"

He sat up abruptly, his nostrils flaring, her question hitting very well on target. He had been running from his failure, from his fears, from himself and he just couldn't see how to stop. How to gather all the pieces that were missing. "Have you ever felt as if you're on the outside looking in?"

Her hands continued to caress him. With her face against his back she said, "No." She turned him around, her voice soft and filled with knowing clarity.

"That's how I've always felt."

Jennifer didn't say anything, just pressed her face against his chest and then very slowly began to unbutton his shirt.

He let his passion for her take over and it unleashed like a snapping whip. What little control he had slipped away like sand through his fingers, slipped away like the days he had left with her. Jennifer. As elusive as the horizon.

Chapter 13

Two days later, Corey sweated under the sun as he dug postholes for a new line fence. It was brutally hard work and it made his muscles throb with sensation that was a close cousin to pain, but provided no distraction to his thoughts.

He jammed the posthole digger against the relentless ground. The shock reverberated through his arms and shoulders. He cursed and threw the tool down.

"You look like a man with a problem, son."

Corey straightened and whirled. Sheriff Dawson sat on a big bay horse, the reins hung loosely in his hands.

"It hasn't got anything to do with the law, Sheriff."

"No, I already know that. I ran a check on you already. It has to do with Ms. Horn."

Corey snorted with wry amusement. "If you came all the way out here to discuss my relationship with Jennifer then you've wasted your time."

"I came to tell you, son, that she'd be better off if you left." His voice was accusatory.

"I know. I figured that out all by myself," Corey said with hard steel in his voice.

"Then why are you still here?"

Corey picked up his shirt and shrugged into it. "I don't know," he said with a fierceness that caused the sheriff's eyebrows to rise.

"Look, son, I'm not about to tell you what to do, but this feud you have with the Butler boys ain't going to go away. In fact, if you ask me, you're the one who caused it to grow into this ruckus. She's had property destroyed, animals shot, threatening phone calls and all because of you."

Corey knew the sheriff was right. He'd just come to that conclusion himself. "I know that, too, Sheriff, and I've decided to leave tonight as soon as I get back. You make sure the Butler boys know that." Corey approached the big bay and looked up at the man sitting astride it. "And you listen good, Sheriff. I want you to watch out for her, because if I hear different, I'm coming back and the Butler boys aren't going to be the only ones I'm going to be looking for."

"I got your drift, son." Without another word, the sheriff turned his horse and rode off.

Corey retrieved the canteen of water off Monster's saddle and took a long drink, pouring some of the water over his sweaty, dirty face.

He had deliberated long into the night about the part he'd played in this feud. In protecting Jennifer, he'd made Butler's advances continue because the quarrel had become personal. Butler hated him. That was evident, but Jennifer had been a prize to Butler, and in his eyes she had spurned him for an Indian. Prejudice was ugly. Corey knew that.

He had seen his share of it on the circuit and in the little towns he'd visited.

All this fighting. Jay wouldn't rest until he had bested Corey. He would continue to harass Jennifer until there wasn't any reason for him to do so. That would mean Corey had to leave. It was past time, anyway. Long past due. Yet that didn't stop his heart from breaking or his gut from clenching at the thought of leaving Jennifer and Ellie. There were no happily-ever-afters for him, but then he had never expected there would be.

Now that he had made the decision to go, he had to stick to it. He wanted to just disappear. He wanted to slink away like the dog he was, but he couldn't leave them without a word. He couldn't bear the thought that he would leave them as Sonny had. He would tell them he was going. He owed them that much.

Tucker knew that something bad was going to happen. He hadn't wanted to stay with his father. He never wanted to stay with his father, but his secret, the one he'd kept all these years, had to be protected. He eyed Jay as the man took another long drink of the bottle of whiskey he held in his hand. His father and uncles had been bad-mouthing Corey Rainwater almost all day and into the evening, sucking courage from the bottle. Jay and his brothers were nothing but vicious bullies. Tucker knew the time had come when they'd decided to do something about Corey, instead of just talk about it.

"Tucker, come here," Jay snarled.

Tucker squared his shoulders, his mouth tightening, and got up from the floor where his father had made him sit. Whenever he was in this house, he was never allowed on the furniture. "You're going to come with us and see how real men take care of a coward."

Tucker had made a point of resisting Jay just because it irked the man so much. He had no intention of going to the Horn ranch and hurting anyone that Ellie cared about. She probably already thought he was a lowlife just by association. He had no intention of proving it to her. "No." His answer was clipped and filled with a surprising anger that had suddenly surged from somewhere deep inside him.

Tucker knew that Jay hated his guts. His father took every opportunity to humiliate, berate and shame him. Tucker didn't care because he had learned long ago that he could rely only on himself. He didn't care if Jay beat him to death, he wasn't budging.

Jay's face turned red then blue and he let out a howl of rage and hit Tucker so hard he slammed against the wall, his head hitting the plaster, cracking like a gunshot in the room. Darkness played around the fringes of his consciousness until it overtook him and he slipped down into the blackness.

"Damn, Jay," Clovis said indifferently, "I think you've killed the little bastard."

Jennifer made her way to the barn looking for Corey. When she didn't find him there, she headed for the cottage. He'd been gone for two days riding fences, but she knew better. He was trying to avoid her. He was trying to figure out a way to tell her that he was leaving.

Her hand was on the knob when a shadow stepped out of the darkness and grabbed her, wrapping his hand around her mouth so that she couldn't scream. The hand tightened when she struggled, a voice she knew as well as her own sending rippling chills down her spine.

"Hi, Jenny honey. Surprise."

Corey let Monster walk the rest of the way. His heart heavy and filled with agony, he was in no hurry to get back to the ranch. He'd made the decision to leave because he felt that his presence was making matters worse. Corey had to believe that when he left this time, the attacks would cease. His continued presence only seemed to escalate the feud. Leaving was his only choice.

Soul-searing pain engulfed him at the thought of never seeing them again. He clenched his jaw against the onslaught that ripped at his heart. Oh God, never to hold Jennifer again, touch her, see her fiery hair spread out on his chest. Never to hear her laugh or strip off a piece of his hide with her formidable anger.

He was destined to be alone. He'd known that a long time ago. Safety and security were for someone with a normal life. Some other man who could give Jennifer one hundred percent of himself. He just didn't know how to break the silence, breach that impenetrable wall. The silence was trapped inside him and he couldn't let it out. He would hunger for Jennifer until his sorry life ended, which he surmised wouldn't be too long from now.

He didn't seem to care anymore. The fight seemed empty, for without Jennifer, the light would go out of his life. He dismounted at the barn. The ranch was quiet, eerily so. He looped the reins loosely at the corral gate, the hair on the back of his neck suddenly raised.

"Corey."

His name was a whispered plea. Her voice filled with fear, love, and laced with dread. He whirled and his blood ran cold. Then in an instant his blood burned with a rage that terrified him.

Jay Butler stood with his beefy arm around Jennifer's neck. His four brothers flanked him. The vicious look in their eyes told him what he needed to know. They had come here to kill him. He could see it in the depths of their cold, bigoted eyes.

Jackson and Clovis intercepted Corey as he lunged at Jay, just missing his arm by inches. Corey struggled with all his strength, but two jabs to his recently healed ribs took his breath away. He got back on his feet and growled low and threatening when he saw Jay's hands on Jennifer, and he saw that if he put up a fight, Jay would hurt her.

Jay sneered. "That's right, be good and we don't hurt her too bad."

"Jay, hurt her and there won't be a place on this earth that you can hide from me," Corey said in a harsh, raw voice.

Jay stepped back at the chilling tone, then said, "You bested us for the last time. You should have left when you had the chance."

"Yeah," Emmett said. "Now we're going to mess you up real good, chief, and then have some fun with your half-breed-loving woman." Stuart laughed at his brother's remark.

Emmett grabbed Jennifer's hair and jerked her head back. "You like breeds, bitch. Let me show you what a real man can do."

Through the fear and desperation, her temper flared and without realizing the consequences, she reacted to Emmett's vicious words. She had to give Corey a fighting chance.

With all the force she could muster, she lifted her knee, catching Emmett in the groin. She would not be a hostage to keep Corey in line. She realized with cold dread that they were going to kill them both. She saw it in their eyes. He let go of her hair with a painful curse, dropping to his knees in the dust, choking out the contents of his stomach into the dirt.

Then she bit down as hard as she could on Jay's hand. When he let her go, she turned and pushed Jay into Stuart and when they staggered back, she ran. There would be no way that she would be used to hurt Corey, she vowed again, running for both their lives. Corey's only chance to defend himself would be if she was out of the picture. She deftly slipped through the corral fence as quick as a flash.

Jay swore viciously. "Hold him here until I get her and bring her back. I want her to see him humiliated and begging for mercy."

He charged after Jennifer and Corey struggled, but he was held too securely.

"Excuse me, gentlemen, but I would appreciate it if you would get your hands off our foreman." Ellie's polite words broke into the thick, charged air.

Five heads whipped around and five mouths gaped open as fourteen-year-old Eleanor Jean Horn cocked the rifle she was holding with a metallic, unmistakable sound.

"Now, now, little lady, you better put down that gun before someone gets hurt," Jackson said, letting go of Corey's arm.

"Someone will get hurt for sure, Mr. Butler, if you don't let him go." Her voice never wavered, her hands as steady as a rock. When they didn't do as she asked, she pulled the trigger, hitting very close to Emmett's foot. A smile curved her mouth when he yelped and jumped away. Very deliberately and without taking her eyes from Emmett's, she cocked the gun again. "Let him go now or the next one will be extremely painful!"

When Emmett took a step toward her, Ellie smiled nastily and without missing a beat said, "Go ahead, Mr. Butler, make my day!"

A siren in the background caused them to back off. "Face down in the dirt and don't move a muscle." Ellie watched closely as all four of them lay down in the dirt. Thank God the sheriff had called her. Of course, he'd told her to hightail it out of there, but she couldn't leave her mother and Corey at the mercy of the Butlers.

Corey turned and frantically searched the corral, his eyes lighting on a scene straight out of his worst nightmare. Jay had Jennifer by the hair up against the far wall of the barn. His hands were on her. In the corner, a large shadow moved and fear squeezed Corey's heart. He was paralyzed, recognizing the shadow as it lumbered into the moonlight, its small dark eyes fastened on the movements of Jay attempting to strip off Jennifer's blouse. Fury mixed with fear.

Jay wore a red shirt that looked even brighter in the moonlight. Unable to move, unable to breathe around the fear in his gut, Corey watched in horrified dread as the bull pawed the ground. A bull that Jennifer had had to single out of the herd because he was too aggressive. A bull that had to be isolated because he had killed other males. A bull that was the rodeo's dream.

A killer named Marauder.

Corey let out a ragged groan as the bull charged, his bellow loud on the still air. "Butler, look out!" Corey shouted, but it was too late. Much too late.

Jay turned too slowly. The bull impaled him on his horns and threw him into the air, shaking his head and stamping around the ring in a frenzy of rage. Jay stood shakily on his feet, blood soaking into the red shirt. With a stumbling run, he headed for the fence, leaving Jennifer behind. Marauder stood still for a moment, then he pawed the ground, churning up the earth and nausea twisted Corey's stomach. The scene was so familiar. With another bellow, the bull surged forward, hundreds of pounds of enraged muscle and sinew, death shining off the wicked horns. He gored Jay again, then in a rage trampled Jay's broken body.

Ellie watched in stunned horror as the bull mauled Jay, and with a sickening feeling deep down inside, she knew he was dead, and with a frightening dread, she realized she was glad. She also realized that she would never be the same again, and that Tucker would never look at her the same again.

With the bull distracted, it gave Corey a chance. A very slim chance. He had time to save Jennifer. Jennifer's eyes never left the sight of the horror of Jay's death. A scream issued from her throat and the bull abandoned Jay's body, his head lifting once again. Those small, black, enraged eyes locked on Jennifer.

Corey moved, not even knowing how he mounted Monster, not even feeling the horse leave the ground as he sailed over the corral fence in a breathtaking graceful leap, ignoring the jarring impact when Monster's front hooves hit the dirt of the corral. With speed and agility, big muscles flexing and lengthening, the horse raced toward Jennifer at the same time the bull charged.

Corey leaned down low over the saddle, reaching out with his hand. Time seemed to slow and the far wall looked a million miles away. He prayed, something he used to do as a boy. Something he hadn't done in a long, long time. Prayed to a God who had abandoned him in his need. Prayed as he'd never prayed before.

He reached her a split second before the bull, scooping her up and over the saddle with a desperate move that almost unseated him and pulled the muscles of his back. His hip burned and ached as if a hot brand were pressed against his flesh. The wicked horns of the bull missed the hindquarters of Monster by mere inches and the big gray horse, pale as a ghost in the light of the moon, sprinted toward the fence in a run for his life. The bull ravaged the barn wall with his horns, enraged at missing Jennifer, giving

Corey a few more precious minutes to reach safety. Then, with another bellow, the bull turned and gave chase.

"Jennifer, hang on!" Corey yelled, knowing he was taking a big chance in forcing Monster to jump a fence with two riders. Jennifer was in a precarious position, he could lose her, but he had no choice. The stallion increased his speed, giving all he had in response to Corey's urging. The bull gained, but with the extra burst of speed, the animal's horns missed again.

Corey felt Monster prepare himself for the leap, judging the distance and the height, and then, as if the horse had grown wings, they were flying. Corey felt the sheer power of the animal throughout his body. The impact was jarring and he felt Jennifer slip, but she clutched at his leg and held on.

That night Jennifer sat at the window seat. Knowing now that it was just a matter of time before Corey finally left. Now that Jay wasn't a threat, there was nothing to keep him here with her. She could feel the distance he was already putting between them. She wished she knew what to say, how to get through to him.

She'd seen him walk down to the paddock and lean against the fence, his head bowed as if the weight of the world was upon his shoulders. Her heart ached as she watched the light wind ruffle his dark silky hair, her fingers tingling with an uncontrollable urge to feel the soft strands. She watched him push it back impatiently, as if it was the thing that annoyed him.

She could see that he was in torment. Even now, his body looked ready to flee. She saw his muscles tense and he shifted, leaning all his weight on his hip. Then she saw him flinch and rub the flesh beneath his tight-fitting jeans. He was in pain and she fought back a knot of emotion that clogged her throat. With a fierce caring and an anger that was irrational, yet strangely justified, she continued to watch him.

He gripped the fence and kicked the bottom rail, then leaned his head against the top rail and her heart surged with so much feeling for this man she could barely contain it. He pulled a long knife from his boot and she watched him test the edge with his thumb. Suddenly something inside her went cold.

He grabbed his hip again, his muscles bunched and he moved away from the fence with that same graceful prowling stride she'd seen him move with countless times. Panic fluttered in her like a thousand tiny birds trying to get loose. She ran outside, later not even remembering her desperate run through the house. He was going to do something irrevocable, unspeakable. She could tell. He was going to the bunkhouse to destroy something in himself with the act and she wasn't going to let him do it.

The slashed canvases flashed in her head. She remembered the pain that finding those had caused her. It was as if in his need to heal himself, he refused the means by which to do it. Countless times punishing himself over and over again. Spiritually, irreversibly, permanently.

Corey had stood at the fence replaying the bull goring in his head over and over again until his hip ached with the remembered agony. The destructive force inside him was restless and savage tonight. He wanted to hit something, crush something with his hands. He wanted her. She was all that was good, beautiful and bright. Color in a gray world. Vibrancy in a dull, dark void. Fulfillment where there was only dissatisfaction.

His hand gripped tightly around the handle of the long blade in his hand. Dark destruction was all he knew. It was in his genes passed from father to son. He didn't want to be like his father. That was the deep, imbedded, innate fear that ate like acid, burned like a white-hot fire with scorching, searing, relentless pain.

He strode into the cottage, leaving the door open because as soon as this was done, he was getting on his bike. He was going to get far away from them both, before he hurt them, before they found out what kind of monster they had given their trust.

He stopped in front of the canvas and just stared at the soft brush strokes, the beauty of what he had depicted. The coalescence of all he had ever wanted since he'd first laid eyes on Jennifer Horn.

He stood before the canvas and felt deep, tortured pain and ruthlessly he squashed it. Banished it to somewhere else as he'd done as a child, though as an adult he knew that the pain never went away until it was dealt with. Later, he promised himself. Later, he would deal with it. Later, when all he had to comfort him were elusive, sensual memories of Jennifer, of holding her, of the sheer beauty of finding a woman he could be friends with as well as lover.

And always the dream would haunt him. And before him was the dream. His most coveted wish brought to aching life. His arm raised as he looked at the masterpiece that sat before him. He knew he was good, but that didn't seem to assuage the dark acidlike pain. He was even better than his father. That was what he had told him. *You inherited my skill. You inherited my weaknesses, as well. You'll grow up to be just like me.*

Just like me. He closed his eyes, fear rising out of a dark, deep fissure in his heart. With a clarity that was terrifying, he saw Jennifer's face bruised and battered. His heart squeezed with tight, unrelenting agony. He stiffened and cried out, the picture shattering in his mind. Destroy this and destroy himself. He didn't want to be like his father.

The knife came down and her hand closed around his wrist, stopping the very tool of his own destruction. "No, Corey."

"Yes," he said hoarsely, knowing that he could easily break her hold. He could easily hurt her with his superior strength. He could shove her away and continue to do what he must.

He didn't want to be like his father who had hurt his mother countless times and who had beaten him, telling him over and over again how much he was like him.

"No, Corey," she repeated. She didn't look at him because she needed this unsteady anger. She knew if she looked at him it would dissolve along with her determination. Instead, she looked down at the first painting that hadn't been slashed to ribbons. She looked down at true genius, true and genuine artistry. Smooth, masterful blending of colors gave the painting a rich, lifelike quality so that the people in it seemed real. It was the most beautiful painting she'd ever seen, touching her in a place that ached for him.

Tears scorched the backs of her eyelids. Scalding tears that wanted to fall. But she couldn't...she wouldn't let him see her this way. Calmness and tenderness were what he needed now.

She looked at the canvas again and was so very glad he hadn't had a chance to destroy this painting. It was a beautiful replication of the three of them, and she smiled through her tears at the perfect copy of Two Tone sitting in Ellie's lap. Ellie looked straight out at her, but the Jennifer in the painting was looking at Corey and he at her. His left hand was on her face and the turquoise band on the third finger of his left hand made her breath catch.

"Corey...." The sob caught in her throat. "This is what you were destroying? Why?"

His face twisted in pain and he bit his lip until it bled. "It's fantasy, Jennifer. Just pure fantasy." He looked like a wild thing, his eyes wide and unfocused. It scared her and she felt a chill. What would he have done this time after he'd slashed the painting? The thought sent shivers up her spine.

"This is what you want, isn't it? To be part of us?"

"Yes," he whispered, then in the next breath denied it, "No. No." His anguished voice beat the air like birds' wings and she heard the sheer desperation in his words as if denying what he'd just told her was the only thing that would keep him alive. His hair whipped around his face as he ripped his wrist from her grasp and knelt to pick up the knife. When he rose, the dark determination on his face scared her. He'd been doing this over and over again. Destroying his dream, his hope, and in that instant she realized how much he must love her and Ellie. How much it hurt him to do this. She couldn't let him. "No! Corey, please," she cried, and stood in front of the canvas, reaching for his face. Drawing him down, she kissed his mouth, tasted the coppery tang of blood, the stark fear and the seething anger. He tried to avoid her, but she held him firm. "I love you, Corey. Ellie loves you. We both love you so much. Don't do this to yourself, please."

He jerked against her at her words, a sob catching in his throat. "I don't deserve you." His voice cracked, his chest expanding in ragged agony.

"The hell you don't. I've never met anyone more giving, more beautiful." She kissed him again and tasted the salt of his tears. "I love you. I'll only ever love you."

"Jennifer," he crooned, his hot seeking mouth capturing hers. A violent shudder coursed through him as her hands caressed his face, moving along his firm jaw, sliding deeply into his hair. "I can't. I don't know how." His voice broke, the words rushing over her lips.

She grabbed handfuls of his shirt and shook him. "Of all the stubborn... Corey, what do you think you've been doing? You taught Ellie to barrel race, you held her on her birthday when she was upset over her father, you shared your own life experiences with her, you've supported me, stood by me, protected me and saved my life. You've fed Two Tone, you've taken us to dinner and the movies. What do you think all that is? It's being a family." She shook him again for emphasis.

He pulled away from her to look in her face. She could see how much he wanted to believe her. His eyes closed and his throat worked spasmodically.

Her hand clasped the one with the knife. She could feel the trembling of his body where her fingers were wrapped around his hand. She reached up and very gently pried his fingers from the handle of the knife. He put up no resistance. His hand stayed open as if waiting to be filled, waiting to be needed.

She dropped the knife, slipping her hand into his, and he closed his fist around her almost painfully. She drew him up the stairs into the bedroom and began unbuttoning his shirt. He didn't protest. It was as if the fight had gone out of him, as if all of him had finally drained away into nothing.

"*Jennifer,*" he drawled softly, leaning his head against her forehead while she stripped his shirt from him.

Then she looked up and over his shoulder and her breath caught in her chest. Strong emotion clogged her throat with a rawness that left her feeling as if some protective layer had just been peeled from her body. It was another canvas, but the picture depicted was not of the three of them.

He sat on his motorcycle with her completely naked straddling his lap. In the painting, stark tenderness ravaged his face as his desire-dark eyes watched her moving over him, savage gentleness outlined in the long smooth fingers of his hands where he clutched her hips. And she could almost hear his words. "I'm hurting for you, darlin'. Give me what I need."

His naked leg was delineated with heavy thick muscles bunched in seductive male beauty as he used it to anchor both of them on the bike.

Then she looked at herself in the painting. Is this what she looked like in his eyes? This sensuous, breathtaking, wild woman with a mane of blazing hair falling down her back? Her lips were parted as if she was crying out her release into the night sky. The painting stirred intense emotions in her that she hadn't believed possible. Emotions she couldn't even begin to name. It aroused her with a rush of heat and honey.

In the portrait her head was back and her eyes closed as she absorbed the sensations he was stroking in her. Her face was rapt with love for him.

Her voice was unsteady and thick with tears when she was finally able to speak. "Corey, my God, it's beautiful."

He didn't know what he expected her to say. Wondered while he was creating this replication of his most erotic fantasy whether she would find it crude, disgusting, dirty. He closed his eyes, realizing that she had found it none of those. In her eyes, he realized he could do no wrong. It pushed the darkness back, the need to destroy evaporated.

She made a little sound so soft he would have missed it if he weren't in such harmony with her body, with her feelings. "Don't. Dear God, don't cry, Jennifer. I'll come apart."

She went back to removing his clothes and when his

body was bared she pushed him onto the bed, then went into the bathroom and retrieved a bottle of lotion from the medicine cabinet. She returned to find him lying on his back staring up at the ceiling.

"Turn onto your stomach," she ordered. He complied without any protest and it wrung her heart. She straddled his hips and finally he said, "Jennifer, you don't have to."

"Shh," she scolded, and poured a generous amount of lotion onto her hands. With soft sure strokes she worked out the kinks in his shoulders, kneading his hard muscles, trying to loosen all his aches and pains. She worked her way down his back, her hands gentle and reassuring.

He relaxed into the bed. She could feel every small release of tension, the soft rush of his breath. She worked his lower back, wringing a moan of pleasure from him. Then with infinite tenderness, she stroked over his scar-rough hip. He flinched at first, but then let go, his body once again sinking into the bed. For a long time she massaged his thick hip muscle, trying to show him with her hands that she understood how much it must have hurt. How vulnerable, scared and alone he must have felt.

Then she began on his other hip. When she finished, she got off him and said softly, "Come on, let's go."

He turned his head to look at her and understanding lit his eyes with hot turquoise heat. Without a word he got up and pulled on his jeans and boots, grabbing his mackintosh and shrugging into it, following her out of the cottage.

The bike made a sharp rumbling noise and they took off down the road, emerging onto the highway. Her hands were tight around his waist, and she yelled into his ear to turn off. They followed the old rutted road slowly and carefully by the bright light of the full moon.

Finally he stopped the bike, put down the kickstand and turned as she got off. Silence sweet, pure and clean filled the beautiful meadow, the dark mountains silhouetted against the bright backdrop of the sky.

"Back up," Jennifer coaxed with sugar sweetness in her voice.

"What?"

"Slide that sweet, tight backside backward." Their eyes met in the semidarkness, a flash of heat, a potent sizzle of electricity, and Jennifer shivered. She threw her leg over his and straddled him.

"Are you cold, darlin'?" he asked in a voice desire-filled and husky-soft.

"No. I'm hot, so hot, Corey."

His mouth found hers, touching her lips with wonder, with such awe she felt choked up again. "So gentle, so fierce, my sweet warrior. It's time to lay down your weapons and surrender. Many battles you've waged, but now you've lost the war."

"To whom?"

"To me. I claim victory."

He moaned, the touch of her sweet mouth sending soundless shudders of pleasure down his body. His hands came up to her moon-soaked hair, the strands like living coils of flame against his flesh. He would let her think she had won because nothing had changed. *Only that she loves you, you fool. She loves you and you're going to leave her.* She would get over him. She and Ellie would find happiness with someone else. Someone who didn't have the potential for violence in him.

She looked down at him, at his upturned face and she wanted to see that look that he had painted for himself. She wanted to make his fantasy a reality.

She slid off his lap and grasped the edges of the open mackintosh, pushing the coat off him. Then her hands went to the buttons of her shirt.

Corey surged off the bike with the innate ability of a predatory cat. He caught her in his arms, hugging her fiercely to him. "You're turning me inside out. I feel raw and vulnerable."

"And afraid?"

"Terrified."

"I'll teach you not to be afraid. Let me teach you."

"I didn't know what a relationship could be until you. You're everything I've ever dreamed of. You don't have to do this."

"What makes you think I don't have fantasies of you, Corey?"

"Tell me," he gasped, his breathing irregular and harsh.

"I know it's not painted this way, but leave your hat on."

His eyes blazed and his breath caught, his voice so gruff it was barely audible as he whispered against her mouth, "Jennifer, I'd be so lost without you, darlin'."

"So why don't you tell me your fantasy," she whispered back.

"I dream of you doing to me only what a woman can. Only what she wants to do. What a man would give his heart for."

His bare chest, smooth and sleek under the moon, drew her hands. "Are you willing to pay the price of your heart, Corey?"

"Jennifer, you already have my soul. I lost it the moment I looked into your eyes."

"I love you, Corey. Tell me what you want me to do."

"Touch me, Jennifer. My chest, my body, anywhere you want."

Slowly she smoothed her hands over his chest, massaging his hardening nipples first with her fingertips then her tongue, biting him gently and suckling his hot sensitive skin.

Her hand went to the hard ridge of flesh beneath his jeans. She caressed him through the fabric, liking the small anguished moan that rumbled in his chest. She felt as if she were holding sheer power, controlling formidable strength beneath her hands.

"Now what, Corey?"

"Take my pants off."

She did, easing his zipper down and pushing the denim and cotton briefs over his lean hips, careful of his damaged one.

"Jennifer," he moaned.

She pushed him backward until his backside rested on the bike. Then as quickly as she could, she stripped. He reached out for her, but she slipped out of his grasp to kneel in the fragrant grass.

His maleness jutted forward, so great was his need for her. She cupped him, taking the smooth soft skin between her palms, causing his whole body to buck forward straining, begging, demanding. She kissed the hollow of his hips with her lips and tongue.

His hands went into her hair, kneading her scalp with his strong artist's hands.

Unable to restrain her desire any longer, she gave him his most erotic fantasy. He cried out, his hands turning to fists in her hair, his pleasure building with each movement of her mouth. When he couldn't stand any more of the torturous pleasure, he reached down and grasped her upper arms, jerking her to her feet.

Swiftly he straddled the bike and pulled her over him. This was what he dreamed about late at night in his private torture, her straddling him in the dark of night, trusting him, holding him, loving him.

Jennifer got her wish as she peered into his face and saw the look she'd been craving. "Corey, love me, please."

His hands came up to cup her breasts, taking first one hardened nipple into his mouth then the other. Her hands dug into his shoulders, the only thing that kept her anchored to the ground. He worshiped her with his mouth, sensations strong and hot pouring through her body. She squirmed on his lap. Her head fell back and her lips parted, unable to bear the fire he was building inside her.

He buried his face between her breasts and his hands traveled like liquid flame down her body to wrap around her waist. With a guttural groan of sheer carnal desire, he lowered her. His arms bunched as he lifted and lowered her. She felt as if she'd lost control of her body—as she accepted the savagery of his lovemaking, merging and meeting him on the same plane.

She could feel his back muscles flex as he held them both on the bike and thrust his hips while lifting her in the delicious up-and-down motion. He was so powerful and so thoroughly male, taking her higher and higher with quick, wild thrusts. The scalding pleasure detonated in them suddenly with a powerful backlash of force. He poured himself into her as she spasmed around the slick heat of his arousal and they knew pure rapture.

They held on to each other in the aftermath, enjoying the soft warm breeze against their bodies and the glorious feel of each other.

Jennifer held on to him, knowing this was a night she would never forget as long as she lived. She would never forget the fierce rush of emotions, the aching need that only he could assuage. The sheer power of their joining. A union of two parts to make a whole.

They dressed quietly and rode back to her house in silence. She took his hand, not sure whether he wanted to come into the house with her, but after a moment's hesitation, he followed her.

The house felt chilled to her after the heat of their love-making. She shivered and wrapped her arms around herself, more for comfort than for cold. She needed to be prepared to hear that he wasn't staying. She knew it, but it wasn't the same as accepting it.

"Are you cold? Let me get you a blanket," he said.

"In the chest under the window in my room," she said distractedly, wondering when he left whether she would ever be warm again. She walked over to the counter, opened the cupboard and pulled out the coffee. Suddenly she remembered the book. Dear God. The book.

He ran upstairs and pulled the blanket out of the chest. Something heavy fell to the floor with a thud. Confused, he knelt down and picked up the heavy object. It was a book. He turned it over and his heart froze in his chest. The silence shattered with a roaring, tearing sound, shaking his already crumbling foundations. His breathing stuttered and stopped. With a hard gasping sound, he drew in a ragged breath as if it would be his last.

She knew.

Chapter 14

Like a haunting litany, the words reverberated in his head. He touched the title of the book and a harsh strangled sound escaped his throat.

No one knew. No one. He'd managed to keep his secret from teachers, doctors, social workers and friends at great personal cost.

He went downstairs slowly. He'd kept it from everyone, but not Jennifer. Sweet, beautiful Jennifer knew his shameful, horrible secret. He wasn't normal.

He'd had no reference point for what it was like to be normal, which frightened him because he was always so afraid he would do something wrong. He'd tried as a child. Tried comparing his family with others, but all he got was confused because other families didn't seem to be quite so chaotic.

Jennifer was standing at the sink when he finally reached the kitchen. "How did you know?" he said hoarsely, his voice breaking with disbelief. He hated it. His knees gave way and he collapsed into the nearest chair, his body feeling numb and distant, as if his brain were displaced.

"I noticed hints. The way you wanted to be touched, but were so terrified of it. Your fervent protective instincts. And when you said you hated your father, I had to wonder why. I already knew that you were running from something painful. At the time, I thought it was the bull, but then I realized later that it was so much more. I wanted so desperately to understand. But I couldn't find anything in that pathetic excuse for a library, so I called a friend in Houston. She sent me the book and I read every damn sentence and I ached, Corey. Please don't be angry."

He couldn't speak for a moment. She cared enough to ask someone all the way in Houston to send her a book because she suspected that he had been abused. She had cared enough to go to great lengths to understand him. It was too much. Too much for him to take in. "Angry?" His voice came out broken. "Angry?" he said again. "I'm not angry, Jennifer. I'm stunned, ashamed, so many emotions I can't even begin to tell you about them all."

"I'll sit here all night if you want to tell me about each one in detail."

"Oh God, Jennifer." It was too much for him to take in at one sitting. He got up and bolted across the kitchen, his hand on the doorknob, so close to breaking down in front of her. That would be the ultimate humiliation. The silence that had been so carefully maintained was now gone and he had to face it. But he feared that he could not.

"Don't go. Please, Corey, don't go," she pleaded.

Her voice was like a glass fetter to his legs. So easily he could break the fragile bonds, jump onto his bike and escape into the night. Ride until the fierce emotions eating at him like acid were blown away by the wind. Ah, but he could never forget. He would never forget her or her caring love.

Jennifer leaned forward. "I wanted to talk to you about this, but I didn't know how. I didn't know the right questions to ask... I went into town specifically to get a book, so that I could understand. I remember that first day I met you. There was such pain in your eyes. Such loneliness and sorrow."

He leaned back, closing his eyes trying to sort all this out. He felt naked and exposed and at the same time so unbearably safe he didn't know how to react. He'd expected to feel vulnerable and alone when the silence finally broke, not this warm place in his heart that radiated heat to all the dark, lonely parts of his body.

"I'm not the type of woman that trusts easily, since Sonny. But there was something about you that reached out to me. I just couldn't ignore it. My heart is yours now, and I want to know everything there is to know about you. Your past is part of you. What made you who you are today. I really want to know."

"I remember lying on my bed as a small child trying to understand why my father hit me," he told her. "I can remember the stinging pain, the bruises, the swollen faces and blackened eyes I'd suffered. I remember hurting on the outside and dying on the inside. Hundreds of lonely nights that increased the emptiness and the anger inside me."

"And you thought it was all your fault?" she prompted. She moved forward, pressing her body against his back, gathering him to her.

His eyes opened, his breathing ragged. With an intensity that broke the sudden tense silence, he demanded, "How did you know?"

"You're not alone, Corey. Ellie and I love you. We love you very much." She held on to him. "Why don't you tell me why you were going to slash that painting. Why you slashed all the others."

He broke away from her, rounding on her with a growl, *"I don't want to be like my father!"*

"What does slashing those paintings have to do with that?" she demanded in a tense voice, not flinching or budging an inch.

Corey felt sudden and glad relief. There was no pity in her eyes, just a savage protectiveness and unrelenting need to know. "He painted, Jennifer. I think he hated me for my talent. He used to tell me I was better than him. I haven't painted for years, but when I came here, I so desperately wanted…"

"What?" she said softly when he didn't continue, caressing his jaw with her fingers.

"To be normal. To have you. God, you scared the living daylights out of me."

"You would have left if it wasn't for Jay?"

"Yes," he hissed. "I've been running a long time, darlin'. I was running fast so that I wouldn't stop long enough to fall in love. How did I know it would only take a split second and hair so red it defined the word? And a precocious child so like her mother."

Jennifer smiled and it hurt so bad. "The book says that people react to abuse in different ways, Corey. It says that some people abuse substances and others look for what they need in activities. When you lost the rodeo, you did feel like you lost yourself."

How could she know? How could she understand him so well? "I couldn't save my mother and sister and when I was gored I totally lost my balance."

"And after the goring?" Her words rushed out on a note of understanding.

"Everything came crashing down like a house of cards.

After I got gored, I felt like I was starting from square one again. Then the news came. They told me my mother and little sister were dead. I didn't give a damn about my father.''

"While you were in the hospital?" she prompted.

"Yes," he whispered. "My father was a drunken bastard. He blamed everything on the Anglos. And every one of his failures he battered into my skin, and my mother's, and when she had Marigold, hers, as well. I tried to stop him, but I was too young, and then, as I grew older, I saw that she wouldn't leave. No matter how much I pleaded with her. No matter how much money I sent her. She wouldn't go."

She touched his face lightly. "What happened?"

"He fell asleep with a lit cigarette and they all died."

"Oh God, Corey. I'm so sorry. I'm so very, very sorry. You blame yourself, don't you?"

"I should have made her go, but she wouldn't leave him. I failed her and Marigold."

"No!" she shouted. "You did not fail her. It was your parents' fault, Corey. They were the ones who failed you. You were their responsibility. They're the ones at fault. You were a defenseless child in need of love and nurturing. You didn't get that because they were unable to give it to you. You had no choice." She wrapped her arms around him, holding him tight, rocking him gently.

The warmth and need he felt for this sweet, delicate woman overwhelmed him, a balm to his battered spirit. "I don't ever want to let you go. Jennifer, my Jennifer. I don't ever want to let you go."

"Don't then. Ellie and I need you."

He looked into her eyes. Her words were like silken cords that wrapped around his heart, binding him. She loved him and his heart sang and soared. Yet he knew the truth. He didn't know what it was like to be normal. That was why it was all a dream. Elusive. Out of reach.

"What made it worse was the silence," he said after a moment. "I couldn't talk about what was happening to me. I couldn't ask my friends why their families were so different. Asking questions would have opened up too many inquiries, and I felt too ashamed to talk about it to anyone," he said quietly, his voice drifting into a hushed whisper. "I wanted to be normal, Jennifer. I wanted it so desperately."

He lay his head on her shoulder and she buried her hands in his hair, cupping and kneading his scalp.

"I thought if I could be good enough, it would happen. But there was no turning back for my father. The darkness ate him whole and in the end the fire took him. I started fighting back at ten. I probably would have landed in jail by sixteen if it wasn't for the rodeo. I ran away from home and lied about my age. The rodeo saved me, Jennifer. I had money and prestige and no one beat me anymore. I started to send money to my mother. I told her I would support her and Marigold. I even went home when I was eighteen to beg her to leave. Her arm was in a cast and Marigold looked like a zombie. But she wouldn't go. My father tried to throw me out of the house. I hit him, Jennifer. I hit him so hard I thought I'd killed him. I was in such a rage all I wanted to do was stop him from hurting her. My mother made me leave. She told me never to come back. I never did."

"Corey." She grabbed his face and held it between her hands. "You don't understand, do you? You've been a father to Ellie. No one taught you how. You just did it because it comes natural to you."

The silence stretched as she held him, her hand smoothing through his hair. "I want what I saw in that painting, Corey."

He shuddered, his whole body trembling as another sob caught in his throat. "Oh God, Jennifer, don't."

"It's not going to happen, though, is it, Corey?"

"I have unfinished business, Jennifer. I can't make any promises. I should never have stayed here so long and put you in danger. I'm sorry about that. I can't stay because I need to go back to the rodeo," he lied. He wasn't about to tell her that he loved her. The painting had been a dream. Only that. The reality she wanted he couldn't give her because he couldn't be sure of himself and he wasn't going to stay and test that theory.

"Jay was to blame, Corey. Not you. He was the maniac."

"Do you want me to go now, Jennifer?"

"No. I want you to stay for as long as you can. I saw Ellie's light on. Why don't you go talk to her. I'll be in my room when you're done."

Ellie sat on her bed listlessly trying to do her homework. Her mind was not on the math problems in front of her, but on the trapped feelings of frustration and pain at the loss of Tucker's friendship. Later, she promised herself. Later she would talk to him about all her fears and the shame she felt when Jay died.

"Ellie?" Corey's voice broke into her misery and she lifted her head only to see the resignation on his face. He was coming to tell her he was leaving. She could see the knowledge in his eyes, the unhappy slant to his mouth. It hurt, as if she were losing her own father.

"I don't want you to go," she said, tears forming in her eyes and running down her cheeks.

Corey made his way over to the bed. He sat on the edge and pulled Ellie into his arms. Holding her tightly he smoothed his hand over her hair. He let her cry. Great gulping sobs that brought tears to his own eyes.

"Ellie, I'm sorry, little darlin'. It's time that I found out for myself who I am and where I'm going. Do you understand that I wouldn't be any good to anyone without my own peace of mind?"

"I think so," she said softly, not letting him go, her voice muffled against his chest.

"I want you to remember what you told me. Why you had to ride with a broken wrist. Do you remember?"

"I said that I had to do it for me. For myself."

"Well, Ellie, that's what I have to do. I'm not trying to prove anything to anyone. I have to do this for myself." His chest ached with suppressed tears, his throat tight, so tight.

"It doesn't make it any easier, Corey," she murmured.

"I know," he whispered.

"Are you coming back?" Her voice told him that she already knew the answer.

"No."

"Why? We want you to."

He leaned back so he could look into her eyes. "I can't because a long time ago when I was a child, my father beat me, Ellie."

"I'm so sorry, Corey."

He swallowed, finding it hard to go on. "I'm afraid that part of that violence might be inside me and if I stay here with you and your mom, it might come out. Do you understand?"

Ellie met his stare and nodded. "Yes. I understand. I understand because of Tucker."

Corey nodded and pulled her against his chest once more. He held her until his arms were numb, held her after she'd fallen asleep and it physically hurt when he finally laid her down and covered her with the blanket. He whispered hoarsely, "I love you, Eleanor Jean Horn, like you were my own child." His voice broke on the last word.

Gently he kissed her temple, unaware of the tear that dropped from his eye onto the soft skin of her cheek.

A devastating salty farewell.

It was more than he'd hoped for. They loved him. The knowledge sang through him, yet scared him. Terrified-down-to-his-toes scared. Spitless scared.

He didn't want to hurt them. He didn't want to turn into some kind of a monster. He couldn't bear it if he did.

He was going to run again. Run away because it was easier than facing the devastating fear that his father's words had been true after all. He was going to run and never look back. He was going to leave his dream behind.

Later, once he was in control of himself again, he made his way to Jennifer's room, pushing open the door. She lay in bed, her eyes open, waiting for him.

"Come give me the night," she said and he did. It was all he had to offer her.

The morning came too abruptly. Neither of them had slept. Even now Jennifer lay feigning sleep. She felt him leave her and heard him get dressed. Very gently he kissed her on the lips. "Goodbye, sweet darlin'."

Jennifer heard the door close and she lay there, her stomach in vicious knots. She had to let him go. Once again a man was choosing the rodeo over her. She'd been a complete fool.

She never heard the bike roar down the driveway. Never noticed the time passing. There was only sadness and pain. And the horrifying numbness, which seemed to surround her and swallow her whole.

Two days later, Jennifer and Ellie sat on the front porch, listlessly. Ellie sat on the porch swing pretending to read a book, pushing at the worn wooden boards with the toe of her bare foot. She hadn't turned a page in ten minutes. Jennifer sat in a rocker, rocking slowly back and forth. It was better than pacing restlessly, pining for a man who had come to mean everything to her.

Without knowing why, she looked up and met Ellie's eyes.

"He went to Austin," Ellie said. "I saw his entry form. It's a three-day rodeo. Today's the last day. It's not that far. We could go."

She looked at her daughter's hopeful face. Two days had passed and already his absence was like a hole in her heart. She would have to go to him. Somehow she would have to convince him. Somehow she would have to bring him home.

It didn't take them long to get dressed and get into Jennifer's truck. They both smiled at each other before Jennifer inserted the key in the ignition. *We're coming, Corey, and we're not leaving without you,* she said to herself, for the first time that day feeling full of hope and inspiration for a bright future with the man she loved.

He strapped on his chaps, taking great care with the buckle. His hands were shaking, his insides tied up in knots. He'd drawn Widowmaker as he knew he would. It was his last ride. He had the most points and this ride would decide the winner. He had been like a man possessed during the tournament. Widowmaker was the last challenge. He knew it because it was his destiny.

He walked toward the ring and climbed on the fence, looking down at the black-and-white bull. Two days without Jennifer and Ellie had been so devastatingly lonely. He hadn't slept at night. The hotel room was like a prison.

"Trying a little of the hair of the dog that bit you, huh, Rainwater?" A man's voice broke into Corey's thoughts.

Corey met the other man's unflinching gaze. "Yeah. I'm going to bite him back."

The man smiled and Corey straddled the bull, slipping his hand under the rope and binding it securely. That was all that anchored him to the animal. A piece of rope, a bell and sheer unadulterated guts. Sweat trickled down his face and he turned and nodded at the man holding the gate. "Let'em go."

"He'll be okay, Mommy," Ellie said as they sat down, ready to watch the rest of the rodeo.

Jennifer smiled at her daughter and put her arm around her. "Who's the mother here and who's the daughter?"

Ellie smiled. "Do you still love him, Mom?"

"Yes, Ellie. I love him very much."

Just then his name was called and she heard the chute open and her breath caught in her throat. She'd never seen him so magnificent. Raw power against sheer brute strength. She and Ellie watched transfixed as he rode the bull with the skill and determination that was a deeply ingrained part of him. She watched as the buzzer rang, the eight seconds gone and still he rode.

"Mom," Ellie said very softly, "I think he's riding for us now. He doesn't even know we're here, but he's riding for us."

Jennifer knew it was true. It was just like him. When he slipped off the bull with ease and grace, she and Ellie rose with the other people clapping and shouting and giving him his due. Suddenly he turned and stared straight up at her, the deep green of his eyes hot and possessive, and she felt the bond between them tighten and solidify. She blew him a kiss and he stared one more minute before he turned and exited the ring.

Somehow he knew they would come. That was why he'd ridden for as long as he could. For them. He stood outside the gate, breathing hard, leaning against the fence for support. He could walk away from the rodeo because now he had built new foundations. Foundations that were forged by a beautiful woman with integrity and a warm giving heart and a little girl with innocence and grace who had taught him that being a father was a most natural and rewarding pursuit.

Now he needed only them, wanted only them. He looked up to the stands and could easily pick out Jennifer. A woman with fire in her hair and fire deep down in her heart. A fire for him that she had set and he needed to tend and nurture so that it never went out. Burned for all his life. Standing in the bright sunlight, he knew that he would only be whole with her. Her and her sweet daughter. Walking away from his old life, turning his back on the rodeo, facing his fear was something he'd had to do. Now that it was done, he had a life and a home. He had a future.

Slowly, he sifted through the memories. Ellie's need for his approval and advice. The numerous times she had shown him innocent, heartfelt affection.

Ah, then there was Jennifer's understanding, her desire and her love. Jennifer had shown him that touching didn't have to hurt. He craved her with a powerful desire built upon a carefully constructed foundation of love.

A foundation both strong and enduring.

Jennifer and Ellie had taught him what loving was all about.

Corey climbed up to where Jennifer and Ellie sat, watching other bull riders in the ring make the effort to oust Corey. When Jennifer's eyes met his, all the desperation and loneliness of the past two days evaporated. There was no remorse, no accusation, nothing but love in her eyes.

"I decided that what I had to prove to myself was that I could get on him if I wanted to," he said. "I'm willing to try, Jennifer, because I want to so desperately, because I can't imagine going on without you, because I'm more afraid of being without you. Because I love you."

She looked up into his eyes. "Oh, Corey. I love you, too. I love you so much."

He caught her as she launched herself against him, hugging her so tightly he never wanted to let her go. "I love you, darlin'. I was just too lost to know it."

Over Jennifer's shoulder, his eyes met the piercing green gaze of her daughter.

"What do you say, Ellie? Want a daddy?"

Ellie's eyes filled with tears. "Only if it's you, Corey. I sure love you like you were my very own."

"Come here, sweetheart." He drew her into his arms and hugged them both against his heart where they would stay.

"I couldn't have wished for a more perfect family. My two beautiful girls. Come on, let's go home."

"But," Ellie said, "don't you want to see if you win?"

He pulled on her braid and smiled. "I already have."

A week later, Ellie, Jennifer and Corey sat around the kitchen table planning the wedding. When there was a knock at the door, Corey got up and opened it.

"Mr. Rainwater?"

"Yes," Corey answered, as he opened the door farther.

"You are one hard man to find." The small man removed his hat and wiped at his forehead. He stretched out his hand and offered Corey a card.

"Yeah, I like it that way. What is it you want?" Corey took the card and glanced at the black print.

"I'm David Wells. I was your mother's attorney. In her will she left you everything." The man walked past Corey into the house, setting his briefcase down on the table. He nodded to Jennifer and smiled at Ellie before he opened the locks and pulled out a sheaf of papers.

"The house burned down to the ground. There wasn't anything to leave me." Corey's voice got rough, his throat tight. His eyes reached for Jennifer's and the knot of grief eased at her sympathetic expression.

"On the contrary. There was a trust opened up when you were sixteen. There's quite a sum in it now. I'm here to bestow the legal papers on you." The man sounded relieved and preoccupied.

"A trust? What kind of trust?" It must be the money he had sent his mother, he thought in shock. He'd known she wasn't spending it.

"There was a note," the man said by way of explanation. "She insisted that I find you and make sure you got both the note and the money. There is also the matter of your father's work."

"My father's work?" Corey asked, perplexed. He knew his father had destroyed all his work when his hands had been ruined.

"Yes, his paintings are now worth a considerable sum of money," Wells said, still digging in his briefcase as if he couldn't, or wouldn't, look Corey in the eyes.

"I don't follow you."

"Your mother entrusted me with five of his works. After his unfortunate incident, he destroyed most of the stuff he was working on, but your mother saved five paintings to be sold upon his death."

Corey took a deep breath, unable to take it all in. He looked down at the note.

I could never have taken your money, son. I'm sorry
for the way we parted, but it was better for all of us.
Please don't hate me or your father. I loved him and
I just couldn't leave him. Perhaps it isn't something
you can understand, but I hope maybe one day you
will. Do something good with the money, son. Be
happy.

Corey felt something loosen inside of him and he knew
exactly what he wanted to do with the money.

The man cleared his throat and Corey looked up expectantly. "There is another matter that I really don't know
how to tell you, so I'll tell you straight out. When the news
was given to you at the hospital that your father, mother
and sister were dead, well, you see, the search hadn't been
completed yet. It wasn't discovered until later, after you
left that...well...that your sister was not killed. She's been
waiting for you at your Austin house all this time."

Corey couldn't speak, the air seemed to be trapped in his
chest. *"Marigold,"* he got out hoarsely. *"Where is she?"*

"In my car. She's a bit frightened and..."

Corey didn't hear the rest. He rushed past the little man,
through the door and down the steps, joy and awe pounding
in his blood.

When he got to the car, a dark-haired child turned her
haunted green eyes up to his and he pulled the car door
open, dropping to his knees with a soft cry. He touched her
face and the tears welling in her eyes slipped down her
cheeks.

"Corey." She said his name as if it were home and
wrapped her slim arms around his neck. He felt the hot,
wet slide of her tears against his neck.

He felt Jennifer's hand on his shoulder and he just
couldn't move, his chest was full and aching, tears pricking

the back of his eyes. "My God, I thought you were dead. What happened?"

"Dad went into one of his rages because I broke a glass. I couldn't stand it anymore. I just couldn't. I left and I guess he crashed on the couch with a lit cigarette and caught the house on fire. I went to your house and got the key you always said you'd leave for me. I let myself in to wait for you, but you never came. Finally I called the police because I didn't know what else to do." She stood there forlorn and with shadows in her eyes. "Mom's dead." Her voice broke and she dissolved into tears again.

Corey pulled her close and held her, so thankful that she was alive. It was a miracle that they had both survived their father's brutality.

A low grunt broke them apart and Marigold's tear-streaked face broke into a grin when she saw the little black-and-white pig butting her ankles.

"He does that when he likes someone and wants to be picked up. He loves to be held," Ellie said, reaching down and lifting Two Tone into Marigold's arms.

Shyly she smiled at Ellie, her smile widening with confidence when Ellie grinned back.

Corey introduced Jennifer and Ellie and told Marigold that he was going to get married and that not to worry because he would take care of her. His heart warmed when Jennifer chimed in that they both would take care of her.

And as if Two Tone agreed, he let out a loud grunt and settled his rotund body deeper into Marigold's arms, proclaiming her one of the family. All of them laughed through their tears. And when Corey's and Marigold's eyes met, they knew that finally, out of the darkness of despair, they had found a place of warmth and light. A place they could call home.

Epilogue

Three months had passed since Marigold had moved in with them. She and Ellie had become immediate friends. Seldom apart, they shared secrets, Two Tone and the love of horses.

Jennifer had bonded with Marigold right away, which didn't surprise Corey. With her big heart and gentle hands, she had soothed Marigold's fears, bought her a huge wardrobe that Corey was sure she could never exhaust and made her feel warmly welcome in the big house.

Two months ago he had married Jennifer and it still brought tears to his eyes when he thought about how she had looked at him that day. How her eyes had filled with tears and love when he'd slipped the ring on her finger, broadcasting to everyone that she was his forever. Both Ellie and Marigold had been bridesmaids. The whole town had turned out for the nuptials, heralding Corey as a hero for standing up to Jay Butler and his vicious brothers. Corey had even received grudging respect from the sheriff.

The Butler brothers had been charged with attempted murder and assault and were all sentenced to prison terms. Corey had begun to see a therapist and was working through the emotional baggage he carried around with him. Progress was slow, but it was sure.

He had taken the considerable sum of money his mother had left him and contracted builders to erect the community center on the outskirts of town on a plot of land that had been long forgotten. Jennifer had encouraged Corey to make a bid on the land.

Now the center was ready for the finishing touches and the staffing. He'd recruited Ellie, Marigold and Tucker, promising to pay for the boy's jumping lessons in exchange for his help. He also helped Ellie and Tucker mend the rift between them.

Corey sat resting his aching back against the now-dry, newly painted director's office wall. He closed his eyes wearily.

"What do you think you're doing, Rainwater?" Jennifer asked dryly.

"Resting."

"Looks like slacking to me," she said with a gleam in her eye. His gray T-shirt clung to the hard curves of his chest and his dark hair lay loose and wet against his neck. The red bandanna he'd tied around his forehead was also drenched with sweat.

"Whose idea was it, anyway, to open a community center?" He grinned up at her, humor glinting in his eyes.

Jennifer sauntered over to him and crouched. She pointed her finger into the steel of his chest. "I believe that bright idea was yours, cowboy."

He reached up and cupped her face, the turquoise ring on his left hand reflecting the light from the skylights above. "I'm always up for a challenge."

Jennifer smiled and her eyes traveled down his body. "That's never been one of your problems."

"No. You, darlin', are my only problem. One I want to take a lifetime to solve." He smiled and drew her forward, kissing her mouth.

She grabbed his hand and touched the ring on his finger. "You've got a lifetime, because I'm not letting you go." She intertwined her left hand with his until her matching turquoise ring connected with his. He drew her forward between his legs and with a sigh she melted against him.

He buried his face in her hair. "I love you, Jenny darlin'." His voice was thick and uneven.

She turned her head to look up into his eyes, her heart so full it was almost impossible to hold all the emotion she felt for this brave, strong, precious man. She closed her eyes against the instant surge of emotion, wrapped her arms around his neck and hugged him hard. Swallowing against the tightness in her throat, her happiness perfect and thorough, she cradled his face in her hands. With the same thickness and unevenness in her voice, she said, "My heart will always belong to you, Corey. Forever."

"Jennifer, about Tucker—"

"Yes, we can unofficially adopt him, too. Why not? The more the merrier. He's a sweet kid." Jennifer snuggled into his sweaty warmth and turned her face up for another kiss.

"Please, can't you guys get over it," Ellie said as she walked into the room, Marigold trailing behind her. "The rest of the furniture's here, Dad and Mom. Where do you want them to unload it?"

Jennifer got to her feet and Corey rose. The sound of the word *Dad* on Ellie's lips, even if it was with a teasing inflection, made him feel warm and mushy inside. "You know something, little darlin', you didn't knock," he said in a mock-scolding voice.

"There wasn't a door, smarty-pants," Ellie responded tartly, putting her hands on her hips, using the same taunting inflection that Corey had used.

"Yeah, Corey, you can't expect Ellie to knock if there isn't a door, now, can you?" Marigold mimicked Ellie's stance.

"Is there an echo in here?" He turned to look at Jennifer.

"Parrots maybe." Jennifer laughed, her eyes twinkling as she wrapped her arm around Corey's waist.

"I guess I'd better put one in then," he said as he moved swiftly and caught both girls around the waist and swung them around.

Tucker walked into the room with a disgusted look on his face. "Hey you guys were supposed to tell Corey that the delivery truck is here," he said, puffed up with pride that Corey had trusted him with the furniture.

"I did, Mr. Garrison, so there." Ellie's tone was crisp.

"Don't get snippy with me, Ms. Rainwater. I think those guys are getting impatient," Tucker scolded, his eyes moving to Corey.

"Well, I'll just tell them they'll have to wait!" Ellie started to walk out of the room.

Tucker grabbed her by the arm and said, "You better hold on there. Let Corey handle it."

"Don't get pushy. Who died and made you boss, Garrison?" Ellie extricated her arm with all the grace of a princess, giving Tucker a hard look. She wasn't about to let his touch make her feel all weak in the knees.

Marigold, not about to be left out of the squabble, tugged on Ellie's other hand. "Yeah, Garrison."

They exited the doors still arguing heatedly.

"They're going to drive us crazy, Corey." Jennifer chuckled. "Already Marigold and Ellie are as thick as thieves. God help us when they get hormones. Two fourteen-year-olds. My mother and father have really gotten their revenge.''

Jennifer looked up at her husband and her features softened when she saw the look of pure rapture on his face.

"Yeah, isn't it grand?" He beamed, grabbing Jennifer around the waist. "What do you say, Mrs. Rainwater? Want to go rescue those deliverymen before your daughter puts them in their place?"

"Lead on." The surge of love she felt for him made her voice rough.

Hours later, once the painting was finished and the last door was installed, the furniture unwrapped and situated, the five of them sat on the newly carpeted floor and toasted the opening of the Silver Creek Community Center. Corey and Jennifer with champagne and the teenagers with cider.

Jimmy walked into the center with a camera in his hand. "Why don't y'all gather together and I'll take a picture," he coaxed, undaunted by the moans and groans of the teenagers.

It wasn't until everyone was settled on the sofa that Corey realized that he had finally gotten what he had wanted so many years ago and so much heartache later. A family. A wonderful, beautiful, normal family.

When the shutter clicked, the image was caught forever on film.

"Corey," Jennifer said softly as he slipped into bed beside her that night, gathering her into his arms. "I've been waiting for you. I have something very important to tell you. Where have you been?" She reached out for him.

"Showing Ellie and Marigold how to draw faces," he replied. She snuggled into his arms, drawing her warm soft body against his. "What did you want to tell me?" he murmured sleepily.

"Remember the day we, um, lost control in the pantry? Well...we're going to have a baby... I'm four months along."

Corey made a half shout, half sob in his throat, drawing her closer to him, giving her a kiss that could ignite rock. "God, Jennifer, I'm so happy."

They lay together as he stroked her arm and nibbled on her ear. A few moments later he spoke again. "Are you sure you don't mind? I mean about my sister living with us and about Tucker."

"Don't be so stupid. Of course I don't mind. It looks like she and Ellie are going to be really good friends." After a moment of silence she said, "Hey, are you ready to go to sleep yet, I need my rest."

"How much?"

"I'm pregnant."

"Yeah," he said, doing something wicked with his hand and smiling when she gasped.

"But not that pregnant and not that sleepy," she murmured.

Many moments later in the warm afterglow of their lovemaking, Jennifer stroked the hard planes of his chest and asked softly, "Things are working out with the counselor?"

"It's going to take some time and I know things won't always be perfect, but I'm willing to try." He had discovered that he could only be the man he was and he hoped that would be enough. He looked down into Jennifer's eyes and saw that it was enough, more than enough. He smiled.

She smiled back at him, then reached for his lips. With sighs of pleasure, they joined their mouths and their lives.

* * * * *

COMING NEXT MONTH

#781 NIGHTHAWK—Rachel Lee
Conard County
After being wrongly accused of a crime he hadn't committed, Craig Nighthawk just wanted to be left alone. Then he met Esther Jackson, who was fighting her own battles but needed his protection to make peace with her past...and ensure a future for them both.

#782 IN MEMORY'S SHADOW—Linda Randall Wisdom
Single mom Keely Harper had returned to Echo Ridge to build a new life. But when terrifying memories came flooding back, she sought safety in the arms of town sheriff Sam Barkley. He knew the truth about her past, and he was willing to go above and beyond the call of duty to safeguard this troubled mother.

#783 EVERY WAKING MOMENT—Doreen Roberts
U.S. Marshal Blake Foster should have known better than to get involved with prime murder suspect Gail Stevens. But now was too late for regrets. Time was running out to prove her innocence—and his own love—because Gail had fallen into the hands of the real killer....

#784 AND DADDY MAKES THREE—Kay David
Becoming a dad to the daughter he'd never known about meant that Grayston Powers had to marry her guardian, Annie Burns, because Annie wasn't about to abandon the child she considered her own. They insisted it was a marriage in name only...but could they really deny the passion between them?

#785 McCAIN'S MEMORIES—Maggie Simpson
Defense attorney Lauren Hamilton had a weakness for sexy bad boys, and Jon McCain, her rugged amnesiac client, certainly fit the bill. She needed him to remember something, *anything*, to help her clear his name. Because her case—and her heart—hinged on the secrets of this man without a memory....

#786 GABRIEL IS NO ANGEL—Wendy Haley
Rae Ann Boudreau would do *any*thing to serve a summons on a deadbeat dad—even if it meant going undercover as a belly dancer. Vice cop Gabriel MacLaren would do *any*thing to protect his star snitch—but falling for the gorgeous process server who was threatening his case hadn't been part of the plan....

Take 4 bestselling love stories FREE

Plus get a FREE surprise gift!

Special Limited-time Offer

Mail to Silhouette Reader Service™

3010 Walden Avenue
P.O. Box 1867
Buffalo, N.Y. 14240-1867

YES! Please send me 4 free Silhouette Intimate Moments® novels and my free surprise gift. Then send me 6 brand-new novels every month, which I will receive months before they appear in bookstores. Bill me at the low price of $3.34 each plus 25¢ delivery and applicable sales tax, if any.* That's the complete price and a savings of over 10% off the cover prices—quite a bargain! I understand that accepting the books and gift places me under no obligation ever to buy any books. I can always return a shipment and cancel at any time. Even if I never buy another book from Silhouette, the 4 free books and the surprise gift are mine to keep forever.

245 BPA A3UW

Name	(PLEASE PRINT)	
Address	Apt. No.	
City	State	Zip

This offer is limited to one order per household and not valid to present Silhouette Intimate Moments® subscribers. *Terms and prices are subject to change without notice.
Sales tax applicable in N.Y.

UMOM-696

©1990 Harlequin Enterprises Limited

IN CELEBRATION OF MOTHER'S DAY, JOIN
SILHOUETTE THIS MAY AS WE BRING YOU

a funny thing
HAPPENED ON THE WAY TO THE
DELIVERY ROOM

THESE THREE STORIES, CELEBRATING THE
LIGHTER SIDE OF MOTHERHOOD, ARE
WRITTEN BY YOUR FAVORITE AUTHORS:

KASEY MICHAELS
KATHLEEN EAGLE
EMILIE RICHARDS

When three couples make the trip to the delivery
room, they get more than their own bundles of
joy...they get the promise of love!

Available this May,
wherever Silhouette books are sold.

As seen on TV!
Free Gift Offer

With a Free Gift proof-of-purchase from any Silhouette® book,
you can receive a beautiful cubic zirconia pendant.

This gorgeous marquise-shaped stone is a genuine cubic
zirconia—accented by an 18" gold tone necklace.

(Approximate retail value $19.95)

Send for yours today...
compliments of ▼*Silhouette*®
™

To receive your free gift, a cubic zirconia pendant, send us one original proof-of-
purchase, photocopies not accepted, from the back of any Silhouette Romance™,
Silhouette Desire®, Silhouette Special Edition®, Silhouette Intimate Moments®
or Silhouette Yours Truly™ title available in February, March and April at your favorite
retail outlet, together with the Free Gift Certificate, plus a check or money order for
$1.65 U.S./$2.15 CAN. (do not send cash) to cover postage and handling, payable
to Silhouette Free Gift Offer. We will send you the specified gift. Allow 6 to 8 weeks for
delivery. Offer good until April 30, 1997 or while quantities last. Offer valid in the
U.S. and Canada only.

Free Gift Certificate

Name: _____

Address: _____

City: _____ State/Province: _____ Zip/Postal Code: _____

Mail this certificate, one proof-of-purchase and a check or money order for postage
and handling to: SILHOUETTE FREE GIFT OFFER 1997. In the U.S.: 3010 Walden
Avenue, P.O. Box 9077, Buffalo NY 14269-9077. In Canada: P.O. Box 613, Fort Erie,
Ontario L2Z 5X3.

FREE GIFT OFFER   084-KFD
ONE PROOF-OF-PURCHASE

To collect your fabulous FREE GIFT, a cubic zirconia pendant, you must include this
original proof-of-purchase for each gift with the properly completed Free Gift Certificate.

084-KFD

At last the wait is over...
In March
New York Times bestselling author

NORA ROBERTS

will bring us the latest from the Stanislaskis as
Natasha's now very grown-up stepdaughter,
Freddie, and Rachel's very sexy brother-in-law
Nick discover that love is worth waiting for in

WAITING FOR NICK

Silhouette Special Edition #1088

and in April
visit Natasha and Rachel again—or meet them
for the first time—in

The Stanislaski Sisters

containing TAMING NATASHA
and FALLING FOR RACHEL

Available wherever Silhouette books are sold.

Look us up on-line at:http://www.romance.net

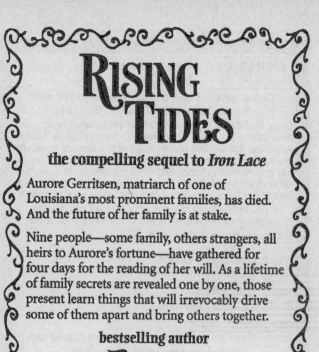

RISING TIDES

the compelling sequel to *Iron Lace*

Aurore Gerritsen, matriarch of one of
Louisiana's most prominent families, has died.
And the future of her family is at stake.

Nine people—some family, others strangers, all
heirs to Aurore's fortune—have gathered for
four days for the reading of her will. As a lifetime
of family secrets are revealed one by one, those
present learn things that will irrevocably drive
some of them apart and bring others together.

bestselling author

EMILIE RICHARDS

Available in May 1997 at your favorite retail outlet.

MIRA The brightest star in women's fiction